Praise for *Ruby Spencer's Whisky Year*

"*Ruby Spencer's Whisky Year* is utterly charming. Rochelle Bilow's evocative writing made me feel like I was in a cozy Scottish cottage right alongside her irrepressible heroine, swooning over the local food, whisky, and strapping, bearded handyman. I finished the book, my heart full and my stomach rumbling, then immediately googled 'plane tickets to Scotland.'"

—Laura Hankin, author of *The Daydreams*

"Rochelle Bilow's debut is a transportive delight! The humor and warmth are like a sip of fine single malt, with all the depth and complexity of flavor to make you plan your own escape to Scotland. If you're in search of a love story to make you feel like you've come home, don't miss your chance to fall in love with this book."

—Denise Williams, author of *Technically Yours*

"This book doesn't just have a phenomenal romance at its heart—and a sexy Scotsman to swoon over—but a truly immersive sense of place, one that you'll never want to leave once you've allowed yourself to discover Thistlecross's inherent charms and the hilarious locals who inhabit this cozy village."

—Paste

"The perfect cozy read for a chilly winter day."

—Culturess

"Bilow has written a romance that should be savored slowly, if only to thoroughly appreciate her poetic prose and immersive sense of place. . . . A charming, lyrical debut about love and self-discovery."

—*Kirkus Reviews*

"Bilow's debut is perfect for readers enamored of Scotland and friends-to-lovers romances."

—*Booklist*

"Food writer Bilow's debut romance is just as charming as its Scottish village setting."

—*Library Journal*

TITLES BY ROCHELLE BILOW

Ruby Spencer's Whisky Year
Effie Olsen's Summer Special

Effie Olsen's Summer Special

Rochelle Bilow

BERKLEY ROMANCE ~ NEW YORK

BERKLEY ROMANCE
Published by Berkley
An imprint of Penguin Random House LLC
penguinrandomhouse.com

Library of Congress Cataloging-in-Publication Data

Names: Bilow, Rochelle, author.
Title: Effie Olsen's summer special / Rochelle Bilow.
Description: First edition. | New York : Berkley Romance, 2024.
Identifiers: LCCN 2023035698 (print) | LCCN 2023035699 (ebook) |
ISBN 9780593547908 (trade paperback) | ISBN 9780593547915 (ebook)
Subjects: LCSH: Best friends--Fiction. | Cooks--Fiction. | Restaurants--Fiction. |
LCGFT: Romance fiction. | Novels.
Classification: LCC PS3602.I476 E44 2024 (print) | LCC PS3602.I476 (ebook) |
DDC 813/.6—dc23/eng/20230828
LC record available at https://lccn.loc.gov/2023035698
LC ebook record available at https://lccn.loc.gov/2023035699

First Edition: April 2024

Printed in the United States of America
1st Printing

Title page art: Lighthouse © Lubenica / Shutterstock
Book design by Elke Sigal

For Julie K.

Effie Olsen's Summer Special

Alder Isle High School Class of 2007 Yearbook

Hey Ern—

I can't believe we made it.

And I can't wait for everything that comes next.

Graduation.

Getting the hell out of here.

Culinary school.

World travel.

I promise not to forget about you when I'm cooking fancy pasta in Italy or whatever.

But you have to promise to come visit.

I'm still low-key mad you convinced me to come to prom. I've never eaten a chicken breast that dry in my life. We looked good, though.

Seriously. Thanks for all the memories. Running track together. Lobstering with your dad. Scooping ice cream with mine (someday you will understand that Grape-Nuts is not a good flavor . . .). Eating Combos until we feel sick. Dumb games of Truth or Dare.

Being there for each other.

Ernie, you rock.

Last chance to come with me. Alder Isle doesn't need you, but I SURE DO!!!!

—Effie

Effie Olsen, you are my best friend, and you always will be.

I know you have to leave, but I wish you wanted to stay.

I'm so proud of you for winning States this year. Those Italian pasta nerds had better be prepared for the best hurdler they've ever met.

Heck, I'm proud of you for everything. For setting a big goal and going for it.

If you ever decide to come back to Alder Isle, I'll find a way to get you the kitchen of your dreams. Including that ridiculously expensive stove from the French company I cannot pronounce.

I'll only buy pizza Combos for the rest of my life.

(Okay I probably would still buy pretzel and cheese in secret.)

I'll take you out on the water whenever you want.

We'll have more adventures than you knew existed on this little ol' island.

I'll be there for you, night and day.

Damn it, Eff. Don't forget about me.

—Ern

Chapter One

SIXTEEN YEARS LATER

Effie Olsen knew it was just after sunup before she opened her eyes. She'd spent the first seventeen years of her life on Alder Isle, and even though she'd been gone for another sixteen, she could still tell time by how the island sun felt on her skin. If Effie had to guess, she'd put it at just before 5:00. The late May morning light was bright and insistent, overly cheery in the most obnoxious way.

Four fifty-nine a.m. was too early for optimism, but try telling Maine that. Or more specifically, try telling that to an island off the midcoast of Maine with a full-time population of fifteen hundred. An island that was once quiet and uncool, but was now ballooning with tourists for much of the year—tourists who'd booked their reservations months in advance for one of the country's best new restaurants. Effie had woken up on an island that was eight miles long and seven miles wide. An island that was hard to get to and damn near impossible to leave. An island that ignored the fact Maine was supposed to have foggy, gray mornings.

Effie rolled over and groaned. Her head was pounding, and her mouth felt dry. Eyes still shut to the world, she reached for her phone on the nightstand, except . . . *Hmmm.* The nightstand wasn't there. Her hand fell to the side of the bed and touched exposed mattress. There was no fitted sheet, and Effie recoiled at the realization. *Ew.* A jersey knit sheet was crumpled down by her feet.

Shitballs.

She understood she wasn't in her childhood room, but there was no good reason for that. Where was she? Her mind raced, although the dull heaviness in her skull made it hard to think. She pulled her knees in close to her chest, curled up like a rabbit in a warren, and tried to piece together the last twenty-four hours.

Her plane had landed at the Bangor airport after flights from San Francisco to New York to Maine.

Her father, Samuel, and younger sister, Ingrid, picked her up with a steaming travel mug of milky coffee and a bag of pizza-flavored Combos. Which was a sweet throwback to her favorite teenage breakfast, but come on, Dad. Heard of granola? Sophomore-year Effie would have happily eaten a whole bag of cheese-filled crackers before 9:00 a.m., but thirty-three-year-old Effie preferred to live by structured, sensible rules. (With, apparently, the exception of waking up in strange bedrooms after a day of cross-country travel.)

On the drive from the airport to the coastal town of Rockland, Effie and her father and sister danced politely around any real conversation until Ingrid blurted out the question Effie had been hoping to avoid. "After sixteen years away, why'd you come home now?" Effie pointed out how she'd come home for Ingrid's high school graduation and for a handful of Christmases. How both Ingrid and her father had visited her in New York, in Italy, and in San Francisco, where she'd been working as a professional chef. She didn't have the heart to tell them that she had returned this summer, for the *whole* summer, out of desperation only.

She didn't have words gentle enough to explain that Alder Isle always felt too small and a little stifling for her big career goals. And she didn't have the courage to tell them she'd just gotten fired from her dream job.

She had too much pride to admit that after years of globe-trotting with a knife bag and a few chef's coats, she was finally, undeniably, very regrettably broke. And that she was fresh out of backup plans. (Even now, in this strange bed, she wondered if she'd find the courage to be fully honest before September rolled around.)

When they reached Rockland, her dad drove his truck right by an enormous queue of cars. Although the ferry had been booked days ago and there was no more vehicle passage available, dear old dad sometimes played poker with the ticket scanner, so they were allowed to squeeze onto the midmorning boat. On the two-hour ride to Alder Isle, Effie successfully diverted every question about herself, instead coaxing Ingrid—a Generation Z financial prodigy who worked as a strategy consultant for one of the big crypto companies—to explain once again what an NFT was, and asking her father to share the updates from Meadowsweet Scoops, his ice cream shop in town. She bit her tongue to hold back questions about her childhood best friend. Effie knew he still lived in town, on the same street he'd grown up on. But she never asked about him specifically when her family shared island life updates. Probing about Ernie would have felt like ripping open an old wound. One that still smarted every time she touched it.

The ferry docked. They drove the half mile into town and then another half toward the library and school. Effie watched out the window as familiar scenery passed. She'd avoided this island for almost as long as she had lived on it, but it still looked, smelled, and sounded the same. Simple houses with graying shingles. Doors in varying shades of sea-foam green, teal, and marine blue. Porthole windows, unselfconsciously twee. Yellow lobster crates stacked five high in side yards. Piles of granite heaped next to front doors, passing as decor. Poppies and irises growing from cracks in the crumbling sidewalks. A pickup bumping down the road with two kids sitting on lawn chairs in the bed. Road dust. Bright sun. Screeching gulls. Dougie's lobster roll truck on the corner. The line outside it. A breeze. Salty air. Effie sighed. It wasn't home anymore, but it felt achingly familiar.

She hated that; hated that she still felt attached to a place she'd tried desperately to disown.

Alder Isle was a perfectly fine little island. If you didn't mind living a perfectly fine little life.

Her dad turned onto Haven Street and pulled the Tacoma

into their drive. Effie stepped out and looked up at the house, scrunched her nose. It was exactly the same. Two stories tall, weathered cedar shakes. The real ones, not the newer style shingles. Four four-paneled windows on the front. A lawn with grass way too long to be considered presentable and half a dozen "projects" scattered around the property, including a riding mower missing the seat. Effie's red Schwinn was leaning up against the garage, but, her father assured her, it had not been there for the last dozen-plus years. He'd put air in the tires and greased the chains and set it out for her arrival. To welcome her home. And because she didn't have a car. It was a vintage cruiser, and it looked its age. But it was hers. Her set of wheels for the next three months. The bossiest part of Effie's brain shouted she ought to be embarrassed about needing her childhood bicycle. But another, more tender part felt a fondness for it.

Effie waved goodbye to her sister, who started off toward the rented house she shared with her boyfriend, a cook at Brown Butter, a wildly popular, Michelin-starred restaurant. Well, good for Ingrid.

Not that Effie was jealous about the house or the boyfriend or even the good relationship her sister had with their mother since her parents' divorce.

She wasn't.

She'd rather live alone, out of a suitcase, for the rest of her life than settle down *here*.

Inside the house, Effie walked up the stairs, her extra-large luggage feeling extra heavy as it thumped against the wood flooring. The suitcase contained the contents of her entire life. She moved often and tried not to become too attached to any one place. It was risky, working in restaurants. She'd never met a restaurant owner she could trust, so she'd become nimble and efficiently self-sufficient. The downside of that strategy was that packing up and moving to a new city or country every year or so was financially devastating. After sixteen years in the business, Effie was financially, mentally, *and* emotionally devastated.

She heaved the suitcase onto the bed, and a bit of her thick, white-blond hair fell into her eye. Annoyed, she rummaged in her pocket for a bobby pin and stuck it in angrily, plastering the lock back into its ponytail. She looked around, further annoyed at the rogue corner of her heart that warmed at the familiar sameness of her childhood room. Same sky-blue shag rug, same white iron bedpost, same crinkly paper lamp hanging from the ceiling. Same collection of cookbooks and Alder Isle yearbooks on the shelf.

Same stupid lobster painting on the wall.

God, Maine was so predictable.

It would never be half as exciting as all the places Effie had traveled. But that was the appeal of this summer, wasn't it? There was safety in the steadiness.

She abandoned her suitcase and padded back downstairs to make a BLT for herself and a TLT for her dad. She used thick, center-cut bacon for herself; tofu for him. Beefsteak tomatoes on toasted white bread. A big smear of Cains mayonnaise. After eating and washing the dishes and leaving them to dry, they walked into town together, to the Meadowsweet Scoops shop. Her father had made a handful of upgrades to the shop, and Effie marveled at how modern and sophisticated it looked. She nodded as he described the state-of-the-art freezer and the elaborate toppings station that was big enough for four flavors of sprinkles. Meadowsweet Scoops had been her parents' pet project. And after they divorced almost twenty years ago, it became his everything.

"I love it, Dad," Effie said, and kissed him on the cheek.

He stayed to open the shop for the evening, and she walked back home, averting her eyes as she passed Brown Butter. She would see it soon enough. Effie let herself in the back door of her house—her *dad's* house, she corrected herself—changed into a pair of sneakers, and ran a quick two miles around the lower island.

She showered, then blow-dried her hair and tied it back into a medium-height tight bun. She hesitated briefly before undoing the pins and letting it hang in a ponytail. She paused above her suitcase, deciding what to wear before settling on a pair of cutoff shorts and a simple button-down. Effie may have been getting ready for a job interview, but she was also back in Alder Isle. No need to make any extra effort. No one else on the island ever bothered to. The permission to do a little less was, Effie realized, a refreshing change of pace.

And also, she didn't want to try too hard. Although the very broke part of her very much needed this job, the very prideful part hoped she wouldn't get it. She forced herself to look at the summer ahead rationally. Over the last sixteen years, Effie had done many things more difficult than cooking in a beautiful seaside restaurant. Even if that restaurant was located in her absurdly small, insufferably chatty hometown. Even if she no longer had any friends here; just ghosts and shameful memories. But hey, at least she'd get to work with the best produce, meat, and seafood Maine had to offer. The thought of fresh lobster, steaming and fire-engine red, made her mouth water. Maybe this wouldn't be so bad after all.

Maybe.

Effie made her way back into town. Back to the fine dining, farm-to-table restaurant that had opened three years ago. It was a Monday, one of Brown Butter's days off, and the parking lot was almost empty.

She entered the dining room. Passed the bar. Walked into the kitchen. She shook the hand of Jarrod Levi, Brown Butter's head chef. She tried not to notice his unruly dark curls tied back into a messy bun. The full sleeve of tattoos on his left arm. His angular jaw and dark eyes.

She tried not to notice the handful of sexist comments he dropped during her interview.

"So," Jarrod said as he led them back out to the dining room and motioned for her to sit on a barstool. "Why do you want to work here?"

Half an hour later, Jarrod offered her the role of Brown Butter's sous chef. His second-in-command. During their interview, he had asked why she'd been fired from her last job, and she gave him an appropriately self-deprecating answer. Told him she hadn't been ready for the responsibility of a head chef role. That she'd gotten in over her head. That to do that job—*his* job—you needed a skill set she simply didn't have. Jarrod had liked that answer. He hadn't said why the previous sous chef at Brown

Butter had left, but that didn't matter to Effie. All she needed was a job for the summer. Despite an angry inner voice that shouted at her to run away immediately, run back to California, or France, or Bali, or literally anywhere else in the world, Effie accepted his offer. Because, despite telling Jarrod she was in it for the long haul, Effie Olsen had no plans to stick around. All she had to do was survive until September and save enough money to leave Alder Isle.

Again. For good.

Fifteen minutes after the interview (currently-in-a-strange-bed Effie cursed quietly at the memory), they were drinking at Son of a Wharf, a shack by Pine Cove that would never pass health code but that had cheap, cold beer and greasy burgers. He was telling her about leaving his job at Eleven Madison Park in Manhattan for Brown Butter a few years ago. She was drinking a beer so fast, she felt woozy.

An hour after that, Effie and Jarrod were taking shots of Jameson and he was laughing loudly. She couldn't seem to stop touching his arm.

An hour after that, his hand was on her bare knee.

Fifteen minutes later, she was shrieking, "MORTON IS TOO GODDAMN SALTY!" and he was slamming his fist on the table, shouting back, "FUUUUCKING THANK YOU! DIAMOND KOSHER SALT OR NOTHING AT ALL!"

It was a little thing, a chef thing. A thing nobody else would have gotten. And it got Effie.

Effie had known from the start that she wanted nothing to do with Jarrod, but in her beer-and-whiskey haze she felt oddly comforted by him. By the fact he knew which kind of salt was the good stuff. By the fact that no one really understood line cooks . . . except other line cooks.

Five seconds later, he was kissing her. She was kissing him. It was hard and intense, and they both tasted like Pabst Blue Ribbon. She was twisting her fingers into his bun, yanking the elastic loose. She wanted her hands in his hair; wanted to get messy and feel wild. He was grabbing her rear, pulling her closer. He was throwing a wad of bills onto the table. She was searching her shoulder bag for an Altoid. He was reaching for her hand, she was squeezing his hand back, they were both stumbling through the dark, late-night streets to the restaurant.

Five minutes later, he was unlocking the back door and leading Effie up the stairs to his apartment above Brown Butter.

And four hours and fifty-nine minutes after that, Effie was waking up sweaty, with an aching skull and hollow heart, in his bed.

Chapter Two

From the way the light pooled on the mattress and warmed her belly, Effie could tell she was facing the window, away from Jarrod. She cautiously opened her eyes, keeping the rest of her body still. *Don't wake up, don't wake up, please don't wake up*, she silently begged him. A digital clock on the sill read 5:02. The windows were clouded with pollen and dust, and there were no curtains. She felt exposed, and flushed hot with shame as she brought her gaze to the floor. There was an empty pizza box, a six-pack of IPA with three cans missing, and a mountain of wrinkled laundry overflowing from a white plastic bin.

Clothes. Where were hers? She was wearing her denim shorts and underpants, but she was shirtless, and her white cotton bra was in a tiny heap by the door.

This was not good.

But was it bad?

She couldn't remember.

Effie turned over and faced Jarrod. He was sprawled on his back, and gave a soft snore. *Shitballs.* He was one hundred percent her type, starting with the tattoos and man bun, and ending with the man-child tendencies toward dirty jokes and inability to clean up after himself. Well, maybe that wasn't *actually* her type. Effie had standards; she was just able to conveniently ignore them. Not that there had been many men over the last sixteen years. Her arms and chest burned as a red blush crept up her neck. She'd slept with a handful of other chefs, but she had never, ever gotten involved with a coworker before. Why, after years working in professional kitchens, had she slipped last night?

Sure, he was sexy in that "dangerous man" sort of way, and *sure*, she'd been far from sober, but still . . . that cocktail of conditions had never triggered such a lapse in judgment before.

Alder Isle, she thought, and pulled the sheet up under her armpits, covering her breasts. Coming back had made her feel emotional and vulnerable. It was the stupid island's fault. She immediately felt itchy and wondered at the state of Jarrod's bedding. Or maybe her body was literally rejecting her hometown, in the form of an allergic reaction.

Jarrod made a snarfling sound and cracked an eyelid. "Oh hey," he mumbled, and rolled over to look at the clock. "Fuck no," he said, seeing the time, and turned over, closing his eyes again.

"Hey. Last night? Did we . . ." She needed to know, so she could calibrate the correct amount of regret for the next fifteen-to-fifty years.

"Have fun?" He opened both eyes. "If you have to ask, the answer's probably yes."

"No. I mean . . . did you . . . Did I?"

"Darlin', I don't know you well enough to know whether you did or not. But give me another few tries, and I'll know whether you're faking it." A little throw-up surged in the back of Effie's throat, and she grimaced.

"Did we have sex or what?" she asked impatiently.

"Nah," he said through a yawn, scratching his ribs. "Don't think so." She stared daggers at him. "Hold on, Jesus," he said, climbing out of the bed and fumbling for his jeans on the ground. Effie turned her face away, already trying to forget the way he looked naked. She didn't want to see him like this, vulnerable and imperfect. The illusion of him last night—hot and unknown—was hard enough to reconcile with the fact he was her boss. She pulled the sheet farther up around herself. *Damnit, Effie.*

"Nope," he said, pulling an unopened condom from the pocket and flicking it in her direction. It landed on the sheet above her stomach. "Seems like we had some self-control, or just fell asleep first." He scrubbed his hand over a jawline peppered with two-day stubble. "How much did we drink last night?"

"I lost track after the Jamo," she said. "Too much."

"Too much, yeah." He raked his eyes over her, as if just realizing she was still there, still mostly naked. "You wanna . . . ?" He gestured halfheartedly at himself.

Would rather die. "I gotta get home," Effie said.

"Cool. I gotta take a piss; hold on." He strode down the hall, way too cocky for 5:00 a.m. She yanked the sheet from the mattress, covering herself as she stumbled to retrieve her bra. The room spun as she clasped the band together underneath the sheet, then pulled the straps up over her shoulders. Her shirt was nowhere in sight, so she tiptoed past the bathroom and into the kitchen. *Ah, lovely.* It had been flung over a saucepot on the stovetop. She retrieved it, making a face at the hem that had been marinating in starchy, cold pasta water all night. She decided to wait for Jarrod in the kitchen rather than venture back into his nightmare of a bedroom, and was just about to sink onto one of the swivel stools when a giant white chest freezer in the corner caught her eye.

"Weird," she murmured. Most chefs she knew—herself included—didn't keep their home kitchens stocked with ingredients. After a long day spent cooking for other people, the menu included two options: boxed macaroni and cheese and cold cereal. She opened the lid and let out an accidental low whistle. The freezer was neatly organized but stuffed to the brim with vacuum-sealed packages. They all contained what looked to be a pound or two of meaty grayish-white fish, gutted and cleaned and ready to cook. Effie picked up a package and turned it over. There was no label, no date. Another curious anomaly: *every* chef she knew was obsessive about labeling and organizing their food.

"Looking for a body?" Jarrod's voice got louder as he got closer, moving toward her from the hallway. She dropped the package with a clatter and released the freezer lid so quickly, it snapped shut on her middle finger. She pulled it out and shook it, then guiltily met his gaze.

"Unless it's hiding underneath the lifetime supply of monkfish, I didn't see one." She hoped her sassy tone covered up the anxious feeling ricocheting around in her stomach.

His eyes narrowed.

She shrugged. "I lived in Maine for a long time. Used to know some fishermen and lobstermen. But if you were stockpiling lobster, I'd assume you'd want to keep the meat in the shell. For presentation, or whatever." She surreptitiously wiped a small pool of sweat from her inner elbows with her opposite forearms. "So, why do you have a crap-ton of fish in a chest freezer?"

Jarrod closed the gap between them in two big steps and crushed his mouth against her neck. "Fuck the fish. Why does your hair look so much better down around your face like that? Why do you smell like rosemary after a night of drinking? Why are you trying to leave so early when I just want to go down on you until I hear my name coming from those pretty lips? Damn girl, why are you so irresistible?"

"Stop," Effie said, the word firm and heavy enough to form a physical barrier between them. She knew he didn't mean anything he'd just said, but it was embarrassingly clear he was just avoiding the question. Whatever. Let him be sketchy with his doomsday-prepper freezer full of second-class lobster. He stepped away.

She spoke. "Obviously this was a huge mistake. I don't normally do this. Never—I never do this." She sucked in a sharp breath and her tone turned stoic. "I'll understand if you don't want to go forward with hiring me," she said, expecting the worst. It wouldn't be the first time her emotions had gotten in the way of her job.

"Ellie," he said, shaking his head.

"Effie," she corrected him sharply. "My name is Effie."

"Sorry," he said, although if it was true, it didn't sound genuine. "Do you know how many classically trained chefs who've worked in France, Italy, New York, *and* California I interviewed this week?"

"You forgot Bali."

"That doesn't count."

"It did to me."

"Fine, and Bali. How many cooks did I interview?"

"One," Effie said. She might have been ashamed in the moment, but she still knew she had a resume to be proud of.

"One," Jarrod confirmed. "And she's got long blond hair and thighs like steel."

One of Effie's hands floated up to touch her hair, the other tugged at the hem of her shorts. She just wanted to get out of there and start the hard work of forgetting this.

"I'm not going to fire you. Or unhire you. Or whatever." Jarrod said.

"And work will be chill?"

"Work will be stressful as shit, because it's Brown Butter and it's a Michelin star. You know that, darlin'." She did. She was not a darlin', but she knew that. She knew that Brown Butter had recently earned its first star from the prestigious international restaurant reviewing organization. And she had, until last month, worked at a two-star restaurant. Despite the two-star rating being one star shy of perfect, it was a breeding ground for big-time stress. "But yeah, we're cool," he finished.

"And you won't say anything about this? To anyone?" She pulled at the elastic hairband on her wrist, snapping it against her skin.

"So long as you don't say anything about my freezer o' fish."

"Nobody's going to care about that. This—" Effie motioned to the uncomfortably narrow space between them. "This is career-ending stuff."

He barked out a laugh. "No, it's not."

"It is if you're a woman."

He looped his index finger through her belt loop and hung on loosely. "I won't say anything. Not about last night, not about the next time I get you in bed, not about the time after that."

"There is no next time!" Effie whisper-shouted, aware there might be prep cooks in the restaurant downstairs. She didn't know the schedule yet; didn't know who worked when. "I mean, I'm here to work my ass off. That's it."

"Sure thing," Jarrod said. His gaze drifted to the buttons on her shirt, which she'd closed up incorrectly in her haste to get dressed. "See you tomorrow, Allie."

She didn't look back as she walked away, undoing and rebuttoning her chambray shirt as she went.

As she reached the top of the stairs, she heard him chuckle, faint but unmissable. She ran down the steps, taking them two at a time, and slammed the door behind her, blinking into the bright Maine morning.

Chapter Three

Until this stupidly sunny day, Effie had never given much weight to the phrase "Walk of Shame." But here she was, literally scuffling home at sunrise. She turned her head toward the harbor as she passed The Gull's Perch. It was open early, serving breakfast for the lobstermen. Effie was sure Gertie was still cooking up pancakes and bacon. She was hungry, but she didn't want to run into the first employer she'd ever had. Not like this.

Back on Haven Street, Effie slipped in the back door. Her dad had never locked it when she was growing up, and he apparently didn't now. On an island with fifteen hundred people, "Why bother?" he'd said. She tiptoed up the stairs, skipping the creaky one at the top. She willed him to stay asleep as she slipped past the primary bedroom into her own, thankful for the rug that muffled her footsteps. It was a dance she'd done dozens of times as a teenager, sneaking in late. She snuck not because she would've gotten in trouble—she didn't have a curfew and her dad had never once grounded her. She snuck because waking him up meant suffering through an hour of chitchat and a mug of his overly bitter, very yellow turmeric tea.

She collapsed onto the navy blue papasan chair and screwed up her face. Deep inhale. Bigger exhale. She let out an effortful howl, like a feral kitten, but no tears came. Effie wasn't a crier. She hadn't cried when her parents divorced and her mom left for good. Effie had been fourteen and angry; her sister, four years old and confused. Effie didn't cry when, on graduation night, her best friend, Ernie, told her to forget he ever existed. She didn't cry during any of the hundreds of times her male coworkers and bosses berated her during dinner service.

Effie didn't cry when, three weeks ago, she was fired from her job as the head chef at Cowboy Bean, one of the hottest restaurants in San Francisco. In California. In the whole country.

Effie didn't cry because if she cried, she felt weak, and her entire career had been one long test of her strength. She wasn't weak. She sat up straighter, which, irritatingly, was difficult to do in a papasan chair. She slowed her breathing enough to calm her mind.

She let her eyes wander over the bookshelves, past the collection of cookbooks and onto the stack of yearbooks. Magnetically drawn to the one with the year 2007 embossed on the spine, she pulled it from the stack and let it fall open on her lap. Her senior year. The book had opened on a page of extracurricular photos, and she smiled as the pictures ignited memories. There was a shot of track practice; of Ernie and her and some other kids, Olive and Luke. Effie remembered teaching Olive how to clear hurdles without losing any speed. In the picture, Effie had her hand on Ernie's shoulder and was stretching her quad. They both looked so young. She flipped to the senior portraits and found Ernie's. She shook her head, her hair shimmering down around her shoulders. *How could I have not seen it?*

She slammed the yearbook shut, sixteen-year-old wounds stinging as sharply as if they'd been doused with an ocean's worth of salt. When she was a kid, her friendship with Ernie had been the only thing on the island that didn't feel awkward and tight; the only thing that felt remotely like home. And now they were strangers. But it wasn't her fault, what happened on graduation night.

She re-shelved the yearbook, and her mind fast-forwarded to a few weeks from now. She pictured her future self at the restaurant pass, inspecting each plate of risotto or striped bass or roasted chicken before it went out to customers in the dining room. Garnishing each one with torn basil leaves and snipped chives. Adding a crack of black pepper. Making it look perfect. Keeping her mind on the food; not getting involved in restaurant drama. Not letting her emotions get in the way. She pictured herself a few months from now, with enough money saved up to move somewhere new. Maybe somewhere in Scandinavia this time. She could vibe with a menu full of tiny tree roots and pickled moss, or at least she could pretend to. The important thing was to keep moving. She imagined herself brave enough to take on another head chef role. It was the title she'd been working toward her whole career. Too bad her first shot at it had turned into such a disaster.

She pictured herself far away from Alder Isle, with a second chance at the top job. She pictured herself happy.

It would happen. She could make it. All she had to do until then was keep her head on straight, do her job for three months, squirrel away those paychecks, and not get distracted. Nobody and nothing, especially not some tiny island, was going to keep Effie down.

However. That new job didn't start until tomorrow, and right now what Effie needed was exercise. Restaurant workers had a reputation for living the hard and fast life—late nights; greasy, salty food at 3:00 in the morning; cocaine and hard liquor—but Effie was part of a smaller faction who fought against that stereotype (last night being a regrettable, if rare, exception). There was no room for that sort of thing if you wanted to rise through the ranks. Rule breakers weren't disciplined enough to stick around the cutthroat, perfection-required environment of a restaurant. She'd learned that fast, and now she lived a rigid and regimented life, in and out of the kitchen. Effie thrived on rules. Rules about relationships (don't get too close to anyone, ever) and rules about routines (stick to them).

It hadn't always been that way. When she was younger, Effie had been wild and free, spontaneous and chaotic; the type of kid who would accidentally put on two mismatched socks and forget to comb her hair for three days. The type of kid who yelled too loud when she got excited, laughed at everything, and spoke without thinking. She'd been a handful; that was the word she regularly heard her mother use. And look how *that* had worked out. Nobody wanted a handful. So, slowly she changed. When she was at work, Effie tried to make herself small and neat and tidy and helpful.

Rules made her feel safe.

Routines helped her feel calm.

It was almost funny how, after less than twenty-four hours back on Alder Isle, she was leaping before she looked—or thought about the consequences.

Almost funny.

She brushed her teeth and splashed water on her face, then took the stairs two at a time down to the yard to retrieve the red Schwinn that was glossier and sleeker than any decades-old bike had the right to be. She shoved her towel into a tote bag and heaved it up over her shoulder. She swung one leg over the bike, then pedaled away from town. She had decided to do what teenager Effie would've done after a hard night. She'd go for a swim.

On the eastern side of the island was a rocky public beach with parking spaces for a few cars. It was never busy, because most people swam at the warmer, smaller abandoned mining quarries closer to town. But if you walked a quarter mile north through the woods, you'd reach another secluded little cove. Locals didn't bother with it; the water was too cold, and the beach was too steep. Tourists didn't know about it. It just so happened to be Effie's favorite place on Alder Isle. When she was twelve, she and Ernie had named it Dulse Cove for the squishy seaweed that floated around its edges. Her breath caught in her throat as she took the curves dangerously fast.

Ernie. Why couldn't her mind stop touching that memory? She'd safely avoided it for years.

Ernie was still on Alder Isle. She was sure of it. He wasn't the leaving type. She'd thought about that when she made the decision to come back. But he had essentially told her to drop dead in 2007, and they'd never spoken again. What was she supposed to do, send him a pin of her location with the message *u up?* There was no way she could avoid him for an entire summer, but there was also no reason to seek him out. They'd see each other when they saw each other. No amount of planning could make that meeting go smoothly. It would be weird, and he would get awkward, and she'd probably say something accidentally mean, and they may even laugh about stuff. If they were lucky.

She jumped off her bike and ditched it behind a large rock, then jogged down the overgrown trail, pulling her tank top up over her head. At home, she'd changed into her swimsuit, a high-waisted bikini with marigold-colored bottoms and a sporty emerald green top. She could hear the waves gently lapping. It was low tide. The air felt heavy and wet, and it smelled like brine and oysters and cold mud.

As she approached the beach, she stopped short. There was a pair of beat-up sneakers and a gray T-shirt by the shore. She wasn't alone. Annoyance immediately tugged the corners of her mouth into a frown. This was *her* spot. *Hers.* Nobody else even knew about it. Nobody except . . .

Effie lifted her gaze from the pile of clothes to the shoreline. There, emerging from the water with glistening skin and dripping hair, was Ernie Callahan.

Chapter Four

It was like her thoughts had summoned him.

Effie blinked and shook her head. He hadn't yet noticed her, and she took the opportunity to study him in the early morning sunlight. Unlike the rest of Alder Isle, he'd changed.

Okay, yes. His red-blond hair was wet and flat, but she could tell it was still styled like a 1990s dreamboat, middle part and floppy sides and all. Although she couldn't see from the distance, she knew his eyes were the same shade of pale gray blue. Like a junco's wing, her father would have said. Did say, once. But that was where the familiarity stopped. Sometime in the last sixteen years, everything else about Ernie Callahan had grown up.

His chest and shoulders had graduated from skinny to muscular and lean, with strong-looking forearms. He had a swimmer's build, finally, to match his water-loving heart. In spite of herself, she smirked when she noticed the touch of pink around his collarbone. That boy always burned so easily. But his abs had never been that . . . *damn*. Effie lifted her hair off her neck and quickly tied it into a low ponytail. She felt hot, and her inner elbows were awfully sweaty. Ernie came closer. He'd noticed the figure on the beach and gave a friendly wave. He must not have recognized her. The Ernie she'd left on graduation night wouldn't be so casually cheerful. She kept staring, too shocked to look away. His waist was whittled down to a narrow *V* with the faintest trail of hair at the band of his swim trunks. She chanced a look at his face, afraid to catch his eye, and saw that his bone structure looked more mature, too. Gone were the cute, toothy grin and chubby cheeks. The man on the beach was all strong jaw and defined cheekbones. Even the explosion of freckles that covered his entire upper half, from forehead to hip bones, seemed sexier, like they'd been chosen as carefully as a fashionable outfit.

She checked herself. This was her former BFF she was ogling. Absolutely not. She had already decided she was not going down that road. Almost sixteen years ago exactly. It was a choice that had cost her their friendship, but it had been the right one. True, they were older now, and more mature. But even the Pop-Rocks-and-Coke sensation dancing on her tongue wasn't enough to convince her that her instinct to tackle him to the ground and kiss him—hard—was a good idea.

Effie shook off the spell his slow walk out of the ocean had cast. Just in time, because now he was standing in front of her, close enough for her to confirm: yep. Same slate blue eyes. Same extra-dense spray of freckles across the bridge of his nose.

"Oh. Hey, Effie."

"Hey, Ern."

"You're standing on my towel."

She took a half step to the left and he reached down to grab it. She felt his breath dance over her knees as he rose to stand, meeting her eyes again. He looked good. She was nervous. None of this made any sense. She suddenly wanted him close, closer than he'd just been. Closer than he'd ever gotten in all the time she'd known him.

But she wasn't going to admit any of that. Not to herself, not to him, not ever. Instead, she said with what she hoped was a lighthearted eye roll, "That's it? After sixteen years . . . that's all I get? 'You're standing on my towel'?"

Ernie tousled his hair with the towel and shook it out. "I haven't exactly been practicing the perfect opener. You told me you were never coming back to Alder Isle, remember?" He let that sink in. "What are you doing here? Visiting your pops?"

Effie's chest splotched with red. She crossed her arms and hunched, drawing her shoulders in close to hide her embarrassment. "I'm back for the summer, actually. I was in California, but . . ." She paused, her lips still parted. She'd already foiled her plan. Everyone had to believe she'd come back for good; Jarrod wouldn't have hired her for such an important job for only a season. But she'd just told Ernie the truth without even thinking. They used to share everything with the promise "No secrets, no lies." They'd seal the intention by drawing an *X* over their chests. But she barely recognized the Ernie standing in front of her; she didn't owe him that kind of bare honesty. She finished in a rush: "I was in California, but I decided to spend a few months at home. Baby sister's growing up, Dad's not getting any younger, all that."

"I know what you mean." A rain cloud crossed over Ernie's face, and it was somehow worse than the chilly, distanced look in his eyes. "How long you been back?"

"A day. Not even."

"What've you been up to?"

"Fucking around and getting into trouble."

And there it was. The tiniest dimple at the corner of Ernie's lip. It betrayed his biggest laughs. The ones that got Effie going, too. The dimple grew now as his eyes got lighter, and he did laugh. It sounded familiar, but older. Wiser and more confident. Still just as gentle. "Oh, Effie. Get over here."

He opened his arms wide with the towel held up behind him like wings. She stepped forward and snuggled in. Their height difference was still the same—her five foot five to his five foot ten—and her cheek landed on his chest as if nothing had changed. Even though, of course, it had. It all had. He used to hold her like this all the time. Except back then, she hadn't known what was in his heart when she was in his arms. She wrapped her own arms around his waist now, and his found their way around her back, the towel covering them both. His skin was chilly from the sea and still a little wet; her shorts clung to her body as they absorbed the seawater. He smelled like Dr. Bronner's almond soap. Like a marzipan cookie.

"Don't be mad at me anymore," Effie whispered into his armpit as he kissed the top of her head. Her stomach surged in a new and unfamiliar way.

He stepped back, just an inch, just enough so he could slide his knuckle under her chin and bring their eyes to meet. Her heart hammered in her chest. She felt shaky but his embrace was strong. "Hey, I . . ."

Absolutely not. Whatever he had to say about the last time she saw him, she wasn't ready to hear it.

"Race you to the water!" Effie shouted as she broke away from him and tore down the beach, expertly skipping her way over the jagged rocks and yanking out her hair elastic. When she got to the seaweed and sand, she stripped off her shorts and turned around to toss them over Ernie's head. He was right behind her, and she scored, the nylon fabric covering his face. She laughed loudly and shook her head, her locks flowing freely as she splashed into the ocean, her knees up high. The water was arrestingly cold; it took her breath away as it hit her stomach. She didn't stop because she knew it was too easy to lose your nerve. Too easy to give up and retreat if you didn't plow through like you had never been scared at all.

He was hot on her heels, chasing her through the first ten yards. Once the grade steepened and the water got deeper, she slipped underneath and swam for a few seconds before surfacing. When she bobbed up, Ernie was gone. She looked around, momentarily worried before feeling both his hands wrap around her ankle and pull her under. "ERNIE CALLAHAN!" she shrieked, the last two syllables of his name bubbling with seawater. They play-fought under the surface, pulling each other close and pushing away, before rising once more, gasping for breath. They were close enough to shore to touch the sandy-muddy earth, and Effie sank down, so she was almost entirely covered by the water.

She licked her lips; she had swallowed a mouthful of ocean

and tasted salt. "You got faster," she said, sinking even lower. She was now in almost up to her chin. His shoulders and chest, dotted with a night's sky worth of freckle constellations, were above the water.

"Did I? Or did you just get slower? What's that mile time now, track star?"

"Kindly fuck right off," she said, laughing. "It's eight minutes, eight-ten if I've had a couple beers the night before. Don't judge. I got old."

"No judgment, Eff," he said, and gave her a sideways glance to see if she'd notice the reappearance of his special nickname for her. How could she not?

"You still pole vaulting?"

"Oh yeah, every morning before work," he said, then quickly added, "JK."

Effie smiled at the abbreviation. They may have grown up, but they'd forever be millennials. She danced her fingertips over the water. He cupped his palms together and squirted some at her face. There was the briefest of pauses when she wondered if she should bring it up—the big fight they'd had so many years ago—but he spoke first. "Wanna get breakfast? The Gull's Perch is still open for another couple hours and I have a feeling that a biscuit sandwich ought to help your hangover."

"Who says I'm hungover?"

Ernie knocked her shoulder with his own. "You don't look as green as the morning after prom, but I know a hungover Effie when I see one."

"I honestly still cannot look at peach schnapps without feeling ill."

"I honestly never could."

She rolled her eyes, and without speaking, counted down on her fingers from five. When she reached one, they both dove underwater and swam for shore.

Chapter Five

Effie never thought she'd be back here, at the corner booth at The Gull's Perch. But then again, in the last twenty-four hours, she'd gone a few places she'd sworn she wouldn't.

"Wow, Ern. You look exactly the same," she lied, finger combing the knots from her hair.

"Thanks?"

"Not the *same*. Clearly somebody's been lifting weights in his spare time." He blushed and dramatically whipped open the plastic-backed menu, pretending to study it intently.

They were in their usual positions, she on the bench with the ripped vinyl seating, he with the view into the kitchen's dish pit. She fiddled with her paper straw wrapper as the teenage waitress filled their tall red cups with ice water. Effie had started at The Gull's Perch as a server, and immediately hated it. Carrying scalding-hot coffee carafes and balancing plates was no problem. But making chitchat with the same twenty, thirty people she'd see ten, fifteen more times that week around the island was awkward. Effie wasn't what you'd call a small-talk kind of person. Unlike Ernie, who liked everyone. After a week of pretending to care about customers' egg preferences, she asked Gertie if she could work in the kitchen instead, and the rest? Well . . . the rest had gotten complicated.

"Hi, Ernie! And Ernie's friend! D'you know what you want?" the server asked, clicking open a pen. Effie assumed the waitress was bored just like she'd been, but she did a good job playing her role. Alder Isle kids were overwhelmingly wholesome. Yet one more reason she had never fit in. They were supremely likable. Like Mouseketeers, with less musical skills.

Ernie raised his eyebrows at Effie, indicating she go first.

"What kinds of muffins do you have today?"

"Hmm . . . there's a fresh batch just out the oven, but I'm not sure what flavor."

From the kitchen, a voice shouted over the clatter of dishes. "Take a bite and find out, Jessalyn. Effie don't mind, do she?"

Effie's stomach flipped nervously as her old boss approached their table. It had been so long since she'd seen Gertie. Jessalyn poured coffee, then went to check out the baked goods. Despite promising to stay in touch when she left for culinary school, Effie hadn't dropped so much as a postcard in the mail for Gertie. She felt guilty now, confronting one of the actual humans who'd been a victim of Effie's effort to erase herself from Alder Isle's story.

Well. Another one of the humans.

Effie had no clue what she'd say, but she checked her instinct to hightail it out of the restaurant and straight onto the docked ferry at the pier. "Gert." She stood and waved, stuck between the bench and the table. "How's business? How are *you*?"

"Business is good, so I'm good." Gertie didn't miss a beat. She reached over and grabbed Effie's hands, rubbing her own thumbs into Effie's palms.

"Girl's got calluses now," Gertie said, cracking a smile. "You still cheffin'?"

"Only thing I know how to do," Effie said.

"Good on you."

Effie flushed, this time with pride. Gertie's praise always meant the most. How had she forgotten that? She was so fixated on hating this interaction, she hadn't realized it might feel good, too.

"Where you workin' now?"

"Well . . . here." Effie directed the words to her sandals.

Gertie looked skeptical.

"Alder Isle, I mean. Not *here*, here."

"You been in town this whole time and I ain't know it?"

"Oh, no. I just got back. Yesterday. Starting tomorrow, I'm the sous chef at Brown Butter."

Across the table, Ernie spat out a mouthful of coffee. It sprayed all over the Formica, and he set his mug down with a clatter.

Gertie tossed a terry-cloth towel to him. He caught it, his ears brilliantly crimson. "Coffee too hot for you, son?"

"Sorry, I just thought . . ." He lifted the mug and wiped underneath and in the crook of the handle. "I could've sworn you said you were working at Brown Butter."

"I did. I am."

"Ahh . . ." Ernie mopped at the table.

"Problem?" Effie sat back down and stared at him.

"No. I mean, not for me."

Gertie cough-laughed, grabbed her towel from Ernie, who was in the middle of folding it neatly into thirds, and retreated to the kitchen.

"Is there something about Brown Butter I should know?"

"Just that," he met her gaze, confidence regained, "I work there too."

It was Effie's turn to struggle with the coffee. She swallowed hard, the liquid burning as it went down. As long as she'd known Ernie, he had wanted to work as a lobsterman. Just like his father.

"I thought you were going to take over for your dad. Inherit his boat, ride off into the sunset with a five-pound lobster sidekick named Claws."

"Things change. My dad had cancer. Melanoma. No doubt from being on that darn boat for five decades without sunscreen."

"Oh, Ern, shit. I mean—I'm sorry. Is he . . . ?" *Still sick.* She couldn't bring herself to finish the question. Her dad had never mentioned Mick Callahan on their calls, and Effie hadn't inquired about either father or son. She didn't want to seem like she cared. But now, she realized, she did. She cared a lot.

Ernie lifted his mug to his lips. He blew on it, breath skittering across the surface. Effie studied him from across the table and realized she couldn't read him. Either she'd forgotten how or he was holding his cards close. "He's okay now, in remission. Salty old bastard is stubborn, if nothing else."

"And we love him for it." Effie reached across the table for Ernie's hand but changed her mind at the last moment and pulled away. She couldn't look at him after that, so she focused on folding her wrapper into a miniature accordion. "Is that when you gave up lobstering, too?"

"Yeah. I did work for him. Right after graduation, up until the wheels fell off. Or rather, the hull got cracked," he deadpanned, and Effie gave him a blank look. "Little boating metaphor that did not land at all. Wow, this is weird. Being back here with you. Making jokes and talking about cancer. Are you sweating as much as I'm sweating right now?"

"No," Effie said. She was sweating on the inside and that didn't count.

But she did feel nervous.

Nervous about being here. Nervous about big conversations. Nervous about the way her heart tightened when her gaze snagged on his.

Why? If it was just because he looked good, why did her entire body feel so fluttery?

"I was going to take over his business when he passed. That man was never going to retire. But then the bills started coming. Do you know how much it costs in this country to be sick? A lot. More if you don't have health insurance."

"Oh . . ."

"I mean, he was an independent lobsterman. It's not like he had some company contributing to a 401(k) and insurance policy. You think he would've been better prepared, after my mom. But . . ." Ernie sat up straighter and placed his hands on the table. "Knowing the right thing and having the resources to do it are two entirely different places to be."

"Did you have to—"

"Sell the boat? Yep. Cages, too. Every little thing."

Effie frowned at her hands. She'd mindlessly shredded the paper into confetti. "The house?" She had always loved Ernie's house. It was right on the water, next to the footbridge to Cleary Island. Tidy, orderly, impeccably clean; it defied every bachelor pad stereotype. Together, Mick and Ernie had converted their old boathouse into a small apartment for Ernie when he started high school. Ernie's mother had passed away when he was five, and instead of despairing, Ernie's dad dug in his heels and did the work of both parents. The Callahan house was nothing like the Olsen house, which was cluttered and chaotic, stuffed to the gills with tchotchkes and curiosities. Her house made her brain hurt. Ernie's helped soothe it.

Mick had often felt more like a parent than her own. When Effie was young, her mom was sullen and withdrawn. Her dad was always working on some creative project or half-baked dream. Making his own candles. Strumming away on the ukulele. A particularly ill-advised foray into welding. Knowing this, Mick regularly invited Effie to stay for dinner. He would serve sloppy joes on fluffy potato buns or tuna noodle casserole topped with extra buttery breadcrumbs because that's how she liked it. He'd check over both kids' homework, and let them pick out whatever movie they wanted to rent, even if it was a school night. Sometimes, after the credits rolled, Effie would bike back home and climb the stairs to her bedroom without even seeing her own parents. But just as often, she and Ernie would fall asleep on the couch and Mick would let them be, pulling a wool Pendleton blanket over them and turning off the lights. He might've telephoned over to her house, but just as likely might not've. Everyone knew Ernie and Effie were inseparable. If they weren't at her house, they were at his. But they were always, always together.

After Ingrid came along and her parents divorced, Effie spent almost every night at Ernie's—by then he and Mick had fixed up the boathouse. With the absence of her mother, the hours after school became a blur of obligations for Effie. First, there was track, where she always stayed late to practice with the other hurdlers. Then, while her father worked the after-dinner rush at Meadowsweet Scoops, she stayed home to babysit her little sister. At 9:05 sharp, once Samuel returned home from the shop, she bolted to Ernie's and let the stresses and obligations of the day melt away, usually crashing into the boathouse with a loud, "Faaaaahck!"

Cursing helped relieve some of the tension. It was also fun to make Ernie blush.

In high school, Effie and Ernie never talked about their parallel experiences having single fathers, despite the fact hers had regularly referred to them all as "Effie and Ernie and their Rad Dads." Not to say she couldn't have brought it up. Ernie would have had the conversation. But there was no way she could have stomached his pity.

But he needed sympathy now. He deserved her ear. She could give that much. "Your house? Did you have to sell that, too?" she prompted gently.

"No, thankfully that was the only thing we held on to. It's not much, but it's the most important. He's owned it outright for years, but it's an old house. Seems like every day, something new breaks, molds, or outright gives up. He could fix everything, you know he's more than capable, but . . ." Ernie spoke the next words into his lap with a self-deprecating smile teasing at his mouth. "I stick around because I like to feel useful."

Effie didn't know what to say next, but at that moment Gertie came back with three plates balanced between her hands and forearms. "Cheez Whiz omelet for you, Mr. Callahan. One sausage breakfast sandwich, extra cheddar, for Effie. And pancakes for the table. The muffins are apple and cinnamon. Not your favorite."

"What's my favorite?"

"Strawberry rhubarb."

How did Gertie remember her order after all these years? When did Ernie develop a taste for Cheez Whiz? There wasn't enough coffee in the world to dig into that second question. Effie's eyes took in the food, on big plates and piled high. Her biscuit was fat and crumbly, and a puddle of hot cheese was melting down the side. A pat of butter was seeping into the pancake stack. Ernie's omelet was glistening with fat. She sighed, just a little. Quietly. This spread was a far cry from her normal green juice, but maybe one day of indulgence wouldn't be the end of the world . . .

"Thanks, Gert," she said as the older woman waved her off and went to check on the fryer.

"Anyway, it's fine," Ernie said. "My problem, not yours."

"Don't say that."

He paused, midway through slicing a bite from his omelet. "Why not, when it's true?"

He had a point.

"So that's why you're not lobstering. How did you end up at Brown Butter? You don't cook."

"You don't know that."

"Well, you didn't in high school."

"I didn't do a lot of things in high school that I do now." The corner of his lip quirked, almost imperceptibly.

Suddenly, Effie *was* sweating.

"Brown Butter opened not long after Pop's diagnosis, and that was right about the time we had to sell the boat and stuff. I'm actually a pretty good cook. I taught myself with all the cookbooks you used to borrow from the library. Which you would know if you'd ever stopped by when you came back for your twenty-four-hour whirlwind visits." She started to protest, but he spoke over her sputtering. "You seriously thought I didn't know all the times you came back? If you believe the residents of Alder Isle don't make it their business to know every person who walks off that ferry three times a day, every day, you have forgotten what it's like to be a resident of Alder Isle." *True.* "It's fine, I'm not offended. Although I always kind of hoped that Facebook friend request you sent me at 3:00 a.m. one night in 2012? 2013? wasn't just a drunken regret."

"Yeah . . . sorry about that. I blame tequila."

"All good. I enjoyed looking through the seven pictures you've posted over the last decade."

"You're one to talk!" She'd spoken louder than she had intended; had almost yelled. "You post *nothing.* I was hoping for some clue as to who you'd become. That you were okay. Engagement pictures with some hot out-of-towner or something . . ."

"Interesting. You know what would have gotten you that information?" He leaned back and laced his fingers together behind his head. "Stopping by the boathouse. Calling me."

"Yeah. Well. You never called me."

"Because you never called me."

He was getting her riled up and combative. She took a couple of shallow breaths and tried to calm her heartbeat. "So. Brown Butter opens, and you . . . ?" Her prompt brought them back to the more recent past.

"I interviewed and got the job. Unfortunately, I'm not a 'real' cook." He made air quotes and twisted his mouth into a frown. "I'm the butcher and prep guy. Mostly, I break down the meat and fish. It comes in whole. I'm sure that's how it is in all restaurants." Effie shook her head—in-house butchery was certainly not standard in all restaurants. Only the good ones. "And then I do stuff like chop onions, peel carrots. It's not so bad, except for the fact I have to work in the basement like a troll."

"Wow," Effie said. Lobstering was in Ernie's blood. It was all he'd ever wanted to do. It was why he swore Alder Isle would be his forever home. Without his boat, what was there left for him to love on this island?

"But it's not as bad as working under Jarrod, which—if you haven't met him yet, I'm sorry to spoil the surprise." Ernie cut another bite with the edge of his fork. "He truly sucks. Be careful."

"I'll be fine," she said, lifting the top of her biscuit and dousing the mound of melted cheese with an irresponsible amount of hot sauce. "I've met Jarrod. He's awful. He's the boss. I'm better than him. But that's restaurant life." She took a huge bite and screwed her eyes up, fighting the urge to primal scream at the Tabasco abusing the back of her throat. As she swallowed, she realized something. "Hey. I meant it, what I said at the beach. That I'm in town for just a few months. I did want to visit my dad; that wasn't a lie." She flicked her eyes down at her knees, embarrassed by the next part. "I'm kind of very broke. I need this job. And Jarrod and the whole crew at the restaurant need to think I'm sticking around for good. Nobody hires a sous chef for just a season. So don't blow my cover?"

"You got it," Ernie said, and despite the disapproval (or was it disappointment?) in his voice, Effie believed him.

They ate the rest of their breakfast in silence, the sound of cutlery against Gertie's chipped porcelain plates loud enough to drown out the chatter around them. Finally, with just three bites of pancake left, Ernie sighed deeply and ran his hand through his hair, the ends flopping into his eyes. Everything felt weird.

Effie shoved the pancake plate closer to him. "You finish these. You know what? I feel like a massive jerk for not knowing about your dad."

"If anything, you're a small-to-medium-sized jerk." She wanted to laugh but kept it inside. He pushed the plate back to her. "I know things were—are?—complicated, but I did miss being your friend. I wish we had kept in touch."

An unmanageable amount of emotions reached a rolling boil

in Effie's heart. She speared the pancake stack with her fork and shoved the whole thing in her mouth at once. "Me too." Her voice was muffled behind the flour, butter, and syrup. She reached for a battered nylon wallet in her tote bag. Extracting a twenty she really couldn't afford to lose, she swallowed and stood. "Brekkie's on me," she said, tossing the money onto the table and turning before it landed. "See you at work, I guess? I gotta go!" She made for the door quickly, but not quickly enough to miss Ernie's irritated groan.

"Yeah," he said as she gave a quick wave to Gertie and beelined for the door. "What else is new?"

Chapter Six

Ernie, Ernie, Ernie. Ernie. ERNIE GODDAMN it all to hell. He'd been her best friend for years, and now . . . Spending just an hour with him had given her whiplash. She wanted to curl into his arms, and she wanted to tear off his gray T-shirt and press her mouth against his skin and she could not, should not, *would not* do any of those things. She had to get him out of her head—out of her system entirely—or this whole summer was going to be a disaster.

She needed to think. Instead of heading home, she turned the bike's front wheel toward the path to Cleary Island. It was a deer tick of a landmass, barely registered on a map, but it was home to a nature preserve and a few houses overlooking the harbor. It was a private sort of place, nice if you didn't mind the gulls. She rode over the bridge and ditched her bike, walked into the scrubby bushes past the wild beach peas all the way to the rocks. She climbed onto the biggest one, then lay flat on her back and screamed.

When she sat up, she heard country music from the water. Dougie was out on his boat in the cove, and he waved. "Fuck's sake," Effie said, and waved back. You were never alone here.

She massaged her temples. For such a small place with nothing to do, things always got complicated real fast. She let her mind turn over her ticket for the express train to Stressful Memories Town. What stop was she getting off at? Right. Graduation night.

The night Ernie ruined everything. Years of shared history.

They had become best friends at age six. It was October, a year into the new school year, and Drake and Parker were bullying Ernie by the swing set. She hadn't caught the beginning of it, what they were shouting about, but it was something about scrawny arms and a dead mom. There were two things Effie hated at the time: the classroom chore chart and Drake Ploughman. So she marched right over, stomped on his toe, took Ernie's hand, and ran like hell. The principal had called her father, who had laughed and given Effie a high five, which somehow made her feel worse. Ernie had written a note of apology to their teacher, even though he hadn't done anything wrong.

In hindsight, she thought, that was classic Ernie and Effie. He was too sweet for his own good. She was too salty for even this seaside town.

After that, they grew up alongside each other. Biked all over, even up to the northern part of the island and its privately owned peninsulas. Monkeyed around on the playground jungle gym.

Had hot-dog-eating contests. Effie always won those, although Ernie kept challenging her. They toasted s'mores over his dad's Weber grill. Stifled giggles and made gagging faces across the table when her dad cooked them blackened tempeh casserole. When they started high school—shortly after the divorce—Effie started skipping classes to swim at the cove, needling Ernie for being too scared to come along. He never did, but he always covered for her. "Out sick. I saw her dad's note," he'd lie to the teacher, crossing his fingers behind his back. In the spring of freshman year, Effie surprised everyone by joining the track team. Running made her feel free, and she was good at it. Ernie wasn't fast, and he didn't particularly like running, but by that point, they went everywhere together. He started pole vaulting and they cheered each other on during meets.

When they turned sixteen, they began sneaking beers from Effie's dad's fridge and stashing them in Ernie's boathouse apartment. Her father knew, probably, but he wasn't much for interfering. Or parenting. They never got wasted because Ernie made them promise they'd only drink two a piece, max, but Effie loved the illicitness of it. Breaking rules made her feel more alive. Breaking rules made her feel like she was defying everyone's expectations that she be wholesome, that she be sweet, that she stick around and do what she was told. She had tried so hard to be a good child when she was younger; to make her mother smile and clean up after her father. And look where that had gotten her.

Either she was no good at being good, or it took more than being good to make people stay.

Whatever, it didn't matter. Doing what she wanted was more fun.

And oh, had she known how to have fun. Sneaking off to Dulse Cove, swimming and being rambunctious in the ocean with Ernie. Playing Truth or Dare, giving goofy challenges and asking faux-serious questions. She was the adventurous one who craved Dares. He always asked for Truths. Except for one chilly spring night during senior year, when he refused to play at all. A few months later, on graduation night, she understood his sudden reluctance for games. She realized why Ernie had always been so caring, so selfless, so relentlessly there for her. Why he gave her everything she asked for and then some. Either she had missed the moment his feelings changed from friendship to something more, or it had been a gradual shift. Either way, he wasn't just a super nice guy. He was a super nice guy who had super big feelings for her.

They were party-hopping, riding bikes around the island to their classmates' houses. There were only seventeen kids graduating that year, counting the two of them, but after the fifth white tent and sheet cake purchased at the supermarket in Rockland, Effie rolled her eyes and asked Ernie if he wanted to ditch the rest.

"I thought you'd never ask," he said.

"Great," she said, swiping her finger through a buttercream frosting rose and sticking it in her mouth. "Gross. Too sweet."

When they got to Dulse Cove, the sun was setting, turning the sky a majestic sherbet purple. Effie stopped so hard her breaks screeched. There was his Pendleton blanket spread out near the mouth of the woods, and a woven laundry basket full of supplies on top of it. Her stomach dropped as Ernie smiled at her, then rummaged around in the basket and brought out a bottle of cheap champagne, a brick of expensive cheese, a fancy little knife, and a sleeve of Ritz crackers. He laid it all out neatly on the blanket. Her nausea rose. It was then she understood what was happening. It was then she saw the entire history of their friendship flash by in a new light. But it wasn't until he grabbed her hands in his and whispered, "I love you," that she threw up on the rocks below.

"Effie, I know." His feet were planted firmly on the ground, but the rest of him was shaking. "I know you want to leave. I won't stop you!" He reached out and wiped her cheek with the corner of a paper napkin. She was silent, still. He continued his speech. "I know you never planned on staying here; that you're meant to be a famous chef. I *want* you to go to culinary school. I *want* you to work in real restaurants. The fancy ones. I want you to learn from them and show them what you know, too. You're really good at everything. But most of all, at teaching people." He was losing his composure, shivering in the heavy night air, but he firmed his chin and swept a knuckle across her collarbone. "So once you're done traveling, I want you to come home. To me. Teach me all the things you learned. Open a restaurant here. Make Alder Isle better." He hugged her close, and her body stiffened. "Effie, we don't even need to try to build a life together. We already have."

It would have been romantic if Effie had felt the same.

If she had *ever* wanted to stay on this island.

If he hadn't just torched the only friendship she'd ever had.

"Why are you doing this?" she asked, untangling herself from his arms.

"I love you." He said it louder this time.

"You don't!"

"I do. It's Drake's fault."

He would not win her over with inside jokes.

There was no coming back from where he'd just brought them. What did she have to say to show him? If she didn't fix this fast, he would convince her to stick around.

"This would never work. We would never work." She picked up the wine and angrily tore away the cage, then yanked off the cork. It flew into the woods with a *pop-fizz.* She poured the entire bottle's contents on the ground with violent *glug-glug-glugs*. When it was empty, she threw the bottle at the rocks. It shattered, glass skidding across the beach.

"You don't love me," she shouted. "You can't. It's impossible."

Silence.

Everything turned cold, the wet air and the spray of the ocean and the hollow feeling inside of her.

When Ernie finally spoke, his voice was quiet, and his eyes were on the ground. "I do love you. And if you don't know that, then we were never even friends."

A thin layer of ice spider-webbed over her chest. Her heart was the harbor in January.

"Get out of here, then." He turned and walked to the road, back to his bike. "Forget about Alder Isle. Forget about all of us. Forget I ever existed." Effie picked up the wire wine cage and crushed it in her palm, the sharp metal leaving welts on her skin. She watched him leave, her chest heaving. He didn't look back. She left for culinary school two days later.

So.

That was everything that had happened, and everything Effie and Ernie weren't saying.

Chapter Seven

On Wednesday, Effie woke extra early and dressed in a pair of athletic tights and a sports bra. She grabbed her earbuds, cell, and her dad's truck keys. After a seven-minute drive, she was at the trailhead on Top Spot Mountain, the highest point on the island. There were miles of trails around Top Spot—residents called it a mountain, but after living in the Alps for a year, Effie refused to. She'd run these trails so many times as a teenager on weekends for extra practice, she knew each turn and tree root by heart. A run would clear her head before the chaos of the workday began. She scrolled through her phone until she found the playlist she was looking for, hit the START button, and set off at a fast pace. She wasn't even a minute in when she rounded a sharp bend in the path and ran into someone. Her phone went flying into a bush as he doubled over in pain.

"Ow," Ernie said, rubbing his jawline. "Effie, watch where you're going! I don't think I've ever come that close to biting my tongue off." He stood up and stuck it out, going cross-eyed as he attempted to inspect the damage.

She yanked her earbuds out then patted the top of her head gingerly, checking for blood. She had slammed into him pretty hard. "Oh God, I think I'm concussed."

"Let me look." He held on to her biceps and frowned into her eyes, checking for vision abnormalities. Her heart surged and she gave a small shudder at the feel of his palms against her bare arms. *We are just friends*, she reminded herself. *This is a friendly mini neurological exam.* He held up his index finger and moved it from side to side, then up and down. Her eyes followed. "You look okay to me, but, Eff, I've got to be honest: I don't know how to tell if someone has a concussion."

"I will probably live. My fault anyway. I wasn't looking where I was going. Working through some anxious energy about my first day."

"Wanna talk about it? I'll listen," he asked.

"No. I'm fine," she said. The retort sounded sharper than she'd meant for it to be.

He shrugged. "Sorry. Was just trying to be nice."

Her harsh edges mellowed. He was nice. The nicest. He always had been. "I'm sorry, I forgot to turn off bitch mode. I was just starting my run. You too?"

Ernie motioned toward his thigh-skimming athletic shorts and Alder Isle Track Team 2007 tank top. "I was a few miles in."

"A few miles? Whoa, look at you, Mr. I Hate Running."

He shrugged. "I guess some things change."

"Tell that to your hair," she said, laughing.

"Cute. Hey. If you want company for the rest of your run, I'm game."

"Okay. But I'm listening to music." She jiggled the earbuds in her fist. Suddenly, the distraction of her favorite songs felt supremely necessary.

"I'm down with that. Show me your playlist." She sighed and retrieved her phone from the bush then handed it over. "Let's see what we've got here," he said. "*Effie's Running Songs*. Straight to the point. I like it." He scrolled for a few seconds before lifting his gaze, a deeply serious look furrowing his brow.

"Problem?" Effie caught her right foot in her hand and stretched. She wobbled a little and he instinctively bent his knees so she could steady herself with a hand on his shoulder.

"I'm not sure if you're aware of this, but there is an upsetting amount of David Guetta on this playlist."

"Oh come on, it's not that bad. How much is 'upsetting,' really?"

"Most mental health experts agree that one remix per week is a safe amount. Counting collaborations, you are at . . ." He checked the screen. "Twelve." He handed back her phone. "Effie, are you okay?"

She tried, and failed, to suppress a big laugh. He grinned.

"Stop! I like techno poppy stuff when I run. It makes me feel like . . ."

"Like you're a Disney cruise performer on uppers for the first time?"

"No, like I'm . . . having fun." Neither one of them spoke for a beat. Effie broke the silence. "Wow, I'm pathetic."

"Furthest thing from it. Your taste in music, however . . ." He hopped up and down a few times, warming his muscles. "What's the pace today, Skrillex?"

"You lead. I'll follow," she said.

He extended his fist. She bumped it. "You may regret this," he said. And then they were off.

Half an hour later, they finished back at the parking lot. Effie was panting hard, her face red and her chest heaving. She doubled over and checked her watch. "That was a six thirty per mile pace. When did you get so freakishly fast?" She stumbled to her dad's truck and steadied herself on the door, her legs wobbly. "And why didn't you warn me?"

He looked at his own watch. "Six thirty-five. You're exaggerating." She rolled her eyes and chugged from the water bottle she'd left on the front seat. "You can consider it punishment for how rudely you ended our brunch date yesterday."

"Wasn't a date. And I wasn't rude."

"You literally ran out of the diner! Kicked up a cloud of dust!"

"Figurative dust, maybe."

He crossed his arms and locked eyes with her. "Say you're sorry."

She sighed and her cheeks got rosy. "I am. Just feeling weird about being home. I guess. I let my anxiety get the best of me."

His arms floated back down to his sides and his stance softened. "See, that wasn't so bad, was it?" His watch chirped at him and his eyebrows raised. "Yikes, it's late. I—we—gotta get to work. See you there?"

Her breath had just finally normalized when he stretched his arms overhead and she caught a glimpse of his sharply cut abs. She sucked in air and yanked on the truck handle, hopping in and waving. "Yep, see you there! Bye!" Her voice was false and cheery and, judging from the amused look on his face, he wasn't buying a single second of it.

After a quick breakfast of black coffee, toast, and an egg, she showered and got ready for her first day at Brown Butter. Today was important. She had to be fully present at the restaurant so she could start learning how things flowed there. The ins and outs of working in any professional kitchen, whether it was a diner or a world-famous restaurant, were the same: Stay organized. Multitask efficiently. Work clean. Don't talk back to the person in charge of you. And if you were a woman, there was also: Don't cry, don't sleep with your coworkers (*yikes*), and don't act, sound, or look like a woman.

About that last one. Effie brushed her hair back and wrapped it into a low bun so tight it made her eyes water. She rolled a white bandana into a thick strip and tied it into a headband shape, then pushed it up just past her hairline. She rolled on a slick of unflavored ChapStick and dropped it in her pants pocket. Beauty portion of the routine: check.

She shrugged into her plain white chef's coat, which she always wore until she was given branded whites from the restaurant, and buttoned it up to the top. Into the chest pocket went a fresh black fine-tipped Sharpie (for labeling and dating prepared ingredients); her favorite metal spoon, long handled with a deep bowl (for tasting sauces, soups, and dressings); and a thin metal cake tester (infinitely useful). She grabbed her knife roll (inside: eight-inch chef's knife, seven-inch santoku, six-inch nakiri, filleting knife, boning knife, utility knife, paring knife, sharpening steel, scissors). She'd spent an hour last night honing each knife to a lethal edge on her whetstone. That was another unspoken rule of working in restaurants: make sure your knives are damn sharp. She looked down at everything she'd put on and gathered, then huffed. Maybe it wasn't just the constant moving that had depleted her bank account. It was also the fact chefs were expected to provide all their own very expensive work tools. She slipped into a pair of black clogs fitted with orthotics and walked the short distance to her *real* home for the next three months.

Effie had resisted reading up on Brown Butter while she'd been away, but she'd known it existed. For the last three years, her dad kept sending emails with links to articles about the new restaurant. And working in the restaurant industry, one hears things. So Effie did know a little about her hometown's shiny new restaurant.

Since it appeared three years ago, it had become a golden child in the world of fine-dining restaurants. It was luxurious, but wore an eco-green halo. It was a good steward of the land and sea, promoting sustainable fishing and farming practices. Unlike many hyper-local restaurants that closed in the chilly months,

Brown Butter operated year-round. The first year, the restaurant slashed prices and offered special deals for locals, but by the next summer, it was such a buzzy scene, it didn't need to. Back in 2020, it opened its doors in June, just one month later than planned. Pandemic be damned, this restaurant defied everyone's expectations from the jump. Even with all the restrictions, all the masks and mandated Covid tests, it got busier and more popular. Every major metropolitan newspaper had written about it. David Chang had visited it on his latest Netflix show. Reservations were now booking a year out. Brown Butter was *hot.* Seventy-five percent of the restaurant's ingredients, like produce, meat, fish, and cheese, came from right there on Alder Isle. The other twenty-five percent were from mainland Maine. One hundred percent local. One hundred percent a cosmopolitan foodie's fantasy.

Over dinner with her dad and sister the night before, she'd learned that Brown Butter was causing the island's infrastructure to buckle under pressure. The ferry was overbooked. The one gas pump on Alder Isle was constantly tapped out. The housing market was, Ingrid said, out of control. The local fishermen had been losing their favorite tables at The Gull's Perch because food tourists kept popping by for breakfast.

Okay, fine. Effie knew a lot about Brown Butter.

She looked around the lot. Chickens were roaming freely and there was a tidy vegetable garden by the porch, enclosed in a rustic wood gate. She rolled her shoulders back and stood up straighter. She clenched her jaw and smiled with closed lips. *Everything is temporary. Especially pain.* Her salary was generous enough that if she lived tight, she could save enough by fall. That's all she had to do: make it through the summer and she was gone. Somewhere new.

She opened the whitewashed barn door to the dining room and reminded herself she'd been cooking professionally for a decade and a half. *How bad could this be?*

Chapter Eight

Brown Butter was in a ramshackle farmhouse. It looked old and wonky because it was. No need for expensive faux antique finishes on the floors when they were actually ancient. The exterior was sided in faded red clapboard that had survived countless nights of angry sea winds. The five-foot-tall windows had real shutters. There was a wraparound porch dotted with tables, ready to be laid for that night's service.

Inside, the formal dining room and bar were dark in a romantic and inviting sort of way. The wood floors were pockmarked but impressively shiny and clean. The chairs were upholstered in oyster-colored linen, and each table had a small ceramic bud vase holding a fern frond. She lifted one of the vases and studied it. The clay had been left rough and was richly textured. Instead of a glossy glaze, it was a natural rusty red. Effie smiled and set it back down. She liked that vase.

Effie looked around, then set her knife roll on the bar and

waited on a stool. Jarrod had said he'd meet her there at nine. It was 8:57. By 9:10, he still hadn't shown, but Effie could hear voices in the kitchen down the hall. Maybe she'd gotten it wrong? Was she supposed to meet him in there? She could have sworn he'd said they'd start with a tour of the dining area, but that was before the Jameson. Before . . . *blergh.* She grabbed her knives and made her way into the kitchen.

Brown Butter wasn't open for lunch, but the place was already alive and humming. She squinted as her eyes adjusted to the bright overhead lights and gleaming stainless-steel surfaces. There was always such a stark contrast between front and back of house. Two men wearing their checkered pants and white coats were standing in front of an indigo-colored Lacanche oven and eight-burner range. Effie's heart stopped for a moment when she saw it. That brand had always been her dream stove, down to the luxe gold knobs. It was sexy as hell, but the main thing was that it drove like a dream. The Ferrari of stoves. Wait, which one was the fancy French car? Bugatti? Whatever, it was a good stove. When she was younger, she used to make Ernie read the catalogues cover to cover with her, fantasizing about the day she'd own a luxe stove of her own. He had offered to buy her one. Even if he could never have afforded it, the gesture had meant a lot. Really, it was just a special way of showing he knew her best. In all the restaurants she'd worked at, there had never been a Lacanche. There had never been an Ernie, either.

She snapped out of her reverie and took in the scene around her fantasy stove. The men were dipping their own tasting spoons into a bubbling pot on the front range and arguing. "Too much salt," the one on the far left with black hair said. Effie guessed he was Sixto, who was dating her little sister. When Ingrid had shared that her boyfriend was also a cook at Brown Butter, Effie had groaned. It was frankly impressive how much she'd forgotten about living in a small town.

"No, c'est parfait," the taller one on the right shot back. "Seafood stock needs salt. It's briny, like the ocean. Correct me if I am wrong, but which one of us trained at Le Cordon Bleu? *Mm?* Which one of us grew up by the sea?"

"Corsica isn't Maine, fucking cabrón," the first man said, turning around and seeing Effie. "You're the new guy? Ingrid's sister?"

"I'm the new guy," Effie confirmed.

"Welcome to hell," he said with a huge grin. She immediately liked him. He would be a good coworker. Now he just had to pass the Acceptable Boyfriend for My Little Sister Test. "I'm Sixto. Entremetier."

"Right on," Effie said. She had worked at the entremetier, or side dishes station, for years. It was a hard place to be, cooking the food that rounded out a meal but rarely received the loudest praise. She already had respect for Sixto, based on his position alone.

The tall man pocketed his spoon and wiped his hands on the towel neatly tucked into his apron strap. "Jean-Claude. Saucier." Effie mentally rolled her eyes as she shook his hand. Of course the French guy was in charge of all the sauces.

She hesitated for just a moment then decided to take a chance. She was technically their boss, even if the power dynamic was all off at the moment. But she was curious about what sort of working relationship these guys wanted to have: collaborative and congenial or . . . not. "Can I try it? The stock?"

One of Jean-Claude's eyebrows disappeared underneath his suave brown hair, but he motioned toward the stove. "Be my guest."

She removed her spoon from her pocket and dipped it in the pot. Both men waited while she tasted, Sixto's arms crossed over his chest. "Well, new guy? Who's right? Too salty, yeah?"

"You really want my opinion?" Effie asked, pretending to be timid. She had to play this one carefully.

"Please," said Jean-Claude, already looking smug.

"It's light. Brothy. Nice for steaming vegetables. But I'm guessing you want a more intense seafood flavor. Next time you make it, give the lobster shells a hard sear in oil before adding aromatics—onions, garlic, herbs. That will create the big flavor you want." She dipped her spoon in a bain-marie of water to clean it, then returned it to her pocket. "It is too salty, though. Sorry."

Sixto clapped her on the back. "This fucking guy! I like it."

Jean-Claude's thin lips turned into a frown. "We'll see what Jarrod says."

"Yeah, do you know when he's supposed to get here? Am I early?"

Sixto snorted. "Homeboy is always late. I'll show you around."

First up was garde manger. The appetizers and salads station was usually reserved for cooks just starting their careers. Brown Butter's garde manger was manned by a stocky twentysomething named B.J. with a mop of curly hair and big biceps. He impatiently told Effie he'd graduated from the Culinary Institute of America two months prior, and had a huge amount of mise en place to get to. Effie nodded, feeling soft toward him. Prepping all her ingredients for the daily mise en place used to feel stressful to her, too. She'd never forget the pressure she'd felt her first few years in kitchens. Eventually, B.J. would learn to manage his stress and have an easier time handling the tasks in front of him. Or he wouldn't, and he'd find another career.

Next, Sixto brought her to the dish pit, an efficiently organized space for washing all the pots, pans, dinnerware, and glasses. Dishwashers rocked. Effie loved them. They worked harder than anyone in any kitchen, and knew all the (literally) dirty secrets. Plus, they held a secret power over the cooks. A dishwasher who didn't like you could make your life miserable. But get on their good side, and they'd always make sure you had the pan, skillet, or set of tongs you needed. Chad, Brown Butter's dishwasher, was a young local. He would be in at ten. Over at the pastry and dessert station, a slight, short man named Dan was weighing balls of dough on a digital scale, then depositing them on a rimmed sheet tray. Dan had previously worked at an iconic restaurant in Berkeley, but he looked less California-cool than highly in need of a CBD edible. Effie understood that, too: pastry chefs worked longer hours than the rest of the line cooks, because their creations were the last to leave the kitchen. And they often didn't get the respect they deserved.

"There's also a rotating crew of interns, but they won't be in 'til later. That's about it," Sixto said, shrugging. "You'll figure out the rest if you're as good as your little sis says you are."

Effie's heart did a twirl. *Ingrid thinks I'm talented?* No matter how padded her resume became, family praise still meant the most. "I'll figure it out. This is me?" She motioned to an empty workspace. He nodded and went to check on a pan of beets roasting in the oven. She rolled her shoulders toward her spine. Her back cracked and she breathed a sigh of relief. *So far, so good,* she thought, unpacking her knives.

The clock above the pass read 9:45. Effie was just about to pull out her phone to text Jarrod when she remembered she'd never gotten his number. Probably for the best.

"Hey, Jean-Claude, I got the chickens all quartered for . . ." Effie heard Ernie's voice ascending from the stairwell. He must have noticed her, because his voice faded, then picked back up with slightly less confidence. "Chickens. For you. To make stock."

She turned slowly, trying to act normal. Trying to act like she didn't know him.

She looked at the man holding the plastic tub full of chicken parts and again felt a wild surge of desire. Maybe she really *didn't* know him. This was not the Ernie she'd grown up with. It wasn't the Ernie she'd gone swimming with the day before. It wasn't even the playful Ernie she had bumped into that morning. How was it possible that the most steadfast, stable person on the entire island kept surprising her at every turn?

Chapter Nine

Ernie deposited the container onto Jean-Claude's station, then walked over to Effie. "Hey," he said.

"Whoa," she said, pointing to his hair. "You look different from . . . two hours ago." *Different* was one word. Effie silently worked another one around in her mouth: *sexy*.

"Yeah?" He patted the top of his head lightly, a look of mild confusion spreading across his face. There was no way he had gotten a haircut before work, but here, at the restaurant, it looked more stylish and grown-up; tousled, and just long enough to catch the hints of blond in his red. "I think you're imagining things."

"Maybe I am." Effie motioned for him to spin around.

He did, then shrugged. "I'm still the same guy."

She looked around the kitchen, feeling panicky and paranoid, but no one was paying attention to them. Her voice dropped to a whisper anyway. "Are you, though?"

He stood a little straighter and his ears reddened. His freckles stretched as his cheeks wore a proud smile. "Far as you know." His voice dropped as he added, "Hey. I don't want to bother you at work. Nobody here knows we're friends, and you probably want to keep it that way. I'll respect your space." She almost protested, but he was right. She appreciated the discretion. He lifted his fist to hers, and she bumped it. They both opened their palms upon impact. "Boom," Ernie said. "You're going to crush this."

"I hope so."

"Know so. If you need anything, you can find me in the dungeon."

He turned and hobbled to the stairwell. He cackled evilly when he reached the door. Jean-Claude snorted. B.J. glanced up from a pile of watermelon radishes and tossed an amused look in Ernie's direction. "This fucking guy! He's so funny," Sixto said from the stove.

Ernie had never been the type to care what other people thought about him, and yet everyone found him charming. She used to tell him it was one of his superpowers. Jarrod still hadn't shown, so she wandered back into the dining area and pulled her phone out of her pants pocket. Was Ernie's number the same? She'd deleted it from her contacts over ten years ago, after a hard night at work and another lesson in the ramifications of tequila shots. She had drunk dialed him and left a rambling message, which he had never returned. The next morning, she drank a green juice *and* a ginger-wheatgrass shot and erased him from her contacts list. But now, as she pulled up the text app and started typing, she found she remembered it by heart.

555-963-0862

What. Was. That?

Not obvious? I was being troll-like. Because I work in a dungeon?

Everyone in that kitchen thinks you're crazy.

Did it make you laugh?

Yes.

We used to do dumb stuff like that all the time.

Remember? To try to get each other to crack.

lol. I remember. I made you laugh-cry during our calculus final.

I still don't know how you managed to sneak a whoopee cushion past Ms. Greenbriar.

Taking it to the grave.

Hey.

Hey?

I'm sorry I was bitchy yesterday.

No need to apologize. It's been a stressful 16 years.

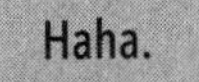

And clearly I have grown to expect that from you.

The bitchiness.

Too far?

Ahhh too far, please feel free to activate bitch mode.

His last four messages came in rapid succession, and reading them made Effie smile.

I'll try to be sugar and spice this summer. Nice Effie only. What time are you off tonight?

4 or 5 usually. You're here until late?

Yep. Wanna have a beer when I'm done?

Normally yes, but I have plans tonight.

With who?

Mind your business, Eff.

Ah, so it's a date.

. . . . .

I'm free tomorrow night, though.

Okay, wanna have a beer when I'm done *tomorrow*?

I thought you'd never ask.

Effie's breath caught in her throat. *I thought you'd never ask.* That's what he'd said, the night sixteen years ago when he confessed his feelings. Had he said it now intentionally?

Did it matter?

I know it's classic, but let's not go to Son of a Wharf. There's a new cocktail bar in town (woohoo). Behind the souvenir shop. Meet you there?

Effie paused with her thumbs poised above the screen. She was playing with fire now, but couldn't stop herself.

Seriously can't wait.

"Fuck me, I had a disaster of a morning."

Effie scrambled to slip the phone in her pocket as Jarrod opened the door with his butt and pushed into the dining room. "Ahh," she said, clocking the big foam cooler in his arms. He'd been shopping for ingredients. "Here, let me help." She motioned to grab one end of it. But as he jostled for control over the cooler, Effie stepped back with her hands up—*Okay, you win.*

His face normalized into a flirty grin. "Heavy. Lots of produce in there. Don't want you to hurt yourself. I'll just throw it in the walk-in. There's more in the car, darlin'," he called over his shoulder. "You wanna make yourself useful, grab the bushel of watercress." She rolled her eyes at his back but headed out to help him unload the vegetables from his market trip.

Fifteen minutes later, she was sitting in Jarrod's office, studying the menu while he went through emails at his desk.

She rubbed the paper between her fingers. It was thick and grainy with visible bits of pulp; one of those little beautiful things that mattered a lot. Printing the menus probably cost a fortune. But that only partially explained the cost of the prix fixe dinner.

For the privilege of eating at Brown Butter, customers paid three hundred dollars. Effie had worked in a lot of restaurants with high prices, but three hundred for just seven courses was bold. Arrogant, even. *Well, if people were willing to pay . . .* It really wasn't her business. Literally or figuratively. And those high prices did eventually trickle down to her all-important paycheck. She read through the menu, pausing to close her eyes so she could envision each dish.

Brown Butter | Sample Summer Tasting Menu

$300 per guest | $375 with wine pairing

Chef de Cuisine: Jarrod Levi

* Please note that our menu is subject to change daily,
as we rely on our local farmers for the bounty we are
privileged to cook with.

norumbega oysters, togarashi, shiso reduction

little gem lettuce, lovage, hazelnut brittle, apple-cider vinaigrette

chilled sorrel soup, goat's cheese cream

charred heirloom squash, swordfish, sun-dried tomato tapenade

daily pasta
(substitute jarrod's lobster ravioli | $45)

maine-raised strip steak, romesco

foraged rhubarb bombolini, meadowsweet
scoops beach plum swirl

Brown Butter | Summer Bar Menu

à la carte

parker house rolls and single-cow butter | $14

maine beef carpaccio | $25

little gem salad | $18

jarrod's lobster ravioli | $45

fried cod | market price

half chicken under a brick | $42

blackberry financiers | $13

Effie flipped to the back of the menu. There was a by-the-glass wine list that started with a seventeen-dollar Txakoli and ended with a list of nonalcoholic house-made juices that included crab apple–beet and honeydew-basil. *Well.* She thought. Incredibly pretentious, very precious. It was just the sort of menu people traveled to experience. *All pretty standard, except for . . .*

"Genius, right?" Jarrod got up from his desk and wrapped his apron strings once around his back then tied them together in the front. "Wait'll you try the shiso reduction. It slaps."

"Yeah, it's good. Just—are you open to a little feedback?" Effie had gotten used to delivering criticism to her male colleagues in the form of a shit sandwich: Detailed compliment, gently worded critique, big-ass compliment. Gilded plate. Sweet smile for dessert. Jarrod chuckled and indicated she continue. He was not going to take whatever she said seriously.

"I love how you don't shy away from herby, bitter, and fresh flavors. That helps brighten a big meal like this. But I noticed the tiniest thing about the lobster pasta. I wouldn't do ravioli."

"It's my signature dish. *Eater* wrote a whole paragraph about it last year. I hired you to help expedite dishes at the pass, not shit on an already-perfect recipe, darlin'."

Her eye twitched at the *darlin'* and she squeezed her hand into a fist behind her back, then released it. "As someone who grew up in Maine, I'm telling you: if you put lobster on the menu, people are going to want to see it. Locals, because they take pride in it. They probably know the guy who caught it. Tourists, because that's literally what they came here for. They want that moment of twirling a forkful of pasta and finding a piece of whole claw meat. It's exciting for them . . . and it is kind of magical. I'd do bucatini instead of ravioli, with a light cream sauce. Lots of fresh chervil for a pop of green on top."

"Locals don't eat here," Sixto shouted as he walked by the office with an eight-quart Cambro container of peeled potatoes.

"Yeah, fair point," Effie said. "Then do it for the tourists."

Jarrod craned his neck to toss a chastising look at Sixto, who was already back at his station, running a knife through his fifth potato. "The ravioli stays," he said, his voice like boots on gravel. "And remember, it's my name on the dish. *I'm* the one who makes it. Got it?"

Effie had other quibbles about the menu, but it was probably not the best time to bring up the fact that no pasta dish, regardless how famous, should cost more than half a chicken. "Sure." She shrugged. He was wrong, but this wasn't her call. And it wouldn't even matter in a few months. It was just one summer.

Chapter Ten

At 11:30 the next night, Effie paused at the entrance to bar. At least, that's what she thought the name of the speakeasy was: bar. One word, all lowercase, punctuated with a period. There was a sandwich-board sign behind the secondhand shop, This Man's Trash, with an arrow pointing to the left, so that's the way Effie went, looking for Ernie.

There was no sign above or on the door, but through the cracked windowpane she could see a crowded room of people holding highball glasses and tumblers. On a Thursday. In Alder Isle. Never in a million years would she have thought.

It'd been a long day and a brutal service. The POS system had gone down, so Brown Butter's servers were scrambling, shoving handwritten tickets in Effie's face as she expedited at the pass. Jarrod was deep in the weeds at the grill and sauté station, and proved to be zero help. She thought he would have jumped in and come to the pass to assist her. It was a lot of work to send the dishes out to the dining room, especially when things began bottlenecking. At least the team had rallied behind her. They were good at listening to orders. *Or maybe*, she allowed herself to feel proud for a moment, *I'm good at giving them*. Eventually, they'd gotten the backed-up plates under control with minimal disturbance in the dining room. "Nice job, Chef," Chad had said shyly, from the dish pit when service was over. Effie smiled at him. She had noticed the way he studied all the cooks when he wasn't scrubbing pots, and made a mental note to schedule a meeting with him later that week. She had a feeling this dishwasher had goals beyond hosing off dinner plates, and she wanted to support him however she could.

Not that she was going to get emotionally involved with any of her coworkers.

She was just doing her job.

After she scrubbed down her station and prepped her tools for the next morning, she stopped at home to change into her favorite pair of denim cutoffs and a white cropped T-shirt. Slid on a pair of tan huarache sandals. Let her hair down. It had felt good to be in a kitchen again, but after a fourteen-hour whirlwind, being off the clock felt even better.

She pushed on the door and entered bar., or Bar, or whatever it was called, clocking Ernie at the corner. Her chest felt tight. Her heart was suddenly being crushed in a vise. Was it the reminder that a decade-plus of growing up looked good on him? Or the fact that he was talking to a petite, curly-haired brunette polishing glasses behind the beer taps? Either way, *ugh*.

"Hey, troll," Effie said, interrupting their conversation and flinging herself onto the stool next to his.

"—so I say to him, 'That's the last time I take advice from a box of quackers!'" Ernie finished his story. The brunette slapped the bar in delight. "Oh, hey, Effie," Ernie said.

"Hi," she responded. She was inexplicably irritated and tried to gloss over it with a joke of her own. "What the duck's going on?"

"Huh?" He sipped from his glass and looked at the brunette with a *What's she talking about?* expression.

"Ducks. Because you said . . . You know what? Forget it. Hi." She directed the last word to the bartender.

The bartender waved.

"Oh, sorry," Ernie said, motioning between the two women. "Effie, this is Lake." Effie tried to hold in a snort. Ernie ignored it. "She works here, obviously, and is a talented ceramicist. *Oh!* You've seen her stuff. She did the vases at Brown Butter. Lake, this is Effie. She rolled into town a few days ago."

"Right on," said Lake, who was five feet tall with a nose ring and perfect teeth. "You've gotta go to Meadowsweet Scoops while you're here. The beach plum swirl is so good."

"Do you have a cocktail list?" Effie asked impatiently.

Lake looked wounded but produced a menu from behind the bar, then went to close out another patron's tab.

As Effie studied the drinks list, she felt Ernie's eyes settle on her with a critical weight. "What? It's been a long day."

"You don't think that was a little rude? She was being nice."

"Yeah, well, Pond could have asked me if I had ever been to Alder Isle before immediately assuming I was a tourist."

"Lake," corrected Ernie, trying to hold in a chuckle.

"*What* is so funny?" Effie slammed the list down on the bar and glared at him.

"You! You are funny. Being mad about people not knowing you're from here. Isn't that what you've always wanted? To be a stranger?" Effie frowned. "It's also honestly very enjoyable to watch you being jealous."

"Drop dead," she said, quickly scanning the rest of the menu. "I'm not jealous, I'm tired. Lake!" she yelled. "How's the bloomin' gin?"

"Phenomenal!" Lake called from across the bar.

Effie looked at Ernie and gave jazz hands. "She says it's phenomenal!" Ernie shook his head. "I'll have one," Effie called back. But after her first sip, Effie realized the bloomin' gin was a mistake. "I do feel a little bad," she said, pushing the drink in front of Ernie. "She worked so hard on it."

"I could have told you that, if you hadn't been in such a hurry to sass me." He fished out one of the daisies that was floating in the glass and inspected it. "It's not so bad when she does it with rose petals. But worse when it's dandelion heads."

"Yikes," said Effie.

"Yikes," agreed Ernie. "Want some beer?"

"I thought you'd never ask," said Effie, helping herself to his session beer.

He grazed his fingertips over his hair. Before she could stop herself, Effie imagined her fingers doing the same thing. Neither one spoke for what felt like years. Sixteen years. "Should we talk about it?" he finally asked, sighing heavily and jolting her back to reality.

"Talk about when you told me you loved me and I had a meltdown and then we hated each other for over a decade?"

"Yeah. That."

"I guess we should. If we're going to be working together and all that. But it's so loud in here. When did Alder Isle get cool?"

"'Bout three days ago."

"Ha."

Ernie paid for his half-finished beer and Effie's abandoned drink. "Come on. I have a few bottles at the boathouse."

She held out her arm, expecting him to loop his through it, the way they used to when they walked to the ice cream shop after dinner. He cocked his head, then shook it a nearly imperceptible amount: *no.* Effie let her arm fall to her side and tried not to look flustered. "Ready when you are," she said, wishing she could take back the last five seconds. They walked side by side, two feet apart, down the road and all the way to his boathouse near Cleary Island.

Mmm. Better." Effie was sinking deeper into Ernie's sofa with an amber bottle of Maine Beer Company. He had held up two options from his fridge and let her pick. She chose the Peeper, a pale ale that tasted like peaches and pine. He was sipping on Lunch, an IPA with malty caramel notes. "Maine beer is the best."

"You don't have this . . . wherever you've been?"

"It's harder to find in San Francisco."

"San Fran, wow."

"And Sicily. Chamonix. Paris. A stint in Bali. Few more."

"You actually did it. All the stuff you said you wanted to."

"Yep. And then I came back to this miserable little island because I missed your beer fridge."

"It's a fridge-fridge. Very responsible ratio of groceries to adult beverages." He cheers-ed her. "But you're welcome to raid it anytime. I won't tell your dad."

"Okay, let's start this conversation here. Why are you acting so . . . nice to me?"

"What do you mean?"

"That was some big stuff before I left. Then I come back, and it's like—I don't know. Almost like none of that happened."

"Okay with you if I sit down?" Ernie motioned from his perch against the kitchen counter to the cushion next to Effie.

"It's not my couch."

"I am aware of that. But is it okay if I share it with you?"

"God, yes. Ernie. You don't have to ask permission to sit on your own furniture."

He looked at her with a glint in his eye. "Have you considered that I'm just the average amount of nice and you're disproportionately mean?"

"My friend, I've known myself to be a salty bitch for years." They both took long pulls from their bottles and sat in tense silence. Effie took the opportunity to study the boathouse. The layout was the same as when they were kids, but it had undergone a glow-up since she'd last seen it. The front door—which was technically the back of the boathouse—spilled right into a seating area, with an overstuffed couch. Draped over the back: the wooly Pendleton blanket that Effie recognized from his father's house. She'd slept under that blanket countless nights after watching a movie with Ernie. It was the very same Pendleton that had made an appearance on their almost-doesn't-count last night together. The couch's leather was soft and looked old, but clean and well-taken care of. Across the room: a simple kitchen with a narrow oven and range. Well-seasoned cast-iron pans hung from a rack on the ceiling. A dark-stained-pine countertop ran alongside the entire wall and two rows of open shelving. The lower shelf held a modest number of bowls and plates. The name Lake flashed brightly in Effie's brain.

The opposite end of the boathouse, the part facing the water, was made into Ernie's bedroom. Unlike the rest of the space, it was closed off by sliding pocket doors, paned with frosted glass. Effie didn't know if that area had changed. She'd never been in there.

"You wanna hear something funny?" Ernie asked. The left side of Effie's mouth turned up in an inviting grin. "I almost bought a ring the week before graduation."

"You're joking. That's unhinged."

"Well, I did say *almost*. I went to the Kay Jewelers in Rockland one afternoon. Instead of English class."

"So that's where you were. You little scamp. I had to suffer through Olive and Josh's *Romeo and Juliet* rap battle all by myself that day. I never thought you'd be one to cut class." Ernie blushed.

"So why didn't you?" Effie leaned in a little, and Ernie leaned farther away.

"Because nothing there would have suited you." Her shoulders slumped. That wasn't the answer she'd expected. "But obviously I'm glad I didn't. Losing my best friend and eleven hundred dollars may have destroyed me."

Effie felt uncomfortable. She knew she should meet him with an equal amount of vulnerability, but she'd never been good at heart-to-hearts. So she set her beer on a coaster made from a bit of marine rope and smiled in Ernie's direction without making eye contact. "I changed my mind. We don't need to dig up all this trauma. Right? Maybe we should play a lighthearted round or two of Truth or Dare."

"Good idea, except you know how that's going to go."

"You'll choose Truth every time and I'll always choose Dare, and neither of us will be any good at coming up with ideas for each other?"

"Yup."

Effie thought for a moment. "Okay. Here's what we'll do: We can only give each other Dares."

"I really hate Dares," he groaned.

"Well, Truths make me wanna puke," she countered.

"Let's just start playing and see what happens," he suggested.

"Okay," she said.

"Okay," he said back.

"You first," she said.

"I choose first, or I ask you first?" he said.

"Um . . ." Effie thought.

"What if . . ." Ernie was stalling.

"Hey Ernie: Truth or Dare?" Effie finally locked eyes with him as she retrieved her beer and took a big swig for bravery.

He set his drink down and held her gaze. "Dare."

"Well, shit! Way to surprise me." She shoved aside an intrusive thought that had hoped for a Truth, so she could ask him about Lake and just how well he knew her. "Let me think for a sec."

While she decided his fate, he ran his palm over his hair again, then brought his hand down to his face and rubbed his jawline with his thumb. Effie closed her eyes, pretending to concentrate on the perfect Dare, but she was trying to ignore the fact that watching his slow, deliberate hands was making her inner thighs feel hot and tingly. "Okay, I've got it. This is gonna be so good. I dare you to streak across the Cleary Island bridge and back. Totally. Buck. Ass. Naked." She put a dramatic beat before her next directive. "But you can wear sneakers if you want."

"I really, *really* hate Dares."

Chapter Eleven

Five minutes later, Ernie was panting hard, hopping back into his khaki shorts and laughing in big, gulping breaths. Effie was applauding from the deck, doubled over and knuckling tears out of the corners of her eyes.

"When Dougie pulled into the harbor and honked his horn . . ." She gasped. "The way that I screamed."

"I'm glad it was good for you. Very pleased that one of us got some pleasure out of that heinous experience." He looped the top button of his shorts and reached for his shirt, which he'd slung over one of the wicker chairs. Effie let her eyes trail down to his abs and the sun-bleached hair at his waistband as he slid the tee over his head. She looked away and hugged herself, feeling chilly.

"For that stunning performance, I'm going to throw you a bone," she said to the boathouse's siding. "Hit me with a Truth."

"Whoa. I need to make this count." He settled onto the chair, and Effie took the loveseat, stretching her legs out on the waterproof cushions. Across the yard, moored boats bobbed on the water. Fireflies flirted past the porch. When Ernie spoke, his voice was soft and tender, and he was holding his hand out across the table that separated them. It was a peace offering, after his refusal to take her arm in the bar. "Are you happy? Since you left, I mean. Working in restaurants, traveling the world?"

She finished her beer and looked at his hand. She did want to take it. Really, she did. He wiggled his fingers and smiled. She smiled back, but busied herself with undoing and retying her ponytail. Now it was her turn to stall. "Truths make me wanna puke."

"I'll hold your hair, if it comes to that." He kept his arm on the frosted glass tabletop. Just in case she needed it. "Are you happy?"

She heaved a big sigh. "Maybe? Sometimes? When I'm actually working, yes. I think? I've been in California for the last half a year or so, and that was cool. Usually, as soon as I get to the next place, all I can think about is leaving. But I would have stayed in San Francisco for a while. A big city full of streets to explore. There are enough people there that you can be anonymous if you want to. Good wine and beer and all that. The air smells like sourdough bread forever and ever . . . It didn't feel like home, but it was exciting. And isn't that better, anyway? It took me a while to get there. After Alder Isle, I went to culinary school in Manhattan. You know that, right?" She was rambling, but he was keeping up. "I did that, no problems. Beyond a stupid amount of debt, obviously. Then I stayed in New York, putting in work in the *Times*'s roster of favorite restaurants. After that, I moved to Bali for a year."

"That is surprising." He was giving her all his attention, and it unnerved her. She had grown used to conversations punctuated by multitasking; communicating with other people was easier with the distraction of peeling vegetables or rolling out pasta dough.

"Yeah, it was my Basic B era," Effie said with a shrug.

"Basic . . . Bali?"

"Bitch, Ernie."

"Ah . . . ?"

"You have to know what Basic Bitch means." He looked at her blankly. "Pumpkin spice lattes and Ugg boots and framed artwork that says 'Good Vibes Only' and sabbaticals in Bali."

"I really don't know . . . but continue."

"It was nice for a while. I cooked at a bougie yoga retreat for Basic Bs with more money than me. A lot of slicing mangoes into animal shapes."

"How does one make a mango into a platypus?"

Effie smacked his open palm with hers. A spark of electricity shocked up through her arm and faded out in sparkling tingles at her scalp. "No mango platypuses. It was mostly swans."

"Boring."

"Tell me about it. After that, I went to Paris. I was ready to get back into the real stuff, and one of my old bosses in New York was opening a new restaurant there. I helped him. Honestly, I did most of the work. Trained the staff, adjusted recipes, made everything perfect. I even chose the font on the menus."

"Now that doesn't surprise me at all. You're a hard worker. When you care about what you're doing, anyway."

"True. The rest of the time I'm a slacker."

"I didn't mean . . ."

She waved away his apology. "After we got up and running, I stupidly assumed I'd be promoted from sous chef to head chef, but no dice. He hired a young guy two years out of culinary school."

"That cabrón."

"Somebody's been taking notes at Brown Butter."

"I have learned," Ernie said, "that the best kind of insults are kitchen insults."

"Oh for sure." Working in a restaurant was like speaking a secret language. It was nice that he was becoming fluent in it, too. "Anyway, after that I was out. Chefs don't work for much, but I wasn't going to give him my pride. So onward to Chamonix, where I cooked at a chalet-style resort for more rich white people."

"Basic Bs on skis?"

"You got *funny* since I've been gone."

"I have always been funny."

She bit her lip. Was that true? "From there, Italy. I started out at this little trattoria. The kind that doesn't even have a name. It's just the place you eat when you're not eating at home. I learned more at that teeny-tiny place than I did in culinary school and all my years of cooking at fancy restaurants combined."

"Why didn't you stay?" he asked. She reached for her bottle and found it empty, so she grabbed his and took a sip. His eyes laughed. "Want me to get you another?"

"Naw, I'll just drink yours."

"Hold on," he said, and disappeared into the house. "Here," he said, handing her a second bottle, the lid already removed.

"See? Perfect example of you being overly nice."

"Nope. Perfect example of me not wanting to share my beer."

She continued. "Mm-kay. So Italy was idyllic, but after a while, not challenging. I felt complacent. Like, I could stay there forever and frolic amongst the grapevines and eat fresh pasta until I turned into a sassy blond gnocchi . . ."

"I'm picturing that, and I like it."

". . . but at what cost? If I'm not pushing myself, I'll turn to dust and die."

"I think technically, you'd die first."

"What?"

"The dying. It comes before the dusting."

"Ah. You're right."

"Continue."

"So I kept an ear to the ground. And when I heard Cowboy Bean was hi—"

"Sorry, *what*?"

"Cowboy Bean. My last job. Fancy farm-to-table restaurant in San Francisco." He was still looking at her like she'd grown a pair of antlers in the last fifteen seconds. "Oh. The name. Cowboy beans are a type of heirloom beans. Got tan and creamy swirls all over them. They look like they're wearing little chaps. Very cute. Excellent beans." She paused and tilted her head, realizing something. "I suppose it could have been named for the dish—Cowboy

Beans. Made with bacon and ground beef. I never thought of that."

"Did you serve that at the restaurant?"

"Not that dish, which is glorified chili. But we cooked with a lot of heirloom and special ingredients. Kind of like Brown Butter does." Ernie chortled, and she knew they were both thinking of shiso reduction and crab apple–beet juice. "Anyway, they were hiring a new executive chef right around the time I was done with Sicily. I applied. And interviewed. Never, in a million and two years, did I think I'd get it. But I did. And then . . . it was full-on the hardest job I've ever had. You know how Brown Butter has a Michelin star?"

"I do."

"Cowboy Bean has two. Double the stress. Double the pressure. Double the responsibility."

"Had you ever worked at a double star before?"

"A two star. That's the industry term, not double star. And no. But I thought I could do it. I'm good, Ernie. I'm really good." She swatted at a mosquito, immediately regretful of her boast.

"Effie, of *that* everyone who's ever met you is aware."

She swallowed hard, feeling his compliment flood her heart. "Thanks." The word came out as a breathy squeak. "But I fucked up."

"You don't have to tell me anything more if you don't want to."

"Is this your first time playing Truth or Dare?"

"It's the first time you've actually chosen Truth, so, kind of."

She swallowed again, this time to conceal a smile that would have come out too tender. They didn't need this stupid game. Nobody knew her like Ernie Callahan.

"Nothing dramatic happened. I didn't accidentally leave the walk-in cooler open and ruin all the quail. I didn't serve a well-done steak to a VIP. I just couldn't keep up with everything. The dining room was bigger than any place I'd ever worked, so there were more covers every night. There were more stations, more people to manage. I was struggling to balance the books because our food costs were friggin' through the roof. I was used to cooking like a beast and doing behind the scenes stuff. Not running the show. I bonked. Basically every night."

Ernie didn't say anything, but she felt supported in the silence. It was reassuring.

"It lasted six miserable months, and then I was fired in a blaze of glory. They told me it was because I was 'too emotional' about the job, and that I 'let my personal relationships get in the way of my authority.' Apparently, I spent too much time trying to 'nurture' my employees and not enough time screaming at them."

"That sounds like some sexist bull crap."

"Was it though? Or was I actually just not good enough?"

"They should have invested more time in you."

"Six months was generous."

"I think anyone would struggle in a situation where they were learning on the job."

"Lots of people figure out how to do it. Just not me."

"Agree to disagree."

"So to answer your initial question: No. I am not happy. I've been living paycheck-to-paycheck my whole life. I work in a misogynistic, toxic industry. My dad paid for my plane ticket home. I'm a thirty-three-year-old woman living rent-free in her childhood bedroom. I'm drinking a beer with the only real friend I've ever had, and it's weird and bad because he hates me, and he has every reason to."

"Why do you think I hate you? You've said that twice now."

"Because I broke your heart."

"I broke my own heart, Eff. It was dumb of me to take that shot. Dumb and selfish. Being your best friend was the greatest thing in the world. I sacrificed that for a fantasy." He paused and thought before he continued. "Not that you're just some fantasy. I didn't mean that. You're real, the realest. You always have been."

She swung her legs off the loveseat and cradled her head in her hands, elbows on her knees. She spoke the next words to her feet. "I hated losing you, too. Being your best friend was the only thing that made sense. It was like we spoke a secret language. All our own."

"I felt that way, too. And I never stopped."

"You still want to be besties?" She had tilted her head so she was looking sideways at him.

"We've got a second chance at the friendship of the century. I don't think we should pass that up, do you?"

She smiled. "And it's not weird that you said you loved me a billion years ago?"

He smiled back. "It's only weird if we make it weird. What I want is to have my friend back. All that other stuff is water under the Cleary Island bridge."

"Yay." It was a casual response, but inside Effie felt immensely better. She'd never considered this plot twist, but all of a sudden, she was looking forward to the next few months. She sat up straighter. "This summer is going to be so fun. The dynamic duo: back in action. What sort of trouble should we get into?"

Ernie closed his eyes and considered her question. When he spoke, he was watching the water lap at the shore. "Take a boat ride out to the big rock near Dulse Cove. Eat fried clams dunked in fresh tartar sauce until our stomachs hurt. Watch the sunset from Top Spot Mountain. Fill our backpacks with cookbooks at the library's summer book sale. Get suntans. Get sunburns. Get up at sunrise to pick beach peas into my ball cap and sauté them in butter and eat them over toast with hot coffee. Drive around town in a pickup with the windows down. Steal waffle cones from your dad's shop and break them apart to use for s'mores. Order a giant lobster roll on a split-top roll from Dougie's truck."

"That's a very extravagant list of activities."

"It's not even the half of it." He'd stood up during his speech and was now pacing on the porch. "We have Mondays and Tuesdays off. You give me every Monday, and we'll make the most of it. Each week, one of us is responsible for planning an activity. We'll alternate."

"Like a field trip?"

"If you want, sure. We could travel, or stay here. Do the stuff we used to, or something entirely new. It doesn't really matter. I just want to spend time getting to know my best friend again." She pointed her thumbs at her chest, and he nodded. "Yup. That's you. I'll start. I'll plan next week's activity. Are you in?"

She nodded wordlessly, looking ahead at the moon hanging low over the harbor.

"I'm glad you came home." Ernie checked his watch and raised his eyebrows. "It's late. Walk you home?"

Effie finished her beer in one long swallow. Her whole body was tingling. Her heart felt full and warm, but her belly was turning over itself. She gave a little shake to recalibrate her nerves, and gave him a classic Effie Olsen smirk. "Yeah. I dare you."

Chapter Twelve

On Sunday, Effie woke up with a buzzy feeling in her heart: there was one more day until Ernie's first item on their summer bucket list and she was dying to know what he'd planned. She'd gotten to Brown Butter early, intent on checking off her kitchen chores before things got busy. None of the waitstaff were in yet, but through the open doorway, she could hear Sixto charring red peppers, the smoky scent curling through the air and coaxing her toward the kitchen. She stopped halfway across the dining room, though: at the bar was a woman she hadn't met yet, arranging large flowers and elegant-looking grasses in tall vases.

The stranger was short and pixie-like, with black-brown hair piled into a messy bear claw of a bun at the top of her head. She had tanned, dewy skin and was wearing a white linen tank with a mauve skirt that grazed the tops of her Birkenstocks. A strand of wooden beads was wrapped three times around her tiny wrist.

As Effie made her way across the room, getting closer, she smelled a mixture of earthy essential oils. Lavender and something.

This woman's presence—her appearance and scent—immediately reminded Effie why she had a difficult time connecting with other women. How were you supposed to, when other women looked like enchanted woodland creatures doing magical flower things . . . and you looked like an exhausted husk of a human wading through Your Mom jokes in a man's world?

"Hello!" The woman glanced up from a bunch of purple plants that looked like pom-poms. She set down her shears—antique-looking, with elegantly long blades—and waved. "We have not met!"

"We have not." Would Effie ever be released from the drudgery of waving to people on Alder Isle? Not today, it would seem. She made a single swishing motion with her hand. "I'm Effie," she offered. "The new sous chef."

"Ohhh, right, right, right!" The woman nodded, sliding a delicate stem into place. She fluffed its tissue-paper-thin petals and pulled the stem upward what Effie perceived to be an indiscernible amount. "I'm Dahlia. I own Ranunculus, the flower shop near Top Spot."

"Right. Right. . . . right." Not every restaurant outsourced its floral arrangements, but the fancy ones did. The florists came, they snipped and fluffed, and then they left. The flower people were not usually named after actual flowers.

"What do you think about this arrangement?" Dahlia asked.

"It's nice. Very flowery," Effie said. Dahlia nodded, expecting more. Effie pointed at the bloom Dahlia had just touched. "What kind is that?"

"Ranunculus! It's my favorite. That may or may not surprise you, seeing as I've named my business after it."

"Mmm." Through the kitchen doors Effie heard Sixto shout a string of four-letter words. She moved her knife roll to her other hand and looked in that direction, ready to be done with the conversation. Angry line cooks swearing to the high heavens, she could handle. Chitchat with ethereal island fairies, not so much.

Before she could mumble out an excuse to leave, the front door opened and Jarrod entered where Effie had just come in. He was balancing five plastic pint containers, one on top of the other. They were all filled with white rice, and inside each one was a knobby black lump.

"Got truffs," he said and paused, seemingly waiting for applause. Effie's eyebrow arched up to her hairline. Italian truffles were nowhere near being a Maine agricultural product. How were they supposed to fit into the 75 percent hyperlocal, 25 percent regional ethos?

Jarrod set down the stack and shook out his hair like he was auditioning for the After part of a Head & Shoulders commercial. He tried again for a better reception: "Fuck yeah, *truffles.* You would not believe how much these cost, but we can upcharge for them if I go out and shave 'em over pasta, tableside. Here, smell." He cracked open a container and shoved it under Effie's nose. Their musky, mushroomy scent walloped her. She liked truffles and felt a little thrill at the chance to cook with them. But she checked her personal opinion and gave Jarrod an exasperated look.

"Those aren't local."

"No, but diners don't know that."

"If they're eating here, they probably do."

"Ellie, trust me—"

"Effie," Dahlia corrected him, frowning over a particularly buoyant cream-colored ranunculus.

Effie looked over at the bar in surprise. Usually it was her against, oh, *everyone* at work. When was the last time another woman stuck up for her? Never? Definitely never.

"Right, whatever," Jarrod continued. "If I go out there and flirt with the rich old ladies and tell them one of our farm partners figured out how to grow truffles, they will practically beg me to tack on an extra twenty-five dollars as a thank-you."

"Practically." Effie crossed her arms, the canvas knife roll slapping against her hip.

Dahlia looked upset. "Truffles aren't local?"

"Nope."

"But I love truffles."

"You can still love them," Effie said. "But I wouldn't advise putting it in writing that they're grown here because they're not."

"You." Jarrod sealed the container and pointed at Effie's chest with a free finger. "My office. Now."

In unexpected alliance with Dahlia, Effie tossed an exasperated look to the florist, who caught it with a stifled titter. "Fine." Effie uncrossed her arms and stalked across the room while Jarrod gathered up his parcels and took a detour to drop them in the walk-in cooler.

Jarrod may have lived dirty, but he worked clean. The tidy office couldn't have been more different from his bedroom. An image that she was still trying to forget. There wasn't a speck of dust on the surface of the desk, and a month's worth of invoices were arranged neatly in two piles. A PAID stamper sat on top of one of them. There was a handsome brass lamp in the corner of the room, and a green velvet armchair sat opposite the desk. Jarrod's own chair was a black walnut Eames. *Predictable,* thought Effie. A few years back, the *New Yorker* had run a profile of the famous chef Bernard Dupont. In it, he'd mentioned he liked Herman Miller furniture. After the article came out, chef fanboys across the country talked about it for weeks. She was certain Jarrod had read it. She set her knives down and slipped behind the desk to try the Eames on for size. She'd never sat in a seven-thousand dollar chair before. This would probably be her only chance.

The leather was cool, and the cushions gently cupped her butt. She surprised herself by comparing it to Ernie's fat old couch. The couch was inviting and comfortable. The Eames was quietly luxurious in a way that made her feel self-conscious. She leaned back, and the chair leaned with her. Okay, the chair was good. She was just about to return to the other side of the desk when her eye caught a file organizer on a cabinet. She scooted the chair across the floor to get a closer look. Each slot held an identical manila folder with its contents written in Sharpie on the tab.

Produce
Meat
Dairy
Seafood
Grains & Flour
Misc.

Plenty of chefs organized their invoices by ingredient genre. She had, during her time at Cowboy Bean. Not that her systems had been the gold standard. Effie wondered when Jarrod would pass the baton to her. In every restaurant where she'd been high enough on the ladder, the ordering and financial duties were shared by sous and executive chefs. Couldn't hurt to start wrapping her head around that part of the job.

As she pulled *Produce* out of its slot, a second folder fluttered to the floor. This one was labeled *Monk*. Weird. She put back the first folder and reached for the second.

"What the fuck, Olsen." She heard Jarrod's voice coming from down the hall. He was almost at the door. The folder fell from her fingertips back into its slot like it was pizza-oven hot. He banged through the door, chucking his own knife case on the desk next to hers.

"Nice chair," Effie said, hoping he hadn't caught her snooping around his files.

"I know." Jarrod stood in front of the desk, crossing his arms. Afraid she'd betray herself with guilty eyes, Effie focused on his tattoo sleeve. It started with a few orange flames licking his wrist and ended in a serpent snaking around his elbow. There was a frying pan and a chef's knife somewhere in the middle. "What's your job title?" He kept his arms crossed.

Oh, hell no. He was not going to play this game with her. He would not intimidate her with a stunning display of toxic masculinity. She held his gaze, her blue eyes Antarctic-glacier-cold. "Sous chef."

"Sous chef, *Chef*," he corrected her. She knew what he was doing; implying that she had left off the title of respect owed to him.

She reached for a little sass in her response. "Nope, it's just sous chef."

Technically, yes. As her superior, addressing him meant adding the word "Chef" to whatever she said. Like, "I'll do that right now, Chef." Or, "Whatever you say, Chef." It was standard restaurant chain-of-command stuff. But Jarrod was just so . . . *No*. The man did not deserve respect.

"The fuck?" He motioned for her to scoot out of the chair. She kept her butt where it was.

"My job title. It's sous chef. Not sous chef-chef."

His lips worked to hold back a growl. "Oh, get your ass out of my chair, Olsen."

She did so finally, flourishing an exaggerated bow to the Eames as she did. As she made her way to the opposite side of the desk and sat in the velvet armchair, anxious bile rose in her throat. Was she going too far? She'd never been so blatantly rude to a boss before. But then, she'd never had a boss as demeaning and slimy as Jarrod. She'd learned the story of Brown Butter's previous sous chef about three hours into her first day: he'd butted heads with Jarrod about practically everything. After eight months, he quit in a blaze of glory—no warning, and, luckily for Effie, leaving no time to be too picky about potential replacements.

Also. Being back home was messing with her brain. It was making her act out in ways that felt unfamiliar despite being deeply ingrained. Once upon a time, Effie had been one hundred percent pure sass. But she hadn't accessed that side of herself in years. She sat up straighter and reminded herself of what really mattered: keeping this job through the summer. Earning enough money to leave. *Do whatever it takes, Effie. Don't get distracted by dumpster trash.*

"Cute as that was, you have got to stop undermining me." Jarrod ran a hand through his hair, curls gone crazy in the foggy Maine morning air. "Every time you speak over me, you're training the staff to value your authority over mine." He paused, waiting for her reaction. She was confused—when had she spoken over him? The night before, at dinner service? When he'd abandoned her at the pass yet again? "Every time you dismiss my expertise, you insinuate your knowledge and skills surpass mine." She suppressed an eye roll. *It's more than insinuation, jerk.* "And every time you question my creative vision, you prove to me that you can't take orders."

This was about the truffles? This seemed to be about more than truffles. She opened her mouth, working to cover up a frown with an explanation. He cut her off. "Can you take orders, Effie? Are you good at that?"

Her frown returned.

"Do you *like* taking orders?" He hadn't sat down; he was

moving to the door, closing it quietly, turning the antique brass knob to seal it against the frame.

"I . . ." Effie's voice trailed off as her eyes followed him. "Jarrod—we—I mean, I—" She fumbled for the right thing to say. Which was what, exactly? That first night had been a mistake. But it had been mutual. Whatever was about to happen next was not. Her heart was pounding, but if she could steer their conversation back to the professional, maybe he would follow her lead. "I'm sorry, Chef." She spoke slowly to iron out the wrinkles in her vocal cords. She stayed perfectly still. Like a deer in the middle of the road. She braced herself for the next part, knowing it would be hard to say out loud: "You're right."

He delivered a wry smile. "*That*'s what I'm talking about. Remember, Olsen: I'm the one with power in this situation. Don't fuck it up for yourself."

"You're right," she repeated, hating the lie but knowing it was necessary to get out of there as fast as possible. "I'm opinionated. Always have been." She gave a little shrug to demonstrate she just couldn't help it. She continued flattering him. Her voice sounded like honey, but the next words tasted like vinegar. "You are head chef, and I work . . ." She gulped. "For you." She stood and stepped away from him, then coolly grabbed her knives. "I take your point, and it won't happen again. I'm sorry to start your day on the wrong foot. Truffles are good. I trust however you want to present them to our guests."

She twisted the knob and got the door open an inch before Jarrod pushed it shut, his arm extended over her shoulder. They were both facing the door, facing the way out. She could feel his heartbeat against her back, that's how close he was. His mouth met the top of her ear, and she felt more than heard the words he spoke next. "You do work for me, Olsen. Don't forget that."

She'd had enough of this. And while he may have enjoyed most of the power, he didn't have it all.

With one swift movement, she swung her elbow backward. He cursed and doubled over in pain. "Just so you're aware," she hissed, "better men have gotten fired for a lot less." She pushed out into the hallway. At the same time, exiting the restroom with a concerned look on her face was Dahlia.

Chapter Thirteen

Dahlia finished drying her hands with one of the luxe terry-cloth towels and tossed it in the vintage hamper just before the bathroom door swung shut. "All good?" Two words that held a world of possibility but surprisingly little pressure. Instinctively, Effie knew she could answer any way she wanted.

She exhaled and the wispy almost-bangs around her temples billowed upward. "All good. Thanks for asking. I appreciate it," she said, realizing that she genuinely did.

Dahlia worried at a turquoise ring on her thumb and shook her head in slow motion. "Really, though? It's just that I know other women who've been alone with Jarrod in his office, and . . ." She cut herself off, letting Effie fill in the blanks for herself. "Wanna take a walk?"

"I'd like to," Effie said, again realizing that she did. "But there's so much to get through before service tonight, especially with the truffles. Jarrod will probably want to create a new pasta dish or something." She pressed her lips together, the words hitting her over the head like a two-by-four. The rest of her morning sounded pretty miserable when you put it like that. "You know what? Yes. I will make time. Let's do it."

"Great," Dahlia said, guiding Effie toward the exit. As they left the hallway, Dahlia lifted her Birkenstock and swiftly kicked Jarrod's door.

I have one piece of advice for you," Dahlia said once they were out on the sunshine-y sidewalk. "If you want it?" Effie nodded, curious what her new friend would offer.

"Ignore the patriarchy," Dahlia said, flashing the inside of her forearm to show a flower-bordered tattoo that read the same thing. *Ignore the patriarchy.*

"Not destroy? Dismantle? Fuck?"

Dahlia grinned. "Being ignored makes them madder. Although you can fuck 'em, too, if you want."

Effie smiled back.

They walked in silence as they passed Ernie's house. Mick was seated at the bay window overlooking the yard. As the women passed, he raised a hand and gave Effie a warm smile. It was the first time she'd seen him since she returned to Alder Isle. She made a mental note to stop by and say hello soon. Although he was technically part of the patriarchy, he was one of the good ones. He'd done so much for her when she was little. The memories flooded her and her eyes felt prickly. Trying to shoo away the emotion, Effie swatted the air, and Dahlia instinctively did the same, assuming mosquitos or flies or bees.

"You don't have to tell me anything," said Dahlia as they crossed the bridge onto Cleary—the same bridge that Ernie had streaked over earlier that week. Effie closed her eyes and let herself recall his ass in the moonlight. She swallowed a smile whole. Dahlia bounced her fingertips across the wild beach-pea bushes. "But Jarrod is toxic, and I know it, and back-of-house knows it, and front-of-house sure as hell knows it." She was at least four inches shorter than Effie and looked up at her now. "You're better than him. More talented and obviously a better human being. At least, that's what the rest of the kitchen staff are saying." *They had said that? About her?* "I'm sure you can look out for yourself, but if you ever need a friend, I am friendly."

Effie let this sink in, the few seconds of silence feeling monumental. "Thanks," she finally said. There was more inside her, like, *It feels like you care, and that unnerves me. I don't know if I can trust you, but I want to try.* Dahlia held out her arms and spun in a circle once. "I love this place. Weird that the best part of Alder Isle isn't on Alder Isle."

"It's nice," Effie agreed. "You're not from here." It was a statement, not a question. Dahlia looked just a handful of years younger than Effie, and if she'd grown up on the island, they would have known each other.

"I am not. But I've been here for a decade." She laughed before Effie could interject. "I know that still doesn't make me a local. But this is the first place that has ever felt like home. It felt like *my* home from the moment I stepped off the ferry." They turned left onto the pathway to the nature preserve that wound around the island and ended at a rocky beach. It was the beach Effie had visited on her first morning back, where she had screamed her lungs out below the gulls and saw Dougie on the water. "Military brat," Dahlia said as she pointed a thumb at her own chest, the descriptor filling in a lot of blanks. "I moved here with a dude, if you can believe that. Moved here *for* a dude, which is even worse," she corrected herself.

"Why wouldn't I believe that?"

Dahlia tilted her head. "Because—oh, right! I forget you don't know me." She laughed at herself. "I assume that everyone I meet knows everything about me because—"

"Because Alder Isle," Effie finished for her. "It's a small place and gossip is the main group-building activity."

"Exactly. So: Kit is my wife," Dahlia said. "You probably haven't met because we live on the north shore and she is a delightfully reclusive painter."

"How . . . did you meet?" Effie wasn't sure what she was trying to ask. She didn't want to pressure Dahlia into sharing anything *she* wouldn't have wanted to talk about with someone she'd just met. Which was practically everything.

"Oh, wow, it's such a good story! I was dating this truly wretched guy who grew up here. He was a lobsterman." Effie's mouth felt dry. *Please don't let it be Ernie.*

"He had moved away from Maine, to the other Portland.

Oregon. That's where I was living at the time." Effie swallowed the lump of fear that had risen unexpectedly fast in her throat. *Phew. Not Ernie.*

"He's about ten years older than me. Convinced me to move back here with him when he got homesick. I was just out of high school and up for whatever. Down for whatever? Across for whatever, I guess, because it was on the other side of the country. He's a sweaty jockstrap of a man, but I might've stayed with him forever if Kit hadn't decided to show some of her paintings at the gallery." Dahlia pointed back toward town. The art gallery was right next to Meadowsweet Scoops. "I dragged him to the opening and fell in love with her when I saw the very first painting. It was of a field of goldenrod and Queen Anne's lace." She sighed, dreamily reminiscing. "Only Kit could have made me believe weeds are flowers, too."

"Did you . . . ?" Effie stumbled.

"Know I could fall for a woman?"

"Yeah, I guess that's what I'm trying to ask. However clumsily."

"If you'd asked me ten years ago, I would have said no. But it's not like meeting Kit changed me. She just helped me see what—who—was already inside. Without doing a thing beyond being herself."

Effie plucked a piece of ragweed from the ground. "Sounds dreamy," she said, bringing the plant to her nose. She sniffed deeply and sneezed. Pollen burst into the air in a violent flurry.

"Oh girl," Dahlia said, taking the stem from her and tossing it in the brush. "Not all weeds are flowers."

They walked and chatted, talking about Maine life—the

good parts and the bad, too—and Effie's travels, until they had completed the loop and made their way back to the bridge to Alder Isle. From across the way, Effie saw Ernie pushing open the boathouse door. He disappeared inside. It was almost noon. In high school, Ernie had gone home every day for lunch. He'd make what he called "DIY Lunchables," but these days on Instagram, you'd find similar creations with hashtags like #epic-charcuterieboard. Effie wondered if he was about to arrange pieces of salami and cheese on an old cutting board, with Wheat Thins fanned out in rows like buttery dominoes. Ernie wasn't the changing kind. He was the kind who brought you a zip-top baggie of cheddar cheese and cherry tomatoes during seventh period history class because he worried you hadn't eaten.

He was the kind who always let you have the last bite, the best piece of everything.

The thoughtful kind.

The surprisingly romantic kind. If you were ready to see it.

Nope. Effie reversed course. The best friend kind.

Dahlia followed Effie's gaze across the water and wore her own smile. "He's an island boy. Works at Brown Butter, too. Ernie Callahan. Though you probably know that. Super, super nice."

"Yeah, we grew up together." Effie worked hard to keep her focus on the ground in front of her as they passed the boathouse. "Although I don't know him very well anymore." The words that left her mouth were replaced with a sour taste, even though it wasn't a lie. She'd spent a handful of hours in his presence since returning; how much could you learn about a person in that time? And yet. Saying that out loud had felt wrong.

Despite being apart for years, seeing him again had made her realize they knew each other better than anyone in the world. Effie would never admit it, but she felt it. And it scared her.

Dahlia pushed open the heavy restaurant door and busied herself with wiping pollen and snipped stems from the bar. "I've got to get back to Ranunculus," she said. "And you have your mice in place to get to."

Effie laughed before she could stop herself. "*Mise* en place." She pronounced it like "meese," the French way. Meaning, having everything ready and organized.

Dahlia grinned like she'd known that all along and held her hands underneath her nose with bent wrists. She wiggled her fingers, like they were whiskers. "Cheesed to meet you, Effie."

Effie mimicked Dahlia's gesture and twitched her nose for good measure. She felt supremely odd and pulled her hands down, back to the safety of her pants pockets. Effie Olsen did not go around pretending to be small woodland creatures. She was not the type to have inside jokes with other friends. At least, she hadn't ever been before.

Well. Except for Ernie.

Although. Somehow, that felt different.

Chapter Fourteen

Although Effie was not the skipping kind, her step was perceptibly lighter as she made her way back to her station in the kitchen. She smiled at Jean-Claude, fist-bumped Sixto, and checked in on Chad, who was picking thyme leaves from a pile of stems. She had asked him the night before if he wanted to start performing some small prep tasks, and he'd agreed with bright eyes and an eager nod. He had a positive attitude, and that was half the job, really. No matter what guys like Jarrod thought. She opened a notebook and scribbled a few ideas for more tasks Chad could handle. She had started to write a prep list for Anika, one of the interns who was working the pasta station that night, when she remembered something. The night before, she'd overheard Nikki, the lead server, grumble to Sixto about a diner's complaint: "I swear, hand over my chest, he said, 'This is the worst ravioli I have ever eaten in my life.'"

Sixto had shaken his head and groaned. "Fucking Jarrod."

The two were huddled by the POS machine and Effie didn't have a good reason to linger, so she hadn't heard what they'd said next. It had been late, and Effie was tired, so she immediately forgot about it. Until now, staring at her own handwritten instructions for cooking and saucing Jarrod's lobster ravioli.

Diners often complained in fine dining restaurants, but they were usually about things like small portions and snooty waitstaff. Effie had never heard a dish being described as the "worst ever." She tried the ravioli herself almost nightly, and found it entirely inoffensive (besides the fact that it should have been bucatini in a cream sauce, as she had suggested to Jarrod). Had something gone wrong with the most recent batch? Maybe the lobster had spoiled. She was mortified to think that Brown Butter might have served bad seafood and decided to investigate in the cold storage. If there was something wrong with their food, she was determined to find out. No way was she willing to put her career reputation on the line for a mass case of food poisoning. Especially not if the head chef knew about it and just didn't care.

Effie found yesterday's half-empty plastic tub of ravioli tucked in the corner, underneath the photo of Christopher Walken. Jarrod had proudly presented the picture on her first day, and she'd pretended to be charmed. But it wasn't an original joke. Most restaurants had a punny nickname for their walk-in coolers and freezers: she'd known a Walk-In Phoenix and a Walk-In Dead. She kneeled on the floor, shivering in the cold, and opened the lid.

It was probably overdramatic to inspect the ravioli right here on the floor in the middle of the afternoon when anyone could walk in (or Walken). But at the moment, Effie didn't care. She was just so sick of men in power acting like psychotic tyrants. If Jarrod was cutting corners with dishes and putting their diners' health at risk, she had to know. She picked up a ravioli and pinched it. It was circular, with neatly crimped edges, like it had been every other night she worked. She peeled it open and huffed angrily. The fish was chopped so finely, and mixed so thoroughly with the cheese and seasonings, it was impossible to know for sure if it was bad. She dipped her finger in the filling and brought a small amount to her tongue. It was cold and claggy and tasted overwhelmingly of garlic. She held it in her left palm as she tore into another ravioli. Same thing. Another. No different. She felt crazy and powerless, and soon she was surrounded by disemboweled ravioli. She was just about to give up when the door opened.

In an instant, Effie's stomach turned, and she shoved half a dozen raviolis in her pants pockets. She pushed the tub onto the shelf, back against the wall. There was no time to latch the lid back on; the door swung open.

Oh, Ernie, I'm so glad it's you." She had been on her knees and collapsed now in a heap onto the floor. A ravioli plopped out of her pocket and rolled a halfhearted foot until it landed between them.

"Nice to see you, too," he said over the enormous stockpot in his hands. "Hang on, this is hot." He set the pot down on a shelf so it could cool. "Jean-Claude asked me to bring it in here," he said, answering the question Effie hadn't asked out loud but had been wondering. It was Jean-Claude's job to make, cool, strain, and store all the stocks and broths. Apparently, he'd convinced Ernie to do some of the work for him.

"So, uh, what's with that?" Ernie lowered himself onto the floor next to her and let his eyes wander to the ravioli. His comforting almondy scent washed over her, and her belly flipped again. "And why are we having this conversation on the floor of a tiny sub-forty-degree room that smells vaguely of fish and onions?"

Effie was quiet for a moment. She wasn't sure how to answer, wasn't entirely sure what she'd just tried to accomplish. And then she realized: if there was one person in this entire restaurant who'd know if something was off with the lobster, it was Ernie.

"You break down all the fish and meat that comes into Brown Butter, right? I mean, you don't get anything in that's preportioned or whatever?"

He studied her, curious about this unexpected line of questioning. "I guess so, yeah."

"So *everything* comes in whole?"

"I mean, stuff has been gutted and whatnot. It's not like a cow walks into the basement and emerges as a steak. What are you asking, Eff?"

"Lobster." The look on his face said it all. Or at least, it said something. "Do you get in lobster whole?"

He set his jaw and shook his head. "That would be the one thing I do not see."

Effie realized how insensitive the question had been. Dealing with lobster would be a sore subject for Ernie, having given up his dad's boat and his own career goals to work here. She put her palm over his knee and felt him tense. She hated to think her touch made him feel uncomfortable, and took back her hand.

"I used to," Ernie said. "For a while, Brown Butter was getting their lobster from the Deacon Lobster Company." Effie nodded; that wasn't uncommon. It was a local company, and most of the lobstermen on the island worked for them. "But after a couple months, I don't know, it just stopped coming in. I asked Jarrod about it, and he told me that he had found 'a guy.'"

"So then you'd get lobster from some random dude?"

"No, then I stopped getting lobster at all. Jarrod fed me some stupid line about my prep not being clean enough. He claimed there was shell in the meat, and he couldn't trust me to do it anymore." Effie felt heat radiating from Ernie's body, and his ears were the color of ripe raspberries. "If anyone in this entire place knows how to clean lobster, it's me. He's a fucking dick."

"Wow," Effie said. "I've never heard you swear before."

"Yeah, well. You haven't been around for a while. Maybe don't seem so surprised when I act like a human being or have my own stuff."

"Fair enough," Effie said, because it was.

They were quiet for a few beats.

"I'm sorry," she said at the same time he asked, "Why did you want to know?"

"It's okay," he answered at the same time she said, "I think I've just fallen into a pile of Brown Butter's dirty laundry."

"That sounds gross, but now I'm intrigued." Ernie stood and

offered his hand to her. It felt nice, being with him in that way. Not just ex–best friends, not just coworkers, but coconspirators. Secret holders. She grabbed the tub from the floor and adjusted the lid on the container. "I've gotta fill you in. But first, I need to get these raviolis out of my pockets and do about a hundred things for my mise. Can I tell you about all this tomorrow? When are we meeting, by the way? And where?"

Ernie's whole body brightened. "We are meeting at the boathouse at eight. In the evening, not morning," he clarified, clocking the horrified look on her face. "Now get cracking on your list so you can get home early tonight. You're going to want to rest up." Her eyes pressed him for more details, but he shook his head to indicate he wasn't divulging any more. He opened the door and held out his hands. Effie deposited the six unraveled ravioli into his cupped palms. He dumped them in the compost bin, then gave her a dutiful salute and walked backward, down the hallway, and into the basement.

Chapter Fifteen

"Hey!" Effie said, shifting her weight from one foot to the other on Ernie's welcome mat. She was holding a mixed six-pack of craft beer. She had spent the morning sleeping in; the afternoon searching job listings for restaurants in Iceland, Denmark, and Sweden; and the last ten minutes doing and undoing her ponytail, trying to figure out how to wear her hair and why she cared. It was five minutes after 8:00.

"Hey yourself," Ernie said back, opening the door a little farther. He was wearing a comfy-looking linen button-down and the khaki shorts he seemed to favor. "Hooray, you brought beer. Is it cold?"

She looked at him, wounded. "What is this, amateur hour?"

He laughed, then reached for his house keys in a bowl by the door. "Forgive me. I should have known better. We'll take it with us. That is, if you're still up for an adventure?"

"I am up for an adventure," Effie said. "Always."

"Walk, bike, or drive?"

Effie looked at the cardboard holder of beer in her hand, removed two, then deposited the rest in his fridge. She met him back by the door. "Definitely walk."

Ten minutes later, they'd reached the parking lot by Dulse Cove. They were holding their bottles from the necks as they meandered away from the water and toward a thicket of trees. The sun was starting its slow slide into the ocean. An alder shook its leaves as a cool breeze picked up. There wasn't another car or person in sight.

"Is this going to get murder-y?" Effie joked.

"Not if I have anything to say about it," Ernie said, leading her deeper into the woods. "You really don't know where we're going?"

Effie shook her head. "I am perplexed."

"Huh. Well you'll remember in a second." They stepped over a lazy stream and turned past a red berry bush. "Now do you remember?"

Effie's free hand flew to her forehead. "Oh, wow. Yes. I do." They were in a tiny clearing no more than six feet by six feet, overgrown with brambles. "Our time capsule."

Ernie nodded and set their bottles on a rock. He pointed to a wooden dowel marking the spot. There was a tattered, faded bandana tied around it in many messy knots. The summer before senior year, when she was sixteen and he was seventeen and they were both hopeful, they'd written down predictions about their lives ten years in the future. If Effie remembered correctly, they had also added little trinkets and souvenirs.

"We're late," she said. "Six years late."

Ernie shrugged.

"You haven't dug it up?"

"Naw," he said. "I was waiting for you."

"You could've been waiting a long time."

He shrugged again. "I know."

She untied the fisherman's sweater from her waist and shimmied into it. The mosquitos were thicker in the grove and had her scrambling to cover her arms. "Did you bring a shovel?"

He pulled a small garden trowel from the backpack he'd slung over one shoulder. "It can't be that deep, right?"

After just a couple minutes of digging, Effie heard metal on metal. Ernie dug around the old tin lunchbox and unearthed it. "It's so rusty. I hope I don't get botulism."

"Tetanus," Effie corrected.

"Know-it-all," he said, and patted the ground next to him. "Let's do it together."

Effie grabbed the latch. He placed his fingers over hers. They looked at each other, and she swallowed. "Ready?"

"Steady."

"Go." The box opened with an ominous creak. Effie half expected a swarm of bugs to fly out, but its contents were neat and tidy. They had written their predictions on index cards and sealed them in plastic zip-top bags. There was a larger, gallon-sized bag holding their treasures. Ernie took that out first and undid the seal. Wordlessly, he handed a folded piece of paper to Effie. She opened it up and made a quiet, tender sound. "My first real dinner."

It was a menu, printed on thick card stock. For her fifteenth birthday, a year after her parents' divorce, Ernie and Mick had taken her to one of Portland's fanciest restaurants. Mick had set up a special menu in advance. The chef had even come out between courses and chatted with Effie about her hopes and dreams to work in a restaurant herself someday. She hadn't thought about that night for years. But now, she could taste the buttery Parker House rolls, the sea bass with bacon vinaigrette and roasted cabbage. She remembered Ernie's eyes shining across the table. The way he squeezed her knee when the chef had said, "Something tells me you're going to make a very good cook, Effie."

She carefully folded the paper back into thirds. "What's your memento?" Ernie threw a balled-up pair of socks at her, and she shrieked. "THOSE THINGS!" They were his lucky pair; he'd been wearing them when their track team took home first place at States. Effie had smoked the competition in the hurdles, and Ernie had taken it all on pole vault. "Please tell me you washed them before we buried this."

"Uhh . . ." He scratched his head, pretending to think about it.

"Gross," Effie said, but she was giggling. "Let's do our predictions."

"Do you remember what they said?" Ernie asked, handing over hers.

"Nope. Do you?"

"Yep."

"Ooh, okay, you go first," Effie said, and leaned back in the grass.

Ernie read aloud:

I, Ernest Sean Callahan, predict that at age twenty-seven, I will be working full time on the boat, having convinced my father to finally retire and relax. (Hahaha JK he'll never quit.) I will be the highest-earning lobsterman on Alder Isle, and thus I will have moved out of the boathouse and into one of the more spacious mansions on the north isle. I will be married to Megan Fox, and we will have so many children, like an obscene amount of children.

"Essentially yes," Effie said. "My turn." Ernie angled the flashlight toward her paper.

I, Euphemia Dove Olsen, predict that by age twenty-six, I will have won a James Beard Award for Rising Star chef. I will have lived in at least five different countries and had different lovers in each one. I will be famous, and I will not give any fucks.

"Also yes?" Ernie took the paper from her and slid it back in the baggie. "Wanna write new ones? For the next ten years?"

Effie wrinkled her nose. "Not really. They seemed harmless and fun at the time but reading that made me feel weird."

"Yeah, I get that," Ernie said, and shut the box, then slid it in his backpack. "Honestly, being here with you now makes me feel weird." Effie looked at him sideways and played with the hem of her sweater. "I'm not saying that to be mean. I just . . . can I tell you something?" She nodded. "The other night, I told you I wasn't mad at you. And that was true. But I was hurt. All that talk about our futures, all the dreaming we'd done. How we'd keep in touch when you went away. How we'd visit each other. More than anything, I felt this huge hole in my life where our friendship had been. I couldn't tell you when something good happened. Or something bad. It was a lonely few years before I got over it. I know we were both at fault for how things ended, but it really sucked to know you had come back a few times and never even tried to contact me." He was speaking quickly, sharing it all without looking at Effie. "Wow. I don't think I've ever called you out on anything before."

"I think that was a first for both of us." She continued to study her sweater. "It wasn't until I started working in kitchens, with bossy men, that I realized how bossy I had been to you. I never really let you have your way, did I?"

"Naw, but it's not like I was brave enough to go toe-to-toe with you over something I didn't really care about."

"What do you mean?"

"For years, like our entire childhood, all I wanted was to tag along with you. You were so fun and spontaneous. It was a thrill to be around. The details didn't matter, as long as we were together."

"Why do I feel like I did something wrong without knowing what it was?"

"Oh, don't feel bad." Ernie retrieved their beers and shook his head. "I guess what I'm trying to say is, when you left the way you did, it created space for me to figure out who I was and what I actually liked doing. Even though it was also hard and painful."

Effie swallowed the urge to defend herself. Ernie had never been the one to guide their conversations. The more he talked, the more she wanted to hold that space for him. "That makes so much sense, and I'm happy for you, despite all the . . . complications. So what did you learn? About yourself?"

His ears turned pink. "Oh God, I hadn't planned this far into the conversation. I have nothing prepared."

"Just tell me some random stuff! Anything!"

"Okay." He sipped and thought. "Well, I did keep going to the library every week. But now I check out books *I* want to read, not just cookbooks. History, mostly," he added. "Big, boring books about obscure battles. Because I am a big, boring nerd."

"What else?"

"Luke has become a good friend since our track shenanigans. Sometimes I help him out with big projects when his construction company has a lot of jobs. I've gotten pretty good at finding my way around a hammer and band saw."

"That's great! And hot! Tell me it's gotten you a date with at least one sexy island transplant."

"You don't actually want to hear about that stuff, do you?"

"I do," said Effie, and immediately realized she didn't. Still, she couldn't stop herself. "You're not dating anyone now, are you?"

"No, not anyone serious." He gave her a sly grin as she pulled her sweater sleeves up around her elbows. "But really, I do have plenty of friends now. You have a way of dominating my time when you're around, you know that?"

"Sorry-not-sorry. Anyone else I know?"

"Actually, yeah. Lake and I hang out." Effie made a face, then tried to cover it up with a pretend sneeze. "Obviously fake," he said. "But nice try. Sixto, too. We have a guy's poker night once a month. Jean-Claude comes sometimes. B.J. has shown on occasion. Luke, obviously. My dad . . ." Ernie's voice rolled into an embarrassed mumble. "Your dad."

"You hang out with my dad?"

"Haha. Yes! Jealous?"

"Annoyingly, a little."

"So . . . yeah. That's it. I'm done with the speech portion of the evening. It felt good to say all that."

"Actually, it felt good to hear." Spending time with Ernie was comforting and familiar, but this new side of him was even better. There was a little residual guilt in her heart, but mostly she felt proud of her best friend, and reassured by his presence. "I was pretty headstrong and intense when I was younger. And I think I avoided seeing you because I was embarrassed about that. I didn't—I still don't—know how to be who I was and who I am. I want to make a joke so badly, but I think I will just say, I'm sorry."

The light was almost gone from the sky. He pulled a small battery-powered lantern from his pack and turned it on. "I forgive you. And I'm sorry, too. I have not been a perfect best friend, either." They were sitting side by side, and he reached an arm around her and hugged her close. Her head hovered above his shoulder awkwardly until he whispered, "It's okay." She nestled in a little closer. He let her settle and get comfortable before he spoke again. "So. I think we were going to talk about lobster ravioli."

"Oh blah. I don't want to think about shithead Jarrod right now," Effie's thoughts materialized in her mouth before she could stop them. "I just overheard Sixto and Nikki talking about some diner who hated the dish. Said it was terrible. I was worried the fish had gone bad, and that we'd accidentally poisoned half the tourists on Alder Isle this weekend."

"I wouldn't be surprised," Ernie said, his chin resting on the top of her head. It was wild how comforting it felt, having him this close after so long. "Jarrod hasn't exactly been discerning in his ingredient procurement over the last year."

"Say more."

"Just that he gets produce from all over. He doesn't even try to hide that. Anything that goes into a sauce or juice or soup is from Sysco. He saves the local-grown stuff to garnish plates. But almost everything I prep is from wherever. He buys Costco chickens when we run out."

Effie's voice wavered. "I'm ashamed of how normal that sounds to me. Every restaurant I've worked in, except for the trattoria, was like that. It's just how stuff gets done in this industry." She smacked at a mosquito feasting on her shin.

Ernie released her, stood, and offered his hand. "It's getting late. So if this is standard operation, why do you care about some customer saying the lobster is bad?"

"Because it's *everything*," Effie said, brushing earth from the seat of her shorts. They started the walk back to town. "Lobster is

Alder Isle's history and industry and pride and joy. It's your job and your dad's job and your passion."

Ernie shook his head. "Not anymore."

"Still. It's the one thing Brown Butter should absolutely nail," she said.

"Yeah. True," he agreed. After a few minutes, he spoke again. "But what can we do about it?"

"Speaking from experience? Not a damn thing."

"That's what I thought. For a while, I considered saying something to him about the sourcing, uh, discrepancies. But it's not like he'd listen to some dweeb being all, 'Hey, man! Lying is not cool!' And then there's my job. I have a feeling anyone who talks back to Jarrod—or blows his cover—will get canned."

They'd reached the boathouse. "Yeah. There's that." Effie stood behind him as he unlocked the door. She hopped from one foot to the other and poked her finger in between his shoulder blades. "But you're not a dweeb."

His smile was indulgent. "Coming in for round two?"

"I . . ." Her gaze landed on the old leather couch and familiar blanket. She wanted to. But the feelings of pride and reassurance she'd felt in the thicket were beginning to morph into something a little more potent. She closed her eyes and the image of his fingers knotted in her hair and his other hand snaking up her T-shirt sent a shiver down her spine. "I am usually round-one-and-done these days," she said, hoping it was too dark for him to notice the color creeping into her cheeks.

"Good call. I should probably get to bed, too. Do you want

to take home the rest of your beer?" She shook her head. "So I guess we do nothing. About the lobster," he clarified.

"I guess we do nothing." She waved and started down the street. He stayed at the door, watching until she rounded the corner. The walk back to her father's felt chilly and sad, and for hours afterward, Effie lay awake, thinking about Ernie's arm around her and wondering how else he had changed, and what it might feel like to find out for herself.

Chapter Sixteen

Two days off in a row felt downright wrong to Effie, who was used to working two weeks straight without a break. But Ernie had assured her most people at Brown Butter actually took their "weekends." Effie had been skeptical, but when she asked Jean-Claude if he put in extra time on Monday or Tuesday, he laughed until there were tears streaming down his cheeks. "For Jarrod? *Mais non.*"

So after her responsibly early night out with Ernie, Effie woke at a reasonable hour and met her sister for breakfast at The Gull's Perch. Ingrid caught her up on all the island gossip that wouldn't have made sense over the phone. To understand some things about small-town life, you just have to be there. Effie was rapt over a saga surrounding a flavored-olive-oil shop that was started by a part-time resident from Boston when she felt a hand clap her shoulder. "Ladies, good morning," Sixto said, coming around the other side of the booth to kiss her sister's cheek. Ingrid blushed a familiar shade of crimson and reached up for Sixto's hand. He was off to Rockland to buy landscaping supplies for their front yard, and didn't want to leave without saying goodbye to his amor.

"Babe, you literally did half an hour ago, when I told you I was meeting Effie."

"Sure. But miss an opportunity to see your beautiful smile—and make you blush? I'm taking every one of those chances I get."

Effie stirred her iced coffee with a straw and averted her eyes so the two could have a private moment. So far, Sixto had aced the boyfriend test. It gave her an idea. "Hey. What are you two doing for dinner?"

Sixto looked to Ingrid, who shrugged. "Trader Joe's spanakopita, probably?"

"Come over," Effie said. "I promised Dad I'd cook lentils with him and—" Ingrid groaned. "And I don't want to go on this journey alone."

"Big sister, I love you. But Trader Joe has never incinerated a pot of dal."

Sixto chuckled. They'd been dating long enough for him to know about Samuel and his lentils. "We'll be there. With wine."

"Lots of wine?" Ingrid pressed her palms together in a prayer position. "Go to the good liquor store? Pinot? Pleeeease?"

Sixto pressed his palms into Ingrid's biceps and gave her a mini massage. "Pinot for my princess. Effie, any requests?"

She waved him off. "Whatever the pinot Princess wants, I will drink. See you tonight, man." One more kiss, this one planted on the tip of Ingrid's nose, and he was gone. "Damn, sis."

Ingrid smiled through a bite of whipped-cream-smothered waffle. "What can I say? An Olsen woman knows her worth."

For the rest of the morning, and late into the afternoon, Effie turned that phrase over in her mind. *An Olsen woman knows her worth.* On the surface, it was sweet: Ingrid had found a good man who cherished her. But its implications were trickier to unravel. What about the original Olsen woman, their mother? (Well, technically Susan was a Taylor. She hadn't taken Samuel's last name. But, semantics.) She had struggled to feel satisfied or even happy in her marriage for over a decade before she finally left. So what did *that* mean? She was worth more than the life she'd left behind? Worth more than Samuel? And Ingrid and Effie?

And what about her? Effie wasn't even sure she knew what it meant to know your worth. Plenty of men had bought her drinks. (Well, technically they were fellow line cooks ponying up for their round after a hard night of service. Still.) But Sixto's generosity seemed to be a minor detail in the story of Ingrid and her beau. How had her sister known he was the one? Known he was someone worth her time? She decided to ask, and pulled her phone out of her back pocket at the exact moment it began vibrating. The caller had a 212 area code, but Effie didn't recognize it. Then again, there were tons of people in New York City it could have been. She declined the call. They'd message if it was important. Right now she had an important-er question for her little sister.

Ingrid

Hi. So. About your boyfriend.

Haha yes he got three bottles. All is well.

That is . . . a lot of wine for four people. But I actually have a question for you.

Ooookay. Shoot.

How does Sixto make you feel?

Um, like in bed?

Ingrid! No!

Stop typing!

Stop! I can see the little typey bubbles!

lol.

What I mean is, emotionally, I guess. You dated practically everyone in your graduating class. What about him is special?

Oh, I see. That's a cute question.

Is it?

Sure. The biggest thing is, I feel respected by him. He values my opinion about everything: work, our home, his friendships. There's trust, too. Not just about faithfulness and monogamy. Well, that. But also, we trust each other to be honest. To have hard conversations, and grow together as a couple. To speak up when one of us is acting like a butthead, and to take that feedback to heart . . . knowing it's only going to make us stronger.

And he is obviously a most excellent cook.

Thanks for sharing. That is all very encouraging. Stating for the record I will not wear a pink bridesmaid dress.

Stating for the record you haven't secured your spot on my list!

Kidding. Obv, you're the maid of honor.

As is my right. See you tonight.

Yaya.

Effie chucked the phone onto the floor and sighed heavily into her papasan chair. For the last sixteen years, her priority had been work. She hadn't put much thought into finding the perfect guy. But what Ingrid had said made a lot of sense. It was the sort of stuff that felt good in her bones. The sort of stuff you could halfway ignore until you'd returned to your hometown and all your former classmates had babies while you had a bag of spatulas and a best friend. A best friend who respected you. Valued your opinion. Trusted you, and had hard conversations. Who spoke up when you were acting like a butthead. The very same best friend you'd lost once, because one of you developed feelings and ruined it all.

"Shitballs," Effie whispered and curled deeper into the chair. She closed her eyes and an image of Ernie's arm around her shoulders flashed big and bright. *That meant nothing*, she scolded herself, and repeated it when her mind hit the next slide: Ernie's beach towel wrapped around them, his lips brushing the top of her head.

No. She wouldn't go there. He'd made it clear that she'd burned through any romantic feelings he had for her. All that was left was friendship. A friendship that, they both agreed, was worth protecting.

"Effie Pantsaroo!" Samuel's voice carried up the stairs, followed shortly by the scent of butter and onions on the stove. "Ready to help your dear old dad make some dinner magic?"

Effie's father tossed her a yellow onion as she crossed the threshold into the kitchen. She caught it easily and whipped it back to him. "Nice!" he said, plopping it on the cutting board. "You've got the moves."

She smiled back. Funny. She remembered how confusing his love could be: smothering, then distant. But she had forgotten how *fun* it was to spend time together. He was good at being a dad when he wanted to. She could play her role, too. It would feel nice to remember. At least for a little while. "I'll make the salad?" she asked.

"Sounds good. I'm on lentil duty."

For a bit, they cooked without speaking. Ari Shapiro's voice hummed from the radio. She rummaged in the old, dented, and dinged refrigerator for vegetables. After grabbing a tight purple head of radicchio, a few bright orange carrots, and a bunch of tiny pink beets, she closed the door and admired the appliance. It was genuine vintage, the color of mint ice cream, with a rusted steel handle. Its edges were rounded, and it was shorter than Effie. These days, you could spend a fortune on modern fridges made to look like this. But Samuel wasn't trying to be stylish. He just wasn't the type to replace anything unless it had broken and couldn't be fixed. And sometimes not even then.

The rest of the kitchen was just as quaint. Between the pastel-colored appliances, the wide-wood-plank floor, the roughhewn cupboards, and the big window over the sink, it was a sanctuary in an otherwise chaotic home. The window was the best part of all. It had an arched top and looked out over the backyard. Effie had never minded washing dishes at that sink, where she could get lost in dreams about the future.

"You and Ernie hook up yet?" Samuel's voice made her jump.

Effie frowned at the pile of vegetables on her cutting board. "What? No . . ." She took a breath. That was not what her dad had meant. "I haven't seen him."

She didn't know why she'd lied. Habit, she guessed. It had started in high school and continued throughout her time away. When they talked on the phone or texted, she glossed over the hard stuff. She told him everything was fine, that work was easy and fulfilling, and that she was happy. If he knew the truth—that her male superiors made her feel small and stupid, that work required eighteen-hour days, and that she was often so physically exhausted when she got back to her apartment, she'd fall asleep on the futon with her shoes still on—he'd make a fuss.

That was another thing Effie couldn't stand. Being worried about. Feeling like a stressful part of someone else's life. So she kept all that inside. She could take care of herself. She'd been doing it for a long time.

"Good kid, Callahan. You two were inseparable . . ." He trailed off as the screen door swung open. Ingrid came in, all chatter and three bottles of pinot in her arms, Sixto right behind.

"Hi, little sis," Effie said. "What's up, Sixto?" Everyone else exchanged greetings. Ingrid rummaged in the hutch for glasses, and Sixto was tasked with cooking rice to go with the lentils.

"You know, it was your mother who taught me how to make this dish," their father said, the wooden spoon hovering above the pot. "She learned when she was on assignment in India back in the seventies." He had a dreamy, faraway look in his eyes. Ingrid looked amused. She had always been more tolerant of their dad's eccentricities than Effie. Ingrid was also the "good" daughter who called their journalist mom once a week. Effie only talked with her mother when one of them needed something from the other. Which wasn't very often.

"Dad!" Effie rushed over and lowered the heat. She shot Sixto a quick eye roll, to which he gave a *Whaddya gonna do?* chuckle. The butter had darkened and was just shy of burning, The oniony smell was now layered faintly with char. "Butter burns quicker than oil. You may want to watch it more closely. And keep the flame lower."

"That's my Effie Pants," he said, unruffled by her chastising tone. "Always teaching me something."

"True! I wouldn't know how to ride a bike without her," Ingrid said. Effie's cheeks warmed and she chased away the tenderness with a grab for the wine bottle, which her sister was dividing between four very generously sized glasses. Samuel stepped aside as Effie poured a splash of pinot noir into the pan.

"Hey!" Ingrid looked offended. "That was a nice bottle."

"Still is," Effie handed it back. The wine had loosened all the browned bits from the bottom, and she used the spoon to scrape them up. The pinot had seeped into the onions and the scent in the kitchen was comforting once again. She handed the spoon back to her dad. "Here. Add a drizzle of oil and keep stirring until the onions are soft. Then add the lentils, some tomato paste, and broth."

He hesitated. "That's not how your mother did it."

"Yeah, well," Effie snapped, swallowing the retort that Susan rarely cooked, on account of motherhood being a *burden*. That was the word Effie overheard again and again during late-night arguments. She turned back to her spot at the cutting board. "She's not exactly my role model."

"Here we go." Ingrid smooshed her face into Sixto's upper arm and plugged her ears. He rubbed her back and added a shower of salt to the rice pot.

"She did the best she could, Effie. And she still loves you."

"Fine, whatever." Effie grabbed a small mixing bowl and began pouring in ingredients for a dressing: balsamic vinegar, tahini, miso paste, olive oil, finely chopped mint.

"Do you want to talk about it?" Samuel said, turning away from the stove and making eye contact with Effie.

"In front of Ingrid's boyfriend?"

"He's family."

Ingrid chugged from her wineglass.

"Dad, the lentils." The room was smelling toasty again.

"I take that as a no."

"Take that as an 'I've moved on.'"

Her father's voice turned gentle. "And an 'I should, too'?"

Effie drizzled the vinaigrette over the radicchio and grated beets and carrots. "I don't know, Dad. It might make you happier.

You guys don't even talk anymore." Effie didn't know if that was true. But she imagined it might be, now that there were no child-rearing obligations keeping the lines of communication open.

"Oh, E.P. I wish I could. But once you love someone to the moon, you can't just float back down to earth. Even if you have to let them go."

"That's sweet, Dad," Ingrid said, handing a glass to him, one to Sixto, and another to Effie.

"I guess," Effie said, ignoring the wine for a moment as she cracked black pepper over the salad.

Samuel reached his arm around Effie's shoulders and pulled her in for a sideways hug. Ingrid came around the other side and squeezed, too. Effie stiffened a little, but her sister's fingernails in her arm made her yelp, then laugh.

"This is a great photo opportunity!" Sixto said, exchanging his spoon for his cell phone camera. "Say, 'Turmeric.'"

They all did, and the picture was lovely. Ingrid and Sixto snapped a couple selfies while the lentils simmered away, and Effie snuggled in closer to her father. "I'm sorry. Just a little stressed about work at the moment."

"Being a member of this family means you show up however you are," he said, brushing her hair back over her forehead. "Stressed, nostalgic, loopy in love . . . who you are is who we cherish." Ingrid was now directing a full-on photo shoot between her and Sixto with the big window in the background. "If I didn't do a good job at teaching you that when you were younger, I'm sorry."

Effie looked up at her father and, for the first time, felt pride at how many of his features her face had adopted. "I wasn't exactly the most pleasant teenager to raise," she admitted. "But it feels good to be back now." Suddenly self-conscious of her vulnerability, she peeled herself out of his arms and began to set the table. "Even if it is only for a summer."

When dinner was finally ready, they sat down at the little round table and clinked glasses. Ready to steer the conversation away from any more big, emotional moments, Effie brought a spoonful of food to her lips and blew on it. "So," she said before taking a bite. "Ingrid. Whiz-kid sister. Genius of my blood. Tell me again how Bitcoin is mined and if it's just an imaginary thing that exists only on the internet."

Chapter Seventeen

The next Saturday night in Brown Butter's kitchen was hot and chaotic. The clock hands had just met at 8:00, and there was a tense tightness in the air. Effie grabbed the ticket the machine had just spat out and scanned it quickly, the paper warm in her hands. "Order in: two tasting menus, one with a gluten allergy." She waited for the rest of the kitchen staff to repeat the order, so she knew they'd heard her.

"Two tasting menus, one liar." The rogue voice was followed by a stifled laugh.

"B.J. . . ." she warned as the machine clicked to life again. Some professional chefs groaned over dietary restrictions and preferences, but Effie didn't mind. It was her job to feed people well, and making sure they felt comfortable with the meal in front of them was the very first step. Allergies, preferences, predilections: she would take care of them all. Effie took the new ticket. "Order in: one little gem salad split between two plates, and two lobster pastas."

"Little gem, two lobbies," the kitchen echoed dutifully.

The tickets kept coming. "Order in: one lobster pasta, VIP at the bar."

"VIP lobbie."

"Order in: four tasting menus; one vegan, one shellfish allergy, one 'fear of parsley.'"

"Four tasting, lotta bullshit," B.J. mumbled into a stainless-steel mixing bowl of lettuce he was massaging with vinaigrette.

Effie shot him a stern look before bringing her attention back to the POS machine. She waited, holding her breath, for another order to interrupt. One, two, three seconds. Four, five, six, seven, eight, nine, ten. *Aaaand exhale.* That was Effie's rule when expediting dinners at the pass: if ten seconds go by without a new order, you can safely assume the servers are circulating the dining room, not adding more orders onto the back-of-house's already giant to-do list. She had at least a couple of minutes to breathe and manage the kitchen staff.

Her eyes scanned the room for signs of trouble. B.J. had plated the salad and left it on the pass. The tower of lettuce leaves looked a little flat, but not so much that she'd make him do it again. When she had started out in his role, eons ago, her boss had told her that every salad should make the diner "feel like a star" when they ate it. It was good advice for a dish that usually got slapped on a plate with little attention. She'd remind him of that later, in a quiet moment. He was now shucking oysters for one of the tasting menus. Hopefully not the one with the shellfish allergy. Jean-Claude was spooning romesco sauce onto a strip steak from an earlier order. Sixto was engrossed in two bowls of sorrel soup, using a pair of long silver tweezers to arrange nasturtium leaves on their surfaces. Over at the pastry station, Dan was using two serving spoons to transform a scoop of sorbet into a torpedo-shaped quenelle. Anika, the intern, was standing with her hand on a wire-mesh basket filled with five raviolis hovering above the pot of boiling water. She almost dropped the pasta in, but looked around the room, pulled her hand back, and waited. *Good job,* Effie silently channeled her way, catching her eye with a nod. Soon, Anika would know intuitively when to fire each new order, but for now she was still jumping the gun or waiting too long. When that happened, either the rest of the orders had to bake under the warming lamp or the pasta sauce got congealed and cold. Working in a professional kitchen was kind of like track and field in that way: you were out there on your own, but your performance affected the whole team. Those were the kind of stakes Effie liked best.

Jarrod was exactly where he'd been every night for the last two weeks: working the grill station. His kind of stakes were actual steaks. His messy curls were tied back in his signature high bun, and his look was intense concentration as he used a short pair of tongs to flip a steak. The meat sizzled as he seasoned a portion of chicken with kosher salt. For the first few days of work, Effie had felt a flash of annoyance at his insistence that he work the line instead of helping her at the pass. That meant the final responsibility of each dish landed on her. The last time she'd felt that kind of pressure was at Cowboy Bean, and it had not worked out well. But she had to admit, Jarrod seemed at home in front of a hot stovetop. And the food he turned out was undeniably good: strip steaks with a glossy golden-brown crust, perfectly done every time. He was kind of a genius when it came to line cooking.

It was the rest of the time that was the problem.

When Jarrod wasn't held captive to the humid, heavy spell of dinner service, he made everyone's lives miserable. Effie had observed him dress down Jean-Claude over a broken hollandaise sauce so aggressively that Jean-Claude walked out of the kitchen in a huff and didn't come back until the next morning. She'd seen Jarrod shove a salad plate under Chad's nose and tell him that a dog could lick dishes clean better than his dishwashing skills. She'd tried, and failed, not to notice as he ran his fingertips over server Nikki's shoulder while she polished wineglasses with a cloth napkin. When he passed by Effie, he kept his hands to himself. He had ever since that morning in his office. But her threat of retaliation hadn't stopped him from cruelly teasing her. Sometimes, he would whisper in B.J.'s ear and cackle as he held eye contact with her from across the room. Or abruptly stop talking with Jersey, the drinks manager, and point her way if Effie entered the bar. She braced herself every time they were in the same room, constantly terrified of what he was saying about her . . . and what the repercussions would be.

She also couldn't shake Ernie's admission that Jarrod was faking ingredients. The problem was more pervasive than anywhere she'd cooked, and now she couldn't *not* see the dozens of little lies. They were told in cardboard boxes of lemons from

Mexico, hazelnuts from Oregon, black pepper from . . . well, who knows where? Even the goat cheese came from Vermont, which was dumb. There was a cheesemaker right there on the island.

But once she and Ernie committed to keeping their mouths shut, it was easy to rationalize complicity. Every restaurant she'd worked in fibbed about their ingredients. At least a little. Even Cowboy Bean sometimes sent interns to the grocery store in a panic when their delivery of heirloom potatoes ran out. It was dishonest, but it was just the way things worked in fine dining. You had to maintain the magic at any cost.

Despite their similarities, every restaurant kitchen had a unique rhythm that hummed, swelled, and dipped throughout the course of a day. Some kitchens kept a steady pace. Some kitchens maintained a constant low-grade stress that set everyone's teeth on edge. Others, like Cowboy Bean, were electric, red-hot. To Effie, working there had felt like burning her hand on the flat-top grill for fifteen hours straight every night. It was intense and awful. But thrilling, too, if you were a certain kind of person. The kind of person who can't stop touching dangerous things.

Brown Butter was different. Brown Butter was under the thumb of a madman. Jarrod's moods swung from flirtatious and conspiratorially bawdy to irate and irrational. The entire staff, from busboys to senior cooks, ducked their heads as soon as he entered the room. Effie had encountered plenty of strong personalities throughout her travels, but she'd never, ever worked in a place where fear ruled. She hated that. Especially because she really liked the rest of the team.

They deserve a stronger leader, she thought now, retying the apron strings at her navel and making her way back to the pass from the dish pit where she'd wandered. A parade of plates, bowls, and platters was now waiting under the heat lamps. It was time to inspect each one before giving the waitstaff the go-ahead to carry them out to the dining room and bar.

But Jarrod got there first. He'd abandoned his station and was bent over two teardrop-shaped plates with rage visible in the pulsing veins of his tattooed forearm. Effie swallowed a now-familiar lump in her throat as she took big steps to meet him. She knew those plates. They were the ones they used for the lobster ravioli. And that could only mean one thing: Anika was about to wish she'd never moved to Alder Isle for the summer.

"INTERN." Jarrod's words were sharp and loud enough to cut through the clatter of pots, pans, and dishes, and the din of laughter from the dining room.

Anika looked up from her station, where she'd been wiping down water splashes from the edge of the stove. Everyone else looked up, too, but quickly trained their eyes back to their own cutting boards. It was bad form to watch someone else get read the riot act. Plus, you never knew when it'd be your turn. "Yes, Chef?" Anika's words came out with the wavering confidence of someone who doesn't know what's coming but thinks it might be bad.

"What's the name of this restaurant?" Jarrod stood with his

arms extended, hands on the pass. Effie stood by. She was ready to step in if needed, but she wanted to give Anika a fighting chance to handle things on her own.

"Brown Butter, Chef."

"Not 'Burned Butter'?"

Anika shook her head. "No, Chef."

"Are you sure?"

"Yes, Chef." Anika was twisting the towel into tight coils, eyes darting from her recently plated dish back to Jarrod's feet.

"Are you really fucking sure?"

"Yes, Che—"

"Then why, Intern, did you sauce these two plates of Brown Butter's signature dish with burned butter?"

"I . . ." Anika flashed a glance in Jean-Claude's direction. Anika's station was pasta. Jean-Claude was the one who made the butter sauce and delivered it to her before service each night. Effie watched. *Was she going to blame him?* "I'm sorry, Chef," Anika finally said, bringing her eyes down to her own clogs.

"That doesn't answer my question."

"I don't know, Chef. I didn't mean to."

"Here's what *I* don't know. I don't know how you got this job when you clearly belong at the fry station at a goddamn Denny's. Re-fire two lobster pastas, do it right, or tonight's your last night here." He threw the plates, ravioli and all, into the dish pit with a clatter. Chad ducked just in time.

"Yes, Chef," Anika said, her hand trembling as she clicked the power burner back on.

Effie made it to Anika in three steps. "Hey," she whispered, dropping five more ravioli into the basket for Anika. "Was the butter burned when Jean-Claude brought it over?" She anticipated Anika's hesitation and met it with reassurance. "You can tell me the truth."

"I don't think so. But now I don't remember."

"Do you have it? Can I see?"

Anika pushed a square pan across the table. Effie smelled it, then dipped her spoon in and tasted a tiny bit. It was perfect: warm, gently nutty, redolent with rosemary and thyme, and brightened by a crack of black pepper and a shock of lemon zest.

"Okay. I know what happened." Effie didn't smile, but she softened her brows so Anika would know she wasn't angry. "You added the sauce to the sauté pan, heated it, then put in the pasta. Am I right?" Anika nodded. "That's too long for already-cooked butter to be on the heat. It'll go from browned to burned like *that*." She snapped her fingers.

Understanding spread across Anika's features. "But if I don't put in the butter first, won't the ravioli stick to the pan?"

"When you transfer the ravioli from the pot, make sure you get a big splash of the cooking water, too. That'll keep things saucy and loose. Then add a ladle of that butter sauce and crank the heat to mid-high. Toss everything two or three times—don't stir, that might damage the pasta—and kill the heat. Plate it up, and you're good to go."

"Thanks," Anika said, lowering the basket of pasta in the water for what probably felt like her thousandth time that night.

"Thanks, *Chef*," Effie corrected. If Jarrod deserved respect in the kitchen, she did, too. She deserved it without the condition of a man's presence.

"Oops. Sorry, Chef."

"No problem. Just a reminder that you don't have to be an unhinged jerk to qualify for the job." Anika smiled. "I'll do it with you this time. Ready?"

As Anika ladled starchy water into the pan, Effie felt eyes on her. She looked up, toward the stairs to the basement. There was Ernie, working late. He was leaning against the doorframe with a plastic tub of vegetable scraps in his arms and a happy, warm smile on his lips.

Chapter Eighteen

Two days later, it was time for Effie's first crack at the bucket list. She had told Ernie to meet her at Meadowsweet Scoops at 5:00 that evening. "Wear something you don't mind getting sticky," she had said, which made him blush, which made her regret her choice of words. She'd tried again: "Something you don't mind getting covered in ice cream." He had understood then.

It wasn't like she'd planned anything crazy. But scooping homemade ice cream for a couple of hours was hard, physical labor. You usually ended up wearing more of it than you expected. Effie and Ernie were both familiar with the job hazards of working at an ice cream shop: they had every summer throughout high school. Samuel paid them a fair wage, plus they got to keep all their tips. During slow hours, they'd mix and match flavors, trying to come up with the weirdest combinations for each other to try. Effie thought it would be fun to revisit their old stomping ground for their first activity on her terms. Also, her father had shared during the lentil and pinot night that he was short-staffed. She'd offered her and Ernie's help. Samuel's face had lit up in such a big smile, Effie made a promise to pop in for a few hours of free labor every week until September.

Meadowsweet Scoops was open from 12:00 to 4:00, then 5:00 to 9:00 every day of the week. Samuel worked almost every shift, and although Effie had suggested he take the night off, he shook his head with a smile. "Spending the evening with you feels like a vacation," he said, waving as Ernie entered the shop, the tiny bell trilling as he pushed on the door.

"Hey, Sam," Ernie said. Effie gave him an incredulous look. At some poker game in the last sixteen years, Ernie had gotten on a first-name basis with her dad. It was kind of cute. Ernie had followed Effie's instructions: he was wearing a pair of paint-splattered khakis and an old Alder Isle Track & Field T-shirt that he'd clearly outgrown. It stretched across his chest, making the outline of his pecs and shoulders impossible to ignore.

"Here. Wear this." Effie threw a cotton apron at him. "Cover yourself up."

Ernie's lip quirked and a few of his freckles danced. *He totally knows what he's doing to me with that stupid T-shirt.* She gave him an evil look. He smiled bigger as he slowly lifted his muscular arms to drop the apron loop over his head. "So. Who's on register and who's scoopin'?"

The bell rang again. Samuel didn't have time to delegate responsibilities before the evening rush started. But that didn't matter. Ernie jumped to the ordering window, and Effie and her dad readied themselves, scoops in hands, behind the big tubs of ice cream. It was their old formation, and within a few minutes they had settled into a groove, working together wordlessly and efficiently. Effie scooped cones and cups while Samuel manned the milkshake and sundae station. The line snaked out the door within minutes of opening, but unlike Brown Butter, all these customers were locals.

As Effie filled waffle cones with buttermilk peach, mint chocolate chip, and graham cracker key lime pie, she watched Ernie interact with the customers. He managed to keep the line moving while also taking time to have a mini conversation with everyone. Effie was surprised to find she recognized and remembered almost all their customers, and she felt a fondness toward her old teachers, coaches, and classmates. Some saw her in the back of the shop and waved. She waved back. For the first time, being on Alder Isle didn't make Effie feel uncomfortable. In her father's ice cream shop with her childhood best friend, she just felt at home.

But. That was the difference between Ernie and her. She was only pretending to have a community here. This was his real life. At the end of the summer, she would leave them all. He was here for the long run. He was an *actual* people person. She was just pretending.

She was salty; he was sweet.

His personality seemed to fill in all the gaps created by hers.

She wondered if he felt the same way.

Oh, Ernie.

Why did you tell me you loved me so many years ago?

Why didn't I say it back?

"Whoa. Nine o'clock already?" Ernie's voice broke her trance, and she looked at the clock as Samuel scooted to turn around the CLOSED sign. "Time flies."

"Thanks to you two, it really did. I don't know how I would have worked that shift alone tonight. You're good kids," Samuel said, picking up the tip jar and handing it to Ernie. "Divide it between you two. And don't spend it all in one place, now." Effie gave her dad a smile she hoped said, *Thank you for everything.*

"Oh man, there's enough in here to split a burger and fries at Son of a Wharf," Ernie said, counting out the quarters and dollar bills.

"Then I'll leave you to it." Samuel kissed Effie's cheek. "If you and Ernie don't mind closing up, I don't mind ignoring the fact you're going to eat at least a pint of ice cream each as soon as I leave."

"Byeeeeee," Effie said, laughing as she pretended to hustle him out the door.

Once they were alone, she felt shy. The question her subconscious had triggered—*Why didn't I say "I love you" back?*—felt like a scarlet letter plastered on her ice cream apron. Surely Ernie could tell something was up. But if that was the case, he graciously ignored it. "So. What flavor are you going for tonight, Ms. Eff?" *Ms. Eff?* She melted, then bristled. Increasingly, everything he said and did felt flirtatious. It made her feel crazy. She had to fix this before it got out of hand.

"Blueberry lavender, duh." She dipped a scoop in the tub to avoid looking at him. "It's only the best flavor."

"Only the second-best," Ernie corrected, falling into place next to her with a scoop of his own. He handed her a waffle cone and took a biodegradable paper cup for himself. "We all know Grape-Nuts reigns supreme."

"No one likes that flavor."

"Right. It's so weird two dozen people ordered it tonight."

"You're exaggerating."

"And you're too stubborn and bratty to admit that your way of living doesn't have to apply to everyone else!" Ernie's voice was almost a shout, and his face had turned red before he'd finished the sentence. "Oops. I didn't mean to say that."

Effie's chest felt radioactive. *Is that how he really feels?* She slammed the freezer door shut and brought her cone to the toppings station, where she tried calmly to coat it with chopped almonds. "And yet you did. I think you're just sour that I've always known what I want, and you don't."

Ernie laughed bitterly. "Oh, that's good." He filled a spoon with gummy bears and held it under her nose. She didn't respond. "Nothing? Really? No sassy retort?"

"No." She licked her cone. *Perfect.* She'd nailed the toppings-to-ice-cream ratio.

"You're seriously not triggered by my adding a cup of gummy bears to Grape-Nuts ice cream? The worst topping in the world, on the worst ice cream in the world. According to you, circa 2005."

"If it's what you want, fine. Just eat it. Stop being mean and awful."

"I'm not. I'm teasing you." He picked up a gummy bear and smooshed it on top of her cone. "There's a difference."

"STOP, you're RUINING IT," Effie shouted, yanking her cone away and flicking the bear off. It landed on his shoe. She hated how she was acting: stubborn and bratty, just like he'd said. But she couldn't stop. Emotions were bubbling up faster than she could swallow them.

Ernie took a step closer so there was no more space between them. "No, ruining it would be doing *this*." He grabbed the cone from her hand and dunked it upside down in his own cup, so that it was studded in gummies and mushy Grape-Nuts.

Her jaw dropped. He was laughing nervously, like he knew he'd gone a step too far. Without thinking at all, she snatched the cone back from him and thrust it in his face. It landed square on his nose, and stayed there for a few seconds before sliding off and hitting the floor between them.

It was his turn to be stunned. "Motherfluffer, are you in trouble," he said, pelting her with handful after handful of rainbow sprinkles.

Effie shrieked as the sprinkles showered over her, settling in the part of her hair and her pockets. She ran to the refrigerator for the squeeze bottle of chocolate sauce and made it back to him in one leap. She wanted to squirt it all over his head, but couldn't reach that high. She aimed for his chest, for his stupid, muscular, manly chest, and covered him in chocolate until he wrenched the bottle from her. He *was* tall enough to coat her hair in chocolate, and soon it was dripping down her face, into her eyes.

She blinked, cemented to the floor if not by syrup, then shock.

"Oh my God. Wait. Hold on. Don't move." Ernie dashed away. She stood perfectly still, waiting for a towel and apology. He returned with a single miniature marshmallow, which he placed on the very top of her head. "There. Now you're perfect."

Somehow, instead of making her angrier, the food fight had unfurled and dissipated the panic that had been building steadily in her chest since five o'clock. She couldn't fight it anymore: Effie began laughing so hard, she had to sit on the concrete floor with her head in her hands. "Mother*fluffer*?" was all she could muster to Ernie, who had slid down the side of the counter and was shaking with laughter of his own.

"I know! I know!" he repeated until his breathing slowed. "I'm so sorry, but I will never forget the look on your face when I put that single dumb gummy bear on your ice cream."

She'd grabbed a towel from the side table and was wiping chocolate tears from her face. "Do you really think I'm a brat?"

"Eff. No." She scrunched her nose. He read her expression, and scooched over to place his hand over her bare knee. She shuddered, and muttered something about the shop always being so cold. "I don't know why I said it. Hold on. Let me think."

She waited, covered in sprinkles and chocolate sauce.

"Okay. I figured it out. Thanks for being patient. When we were younger, I did feel that way. Sometimes. Like I said the other night: you were the one who got your way, your hot take was always the right one. And I didn't care. Except, sometimes I did. And I didn't know how to advocate for myself. I think you just witnessed twentysomething years of resentment in the form of Haribo."

"Oh," she said, feeling awful and small.

He moved even closer and held her cheeks in his hands. She tried to blink away syrup from her lashes so she could see him better. He looked contrite and tender. "I should have found a, uh, better way to process that. But I don't think that about you now. You've grown up. It's really important that you know that." He was still holding her face, melted ice cream slipping between his fingers and dripping onto her thighs. "In fact, all I can think about lately is how *unselfish* you are. The way you're so patient with everyone at work. So generous with your time. For the first time in three years, Brown Butter actually feels like a good place to work, and it's all because of you."

"Really?"

"No lies," Ernie said, squeezing the nape of her neck then releasing her. He drew an *X* over his heart. "That's what I should have told you tonight: not that you were a less than perfect human at age sixteen, but that you're an admirable human now. That I'm proud of you. Proud of who you've become. And on an even more sentimental note, really touched that you chose to share all that with us, here. On little old Alder Isle."

"Thanks," Effie said. "I'm proud of you, too. For how brave you've been. For your pops, and everything you've been through." He smiled at her. They both stood and surveyed the damage. "We should clean this up, or my dad'll fire us."

As they wiped down counters and mopped the floors, Effie felt shy and uncomfortable in their silence. "What're you doing tomorrow?" she asked, surveying the room for any missed evidence of their food fight.

"Oh," he said, his voice lilting down into an apologetic tone. "Just hanging out with a friend. You?"

Lake. Effie hated how the first word that came to mind was another woman's name. So irrational. So stupid. "Nothing special," she said, then looked down at her chocolate-drizzled shoes. "You still want to split that burger and fries tonight? Son of a Wharf is open for at least another three hours. I just have to change first."

His laughter was low and kind this time, and it washed over her completely. He held the door open; she walked out into the thick night air. "There is no one else on this entire island I would rather share a burger with."

Sixteen years ago, she would have believed him without hesitation. She wanted to now. She almost did. If only they hadn't spent so much time apart. If only everything wasn't suddenly so damn complicated.

Chapter Nineteen

One undeniable fact about working in a restaurant is that when you're there, you exist in a bizarre sort of time warp. The days are longer than you've ever known, yet there are never enough hours in each one to get all your work done. This is true if you're front-of-house, folding napkins and polishing wineglasses or taking orders and verbal abuse from customers. It's true if you're back of house, simmering seafood stock and juicing miniature beets and plating lobster ravioli and stress-sweating from places you didn't even know you could sweat. In a restaurant, the clock hands seem to move faster than anywhere else, laughing at you as you scramble to catch up. Those same hands positively race, careening around the face, during dinner service. There's simply never enough time.

Effie had expected the workdays to fly by, but she hadn't banked on the rest of the summer feeling like it was slipping away, too. If things had gone according to plan—if she'd kept quiet and kept to herself—it may not have. But without realizing it, by mid-July she had become a part of the island's social fabric. And that meant her days weren't just filled with cooking, running, and spending time with Ernie, but with budding friendships, too.

She and Sixto had fallen into the habit of sharing a beer together after service. She liked getting to know her little sister's boyfriend. The routine had started when he stayed late one night to get a head start on his prep list so he could take the morning off for a doctor's appointment. There were no personal days in the restaurant industry. She was deep cleaning the kitchen by herself.

"Why?" he asked, genuinely curious.

"Because no one else will do it."

"Chef, you never asked anyone. At least, you didn't ask me. I would have helped." He picked up a rag and a bottle of stainless-steel polish as he said this, causing an itchy sensation to show up unannounced in the corners of Effie's eyes. He was right. She never had. At Cowboy Bean, she was so focused on proving that she was good enough for the job, she became convinced she had to do it all alone.

From that night on, Sixto regularly joined her, sometimes bringing a six-pack of cheap beer for them to share. Together they would degrease the fancy French range, mop the floor, and polish appliances until they shined.

"Before you showed up," Sixto observed one night, "we did a deep clean once a week. Any particular reason you feel the need to do it nightly here? Beyond general overachiever issues?"

"Yeah, I get that," Effie said. She stood on a stool, spraying down the giant vent hood. "But sometimes doing your job means going above and beyond."

"*Your* job, maybe," he teased.

She smiled. Part of her wanted to admit that she was scared. Scared that if she didn't hold it together, she'd get fired like last time. That another stain on her resume would make moving on and moving away even harder. That without her paycheck, she'd be stuck here forever. She had been lucky enough to be hired for this job in spite of Cowboy Bean. Lucky that Jarrod had overlooked it. Or was focused on something else. She instinctively felt that sharing all this with Sixto would bring them closer. But she didn't know him that well. And she was still technically his boss, even if he was dating her sister. So instead she crouched from her perch and clinked her bottle neck to his as she said, "My job, definitely. Ladies. We work ten times harder for ten times less pay."

He laughed very hard at that.

"What?" She hopped down from the step stool.

"Try being Mexican, my friend."

That was a truth Effie could never come close to understanding. In every restaurant she'd worked in, cooks of color did the majority of the heavy lifting. In many cases, they were the ones performing the most important tasks. The ones grilling the steaks and plating the pastas. They were the ones *actually* cooking the food that racked up such high praises in reviews.

"I'm here if you ever need anything," she said, joining him at the grill with a scrub brush of her own. She wanted him, and Chad, and Anika, and B.J., and the rest of the crew to know she was on their team. *I'm here if you ever need anything.* It was the one phrase she wished someone had said to her when she'd started cooking professionally. She was nobody's savior, but she could be a good leader. *I can*—the thought startled, then comforted her—*be a real friend.*

"On a less depressing note, how did you end up here anyway?" she asked.

"On Alder Isle or at Brown Butter?"

"Mm. I think I meant more like, cooking in general. But . . ." She waved her hand around in the air. "Open-ended question."

Sixto told Effie that he'd lived in a city on the Maine mid-coast for years, working as a line cook. When Brown Butter opened, he had just lost his job—the high-end diner he'd been at closed in the early days of the pandemic. Brown Butter was looking for staff, and Sixto took a chance. He told her he liked the fast-paced environment, and he liked running his own station. That it felt like a game, trying to be better, faster, and more precise than the evening before.

"But you know something?" He gave one last wipe to the front of the fridge and stood. "Sometimes I dream about what it would be like if I ran this place. Instead of Jarrod. If the focus was on my traditions and culture, told through the food. Not some big lie about all-local ingredients." Effie listened. This was interesting. Sixto was animated now, and he kept talking. "I wouldn't be mad if I never heard the phrase 'farm to table' ever again. All food comes from farms, right? It doesn't mean anything. I'm sick of this attitude that everything has to be pulled from a garden in the backyard. And I'm sick of lying about it to diners." Effie opened her mouth, but Sixto kept going. *Of course he knew, too.*

Everyone who touches ingredients at Brown Butter knows where they really come from. "You know what we don't grow in Maine? Guajillo chilis. Avocados. Limes. But they're delicious, and they're a part of my identity as a chef. Taking all that away from me—making me pretend to be excited about micro broccoli greens—it makes me less of a chef." He took a big swig of his beer and crossed his arms, looked at the floor.

"I'm sorry," Effie said.

"Don't be. It's not your fault. You're not the one buying tomatoes from Sysco in April and claiming they grew in a greenhouse in the backyard."

"Ew."

"Yeah, they had stickers on each one. But he put them in a wooden milk crate, like that somehow made them authentic. Like he thought nobody would find out."

Effie felt awful. "Well, this sucks." She finished her beer and rinsed the bottle in the sink. "For what it's worth, I think you'd make a great head chef. Anywhere you want. Here, even."

"You're not eyeing that role?"

"Me?" Effie said dumbly, and Sixto nodded, like *Duh.* "I don't think this is a long-term thing for me." She could feel herself slipping down the Professional Boundaries Hill on a toboggan with greased runners, but she felt fine about it. Sixto had shared something personal with her. It was only fair she give him something in return. "I just . . . it isn't . . ." She rummaged around in her heart for the correct words to describe how she felt.

"It's okay." Sixto saved her. "You don't have to explain. Sometimes it's just not right." He shrugged and held his hand toward the door. It was late and they had done enough for now. "And besides. It's not like you owe anything to anyone here."

"Yeah," said Effie as she locked the door behind them. "Yeah."

Work buddies were surprising. But friend-friends seemed otherworldly to Effie. And yet, all signs pointed to Dahlia as the first honest-to-goodness female friend she'd ever had. Ever since Effie was a kid, making girlfriends was uncomfortable and awkward, like walking in high heels. But spending time with Dahlia was so effortless, it felt like being with an extension of herself. Even if the two women couldn't have been more different. Even if Effie sometimes still felt weird around her. It was a new muscle she was learning how to use.

Dahlia came by twice a week to refresh the floral arrangements, and every time since the truffle incident, she invited Effie to take a short walk. Leaving the restaurant was like recharging her batteries, and after the walks she marveled at how refreshed she felt. She was more mindful, more present when working after a break. And if she'd been in a bad mood before Dahlia arrived, she returned to Brown Butter with a laugh sparkling in the back of her throat and fewer creases across her forehead. Soon enough, they began walking together every day, whether or not Dahlia had a commitment at the restaurant. She showed up, and Effie was glad she had. She didn't know if that's how it always was with girlfriends. She just assumed Dahlia was effortlessly magical.

Effie thought about this one morning as they strolled, and laughed out loud.

"What?" Dahlia kept walking and crossed her arms over her sage-colored linen overalls.

"You are just such a surprise," Effie said. "In a good way. Please don't be offended, but I didn't expect to like you so much."

"Ha! That's pretty much word-for-word my feelings about this tiny ol' island."

Effie turned in a slow circle to take in the panoramic views. "When I moved back, I thought I would suffocate with all the small talk. But it's actually pretty charming. It makes me feel wholesome and cute." Dahlia's laugh sounded like piano keys. "And I'm starting to appreciate having one coffee shop, one grocery store, and two bars. I don't get the decision fatigue I used to in cities. Alder Isle is growing on me." They were on the east coast of the island. At their feet: the ocean and a jumble of seaweedy rocks. Behind them: the library with its stained-glass windows cracked open. Effie could smell the books from where they stood, and her heart tugged a little. She used to spend so much time there, reading cookbooks. "It's kind of like a barnacle."

"LOL," Dahlia said. "Kit did a really charming painting of those once. She sold it to some celebrity for gobs of money. I'll ask her if she still has the sketches and we can look at them at dinner sometime."

"I'd like that," Effie said. "Maybe next week, on one of my days off?"

Dahlia pulled out her cell to check the calendar. "HOLD THE PHONE," she yelled, and Effie offered her hand. "No, I mean metaphorically. I just had a great idea. Instead of dinner, do you want to take a salsa dancing class with Kit and me?"

"Uh," Effie said. "Not really."

"I knew you'd say yes! It's just five bucks, in the community church basement. Monday night. I'm pretty sure Ingrid and Sixto are coming, too."

"Dahlia." Effie stopped and crossed her arms. "I think you're forgetting a crucial detail. You need a partner for salsa dancing. You have Kit. Ingrid has Sixto. I don't have anyone."

Dahlia hopped around in a circle and clapped her hands, then did the running man in place. They had just crossed the bridge back to the mainland and Ernie's boathouse was in sight. "Yes, you do."

Chapter Twenty

Ernie was surprised by Effie's choice of a dance class for their next bucket list activity, but he agreed. They met at the boathouse and walked up the road to the church together. "Are you secretly a professional dancer?" he asked at the entrance. "Because I . . . have two left feet. I don't want you to be disappointed."

She looked down at his size thirteens. There was still a little ice cream stain on the canvas. She blushed. "I don't think I am going to be disappointed." He blushed back. "I am not a professional dancer and I have seven left feet," she rushed to clarify.

"Seven? Wow. I can't believe I never knew that about you." He held open the door and followed her inside, down the stairs, and into the basement.

Ten couples had signed up for the class, which was led by Roberto Gonzalez, a dance teacher and salsa troupe leader on the mainland. He was clapping his hands to get the room's attention when Effie and Ernie slid into place next to Ingrid, Sixto, Dahlia, and Kit.

"Welcome to Salsa Dancing," Roberto said exuberantly. "How much experience have you had with salsa?"

Ingrid raised her hand. Effie shot her a warning look. "What?" Her little sister shrugged. "I watched some YouTube."

Roberto nodded slowly as his thoughts materialized in a stream-of-consciousness monologue. "Oh no. No one. I thought I was very clear my class was for advanced students only. Fine. This is fine. Everything is fine. I am still getting paid! Okay. Now: the first rule of salsa is to release your inhibitions." He spun around on his heels and popped his hip. "The second rule is to let the music ignite the passion inside your heart. And the third rule is to let that passion flow freely through your body."

Effie glanced at her friends. Ernie's ears were the color of strawberries. Dahlia was biting her lip.

"I think this is the spiciest salsa ever to come out of Alder Isle," Sixto leaned in and muttered to Effie. An unruly laugh rocketed out of her.

"Oh, excellent. A volunteer," Roberto said, his eyes laser-focusing on Effie, who shook her head violently. *Please God, anyone but me.* "Come up here, to the front. With your partner." Roberto motioned toward Sixto, who took a step back and pushed Ernie forward. Ernie grabbed Effie's hand and pulled her along with him. "Now. Face forward. No, you don't need to touch each other yet. But I appreciate the enthusiasm." Ernie dropped his hand from Effie's waist and his freckles disappeared behind a wave of red. "Step forward with your left foot. Rock back on the right. Return your left foot to where it started."

"Hey, you're dancing!" Dahlia yelled, and tried the move herself, holding on to Kit's hand so they could do it together.

"Quiet, please," Roberto snapped. Dahlia stood at attention, but there was a mischievous gleam in her eyes.

"Now." Roberto brought his attention back to Effie and Ernie. "Step *back* with the left. Rock onto the right. Return with the left."

"Huh?" Ernie said.

"Wait, what?" Effie repeated the first set of moves with the wrong feet.

"When do the hips come in?" Ingrid cupped her hands around her mouth as she shouted.

"I cannot believe my baby sister is heckling me at a dance class in a church basement," Effie hissed to Ernie, who bit back a laugh.

"I cannot believe I am working with such amateurs!" Roberto said. "Go. Back to your places. New volunteers. Anyone?"

Luckily Mrs. Greenbriar, their old teacher, and her husband stepped forward and saved them all. After fifteen minutes of demonstration and practice, they were ready to try the basics with music. "But first, the embrace," Roberto said. "Men: hold your partner's hand at the lady's eye level."

"Problem!" Dahlia called out, doubled over in laughter again. Kit was trying to keep it together, but her eyes were sparkling just as mirthfully behind her curly brown bangs.

"Oh. Uh . . . at the secondary partner's eye level," Roberto corrected himself.

Dahlia and Kit dissolved into a puddle of giggles while Roberto flushed and continued his instructions. "Men. I mean, primary partners: your other hand rests on the lady's ribs."

Ernie's palm settled onto Effie's back. The sensation was light and tentative.

"With *confidence*," Roberto corrected the room.

"With confidence, Ern," Effie repeated, looking up to meet Ernie's eyes. She'd wanted to make him laugh, but he seemed serious. Focused. A little intense. His palm pressed harder into her back, and his thumb swooped down the line of her shoulder blade. She shivered and Ernie instinctively pulled her a couple of inches closer. Their hips were almost touching. Her lower lip dropped slightly. His gaze dropped with it.

"YES!" Roberto shouted, clapping his hands as he circled the room. "The passion!"

"The passion," Effie repeated. Her voice, working hard to maintain an irreverent tone, had become a whisper.

Roberto pressed PLAY on a boom box and the first few notes of music filled the room, layering in a sensual tone.

"Ready to crush this?" Effie asked. Ernie didn't answer, just locked eyes with her and pulled her even closer. There was now no space between them at all. Her heart hammered against his chest. She felt like she was about to come unraveled, and grasped at another attempt at humor. "Wait. Am I leading? Or are you?"

Roberto turned the volume up. Ernie brought his lips to

Effie's ear. "Let me lead, Eff," he said, his voice low and hungry. She swallowed hard.

"Okay." Her eyes fluttered closed, and she took a step back. He stepped forward, filling in the space where she had just been. They both rocked, then replaced their feet. As they repeated the moves in the opposite direction, his palm dropped down a few inches, settling on the small of her back. Effie stumbled.

"Hand lifted," Roberto said, tapping Ernie's shoulder as he walked by. Ernie's palm stayed where it was.

"Hand lifted," Effie repeated weakly.

"I know where to put my damn hands," Ernie said, and grabbed on to one of her denim belt loops with his first two fingers. They were doing the steps in circles now, moving around the room. Dahlia and Kit were somewhere nearby. Ingrid and Sixto, too. But all Effie could focus on was the feeling of Ernie's hands on her, and his sweet almond scent inches from her nose. Her mouth. This was a bad, bad idea. They would break out of this reverie any second. And then Ernie would realize he'd gotten carried away. He'd apologize, and she'd laugh it off. They would admit they'd made a mistake.

But she wasn't sure this time she could get over it.

She opened her eyes and dared herself to meet his. His gray-blue gaze was still on her lips as they spun around the room, his hand now sliding farther down, fingers dancing over her tailbone and brushing her back pocket. *Oh God.* Effie wanted him. She hated how much she did. She hated how much she'd missed his friendship. But most of all, she hated how she was ready to torch it again for one more chance at being more.

. . .

An hour later, the six friends were squeezed around a picnic table at Son of a Wharf. Effie had ordered sparkling water with a lime wedge, already feeling intoxicated from Ernie's hands all over her.

"That was quite the experience," Ingrid said, taking a swig from her cranberry and vodka. "Ernie, I had no idea you were so . . . talented." Effie looked sideways at him. He seemed back to his old self, pink ears and all.

"*Talented* is a word," Sixto said, tossing Ernie an elbow. "But come on, mi amor, we all know I had the best moves in that class."

"True." Kit raised her beer in Sixto's direction. "Still, you have to give it up for Ernie. Top marks for passion."

"Yeah, it was like you became a totally different person in there," Ingrid said.

Ernie shook off their barbs with a smirk directed at no one in particular. Effie's heart seized. "Oh, I don't know," he said. "Handsy secret salsa dancer feels like a good fit." Her phone buzzed in her back pocket, and she pulled it out. The same 212 number from earlier in the summer. She quickly declined the call and set the phone screen-side-down on the table.

"Haaaa," said Ingrid.

"Ha-ha," agreed Ernie. Under the table, he knocked his knee against Effie's. His next words were quiet. Too quiet to have been meant for anyone but her: "Maybe I just needed the right partner to bring out that part of me." Effie sat perfectly still, hoping her silence said everything she was afraid to.

"I think it was the perfect addition to your summer bucket list." Dahlia's voice brought them back to the table. "So what comes next?"

"Oh." Ernie said, his entire thigh now pressed against hers. "I honestly have no idea."

Chapter Twenty-One

The next two weeks went by in a blur as Effie's schedule settled into a predictable routine: wake up, go for a run, work until late, text with Ernie for an hour or so, then fall asleep with the phone on her pillow or still cradled in her palm. She hadn't meant to open the texting floodgates with him. For the first month they had only exchanged a few messages. But then the salsa class happened. He sent her a late-night message when she got home that night.

Ernie

Hey. I should apologize for today.

I forgive you for hiding the fact you're secretly a competition-level salsa-er.

Haha. But actually. Can I be serious for a sec?

You can . . . I don't know if I'll be able to.

I overstepped. The way that I held you. What I said. I'm sorry.

Effie read his text a few times. Although it was a retraction, she kept getting snagged on the words *The way that I held you*. She had been thinking a lot about that, too.

Honestly have no idea what got into me. The music? Roberto's call for passion? If I made you uncomfortable, that's not okay.

You didn't make me feel uncomfortable.

Oh. Then I'm not sorry?

JK.

JK again. I am actually sorry.

Ugggggh.

It's fine. We're both sexually repressed singletons and you got carried away. I forgive you.

Sexually repressed? Speak for yourself.

Uggggh.

Since then, their messages had walked a line between teasing and flirtatious. She wondered if he was using the technological barrier as a shield to say things he wouldn't in person. She knew she was. But no matter how far they ratcheted things up over text, they never talked about it in person. Not at work, not on any of their bucket list activities. Not when she taught him how to make quiche at the Lacanche in an empty Brown Butter kitchen; not when it rained all day and they streamed three nineties movies in a row in the boathouse. On the last Sunday in July, Effie got home from the restaurant particularly late, and realized she hadn't checked in on their activity for tomorrow. It was his turn to plan.

Ernie

Hiiii. You up?

For you, sure.

Oh shit, did I wake you?

A little. I was in and out.

Effie sent an eggplant emoji.

Wow.

WOW.

Heheh. Sorry. It was too easy.
#westillupfortomorrow?

You don't hashtag in a text.

#ido

#nerd #yes #meetmeattheboathouseatnoon

#whatshouldiwear

#youdontwantmetopickthat

#maybeidothough #nightnight
#watchthosehandssalsaboy

You watch them.

Effie dropped the phone like it had bitten her and pulled the covers up to her chin. She slept deeply and woke the next morning feeling groggy. She took her time getting ready, sipping coffee and standing under a hot shower for far longer than was necessary.

When her skin was bright pink and the water started to run lukewarm, she wrapped herself in a towel and wrapped her hair in a second and sat on the edge of her bed. She stayed like that for a couple of minutes, staring catatonically at the wall. Eventually, she lay back and stared at the ceiling for half an hour. How was she going to get through the day? Every text she sent made it harder to be with him in person and not say what was on her mind.

Looking good, Eff," Ernie said as she turned into the gravel drive by his boathouse. "Where're the wheels?"

She looked over her black aviators at him. "I walked. Should I go get my bike?"

He handed her a wicker basket. "Naw, just teasing. I'll drive us to Top Spot and we can tool around on foot from there."

"Are we picking berries? Nice." She did the running man in a circle twice before realizing she had stolen one of Dahlia's moves.

Top Spot Mountain wasn't just Effie's favorite place to run. It was a treasure trove of wild raspberries in the summer. She and Ernie used to eat them by the palmful until they felt sick. Their ride to the mountain now was short and silent, and they didn't speak again until Ernie had parked and they'd hiked in about a quarter mile.

"So." Ernie pointed to the other side of a hill. "They're growing like mad in a patch over yonder."

"Over yonder?" Her basket settled nicely in the crook of her elbow as they walked.

"I'm just trying to act the age my name implies I am."

She cracked a grin. "I love your name, though."

"Oh sure. It's all fun and games until you realize being named Ernest is a dating handicap."

"Come on, that's not true."

He stopped, and she did, too, both their baskets swinging. "Trust me. Women are not exactly lining up to date me. The ladies do not love the old-school names. Too nerdy."

She extended her hand. "Hi, have we met? Euphemia."

He shook her hand, and his face was serious when he said, "Euphemia is a beautiful name."

She swallowed, and felt herself start to break out in a sweat. The basket slipped down her arm. "And very nerdy. I win. Or lose, depending on how you're looking at it. But more to the point: I don't buy your story. Ernest Hemingway seemed highly fuckable."

"Please keep all remaining depraved literary fantasies to yourself for the remainder of this excursion," he joked back. "Almost here."

As they crested the hill, the berries came into sight. There were so many, all Effie could see was a tangle of deep red and thorns. And a certain curly-haired, nose-ringed brunette bartender from town.

"Ernie! Ellie, hi!"

"Effie," Effie said, crossing her arms. She wanted to be mad, but she had purposely gotten Lake's name wrong the first time they met. Fair was fair.

"Hey, Lake," Ernie said, looking nervously between the two women. "What're you up to?"

"Same as you, it looks like." Lake did a dramatic bow, her cuffed denim shorts riding up her tanned legs. Effie stole a glance at Ernie, wanting to see if he had noticed, too. Hard to say. "Well, y'all have at it. I've got about as much as I can berry here," Lake said. Ernie's lips opened for a laugh. "See you next Wednesday night?"

"You bet," Ernie said. "No way I'm missing two weeks in a row."

"Yay!" Lake said, then, "Sorry," as she stepped past Effie and disappeared down the hill.

"Well, get pickin'!" Ernie said to Effie as he plunked his basket down and kneeled, oblivious for a few moments to her shadow looming over him. When he realized she was still standing, he sat back on his heels and looked confused. "What?"

"You tell me." She flung herself down in the middle of the patch, landing on her butt and immediately regretting the smushed raspberry stains. "Are you two dating? Is she these mysterious dinner plans you keep having?"

A low huff escaped Ernie's throat, and he started ripping berries from the canes with such intensity that their little green leaves flew like confetti. When he spoke, his words were directed at the work his hands were doing. "Lake. Teaches. Pottery. In. Her. House. I'm. Learning. From. Her."

"You didn't answer the question, though, Hemingway." Effie plucked a single berry and popped it in her mouth.

"EFFIE GODDAMN OLSEN," Ernie shouted at the exact moment a crack of thunder shuddered through the air and reverberated in their chests. She gasped, then covered her mouth with her palm. That was something she had forgotten about summer in Maine: the sudden thunderstorms. The heavy rain clouds in her heart had made her completely oblivious to the ones gathering in the sky.

Without speaking, Ernie grabbed her hand and pulled her up from the raspberry patch. The first drops had already begun falling, fat and heavy and fast. Effie let herself be led back down the trail, tripping and stumbling. The rain was coming in thick sheets now. Water ran down her arms and legs, pooling in her sandals. Ernie's fingers around her wrist were confident and strong. She was dizzy with the suddenness of it; the way she felt small and safe in his grip. When they reached the parking lot, Ernie yanked open the door, then scooped Effie off the ground, cradling her for just a moment. It was entirely unnecessary, and it felt better than anything in the world. Their eyes locked and his lips parted, like he was going to say something, or pull her closer and kiss her and never stop. She let herself be held, soft like a rag doll in his arms.

"Ernie, I—" she spoke, but the words got lost in the next clap of thunder. He hoisted her higher, then lowered her down, gently, onto the passenger seat and shut the door. When he was safely in the cab, he reached into the back row of seats for a towel and handed it to her. She didn't take it, and eventually he let it fall into her lap. They sat there for a few more moments, just watching raindrops drip from each other's eyelashes. Eventually, Ernie keyed into the ignition and turned on the heat. He massaged his temples and spoke the next words facing the windshield.

"Lake and I slept together once, when she first moved here. It was years ago. We met—you know what, it doesn't matter. We tried each other out. It wasn't a fit. She's a talented ceramicist. She sells her stuff online and in the souvenir shop. Eventually, she started a class here. On Wednesdays, a handful of us get together and make stuff. It used to be a hobby, but once my dad started going through everything, it became more. I like going. I like being there with her, and the rest of our friends, because we have shared interests and good conversation." He ran his palms up and down the steering wheel a few times, then let them settle on his thighs. "We are not dating."

Effie tried to process this but got hung up. "Then why are all your bowls and plates from her?"

He took a moment to catch up to her train of thought. "The stuff in the boathouse? That was me. My work."

"You made that? All of it? I'm impressed." She gathered her hair into a twist and wrung it out on the floor. "Why didn't you tell me?"

"Well," he said, taking the towel back and running it over the back of his neck. "I guess I'm still learning how to be your best friend after such a long break. There's a lot to catch up on. And it's probably time we had a real conversation. That doesn't take place over text."

She cracked her knuckles in faux seriousness. "You're right. It's like I barely know you anymore. Okay, favorite NPR personality."

"The Magliozzi Brothers. Click and Clack, from *Car Talk*."

"They're not on the air anymore."

"Doesn't change my answer." He frowned. "Shoot. That's not the kind of conversation I meant. Truth or Dare?"

She yanked on the elastic around her wrist. "Dare."

He grabbed both her hands across the center console. "I dare you to tell me what you're actually thinking about when we text at night."

She bit her lip. God, his stare was intense. She opted for a half answer. "Um, about making you blush?"

"Mission accomplished. But come on. What are we *doing*?"

"We're friends. Just goofing around."

"It's flirting. Do you talk to your other friends like that?"

"I don't have any other friends."

"Don't go telling Dahlia that. But the point: This late-night texting thing isn't friendly. It's dangerous."

She closed her eyes and let the darkness slow her thoughts. Ernie kept holding her hands. When she reentered the moment, she spoke with a new assuredness. "How honest do you want me to be?"

"Yikes, what a question. Ideally all the way honest, right?"

"Okay. When we saw each other on the beach that first morning, you threw me. To be mortifyingly frank, I thought you were hot as hell before I realized who you were."

"Ah, then you saw it was me, and the hot and fiery attraction went . . ." He made a spiraling, whistling sound. "I get it."

"No. Not at all. Every time we're together I have to stop myself from, like, grabbing you. At first it was because you're superhot." He rolled his eyes, and she shook her head like, *No, don't disagree.* "But it grew. You seem so much more confident now. Like you're this entirely new person. This guy who has all these talents and interests and skills that I never knew about. But you're somehow still the dorky best friend who I missed so much."

"And . . . ? Or is this a 'but' situation?"

"And—stop looking at me like that. And I want you so badly that some nights, after we stop texting, I touch myself until I fall asleep." His grip on her firmed. "But. We can't go there. We tried to and it ruined our friendship." The next sentence came out as a whisper. "I can't lose you again."

He released her hands and tousled his hair. "*We* didn't try. *I* did. And I was eighteen. You don't think things could be different this time around?"

"I don't know. Ugh. Truth or Dare?"

"Truth."

"What are you thinking about when we're texting?"

He didn't hesitate to answer. "I'm thinking about how you've grown up in some beautiful ways. But that you're still the sassy girl I used to know. I'm thinking about how I *didn't* think about you for years, because my life got full and good without Effie Olsen calling the shots. And I'm thinking about how, now that you're back, I can't stay away from you."

"I think you have to, though. Unless this is going to be a one-summer-only thing. Because I can't stay here."

He let out a big sigh. "Can't do a fling. Not with you."

"Okay, then. We agree: there's attraction here, but we're not going to act on it."

"This sucks." He'd been looking at his lap for the last few sentences.

She lifted her hand to rest against his jawline. "Not being friends would suck more."

He held his hand over hers. "Thank you. I needed that reminder. I don't want to lose you again, not when we got lucky enough to have a second chance. As much as I want to . . ." He stopped himself, and Effie felt the first pangs of loss. "I just like being with you. Spending time together. With our friends or just us two. Doing dumb stuff. Making each other laugh. Being near you feels better than anything."

She smiled, feet finally on firmer ground. This wasn't scary. It was the two of them, just like always. Effie and Ernie. "Me, too. But I understand if you don't want to do any more of the bucket list. It is a little date-y."

"No way. I'm not missing a chance to eat Portland potato doughnuts until I feel sick."

"We're going to Portland?!"

He nodded. "Oh heck yes. Next month. With the new guidelines. We keep hanging out. No more flirting. Effie and Ernie circa . . . 1997."

"But with better hair," she said.

"Oh yeah. Hey. One more thing," Ernie said, patting her

hand, which was still on his cheek. She looked at him expectantly. "Please never again talk to me about getting yourself off."

Effie smirked and slid her hand out of his. She almost danced her fingertips over his neck as they broke contact, but she stopped herself. Because they were friends. That's all they were.

Chapter Twenty-Two

Instead of a bucket list activity the next Monday, Effie and Ernie had agreed to help Samuel and Mick organize for a combined garage sale later in the summer. They decided to spend the morning going through their own things, then bring it all down to the Olsens' garage, where they'd begin pricing items. The timing was right: after years of badgering, Ingrid had finally convinced their dad to get rid of their mom's old stuff collecting dust in the attic. Earlier that week, she'd called Susan to double-check that she didn't want any of her clothes, books, or trinkets. Their mother had laughed out loud and said, "All that junk? Sweetie, if I haven't missed those paisley bell-bottoms by now, I'm never going to."

Depending on who you asked, the Olsen family's attic was either a treasure trove of memories or the scariest room in a haunted house. When Effie's mom left, she'd done so with a few suitcases. Everything else she'd accumulated, owned, and loved in

Alder Isle stayed there. Samuel had moved most of it upstairs, in boxes and big old chests, but for years he refused to part with it. It wasn't like she was dead, he had argued. Just gone. On more than one occasion in high school, Effie had come home to find him sitting on the floor up there, surrounded by photo albums or watching old home movies on the ancient television and VHS player. He loved visiting the attic. He found it comforting. Effie, on the other hand, couldn't stay far enough away. As the family equivalent of Switzerland, Ingrid was neutral on the matter.

That morning, as they climbed the steep staircase, Samuel was full of chatter. But he fell quiet when Effie opened the door. They stood there at the top of the stairs for a beat or two, surveying the mountains of stuff. There was more than Effie had remembered. "Right," her dad said without making any effort to move forward.

"Right," Effie echoed. "Should we start with the clothes?" There were a lot. And they seemed less filled with emotional bombs than the photo albums, videos, and letters. Together they settled onto the rough wooden floor and opened a trunk. A moth flew out, and Effie laughed. Samuel did, too. Ingrid's hands plunged into the trunk and brought out a red-and-black off-the-shoulder sweater. And then they began.

An hour later, they had sorted through all their mother's clothes, separating them into two piles: donate and keep. Against Effie's better judgment, Samuel had convinced them to hang on to a piece of clothing neither sister wanted: their mother's wedding veil. It was lacy and sheer, and extravagantly long. Effie and Ingrid both knew the veil by heart, even though this was their first time feeling the fabric beneath their fingers. They'd seen it thousands of times in a framed photo in the kitchen. Effie had spent hours washing dishes at the sink and studying her mother's smile, the elegant curve of her shoulders. Ingrid texted their mother a picture, which caused Effie to bristle. **Do you want me to mail this to you? Feeling sentimental**, the message from Ingrid said. It was punctuated with an upside-down smile face. A few minutes later, their mother texted back: **Beautiful, but no. Would make a nice table runner?** Ingrid neatly folded the fabric and tucked it in a little mountain of items she'd claimed for herself.

Effie ended up with a score of her own: a sundress. "Oh!" she exclaimed, pulling it from the trunk and holding it out so she could see all of it. It was from the late sixties; it had that groovy, free-spirit kind of look. The fabric was soft cotton and patterned in sherbet-colored stripes that ran vertically all the way down the maxi skirt. The top, which joined the skirt where Effie's natural waist fell, was pale orange with two ties to fasten it: one around the neck, like a halter, and another across the back, with a pretty pink ribbon. Effie had never seen anything like it. She'd never *owned* anything like it.

"She'd want you to have it," Samuel said.

"I wish that were true," Effie responded without thinking.

"Effie Pants, she loved you and your sister." Samuel frowned. "*Loves* you."

She balled the dress up and tossed it begrudgingly in the keep pile. "Yeah? She tell you that?" Her father was quiet. If she had to hazard a guess, the last time her parents had had a *real* conversation was the day he finally gave in to the D-word. *Divorce.*

"You're so hard on her. I think Alder Isle was just a little too much for your mother," he said.

Effie was annoyed. How could he be so naive, after all these years? "No, Dad. It's that *we* were too much."

Ingrid frowned. She was so young when it happened, she had only a handful of Mom memories. Effie envied her. She didn't know what she'd missed out on or what she had lost. It was easy for Ingrid to believe it hadn't been that big of a deal, while Effie knew otherwise.

Samuel sighed and moved closer to Effie. For the first few years, he'd held out hope that Susan would change her mind. After that, when it became clear that she very much would not, the matter of his misplaced hope became an Olsen family forbidden topic. They couldn't discuss it—at least not without professional help. Effie wondered briefly about therapy. Why hadn't he done it? Why hadn't they, as a family? It was a tool she had never tried because no one had ever offered it to her. But she knew other people found it useful. Lifesaving, even.

He held out his arms and motioned for his daughters to scoot closer. "Come in for a hug?"

Effie hesitated but only briefly. She leaned in and let her father hold her. He cradled Ingrid on the other side, and Ingrid reached across for Effie's hand. They were all connected, a small and imperfect circle. Between this hug and their one in the kitchen weeks earlier, it was the most physical contact she'd had with her family in years. For the first few moments, Effie's body remained tense. She kept her neck straight; her cheek hovered above her father's chest. But as he rubbed her back, she melted around the corners. By the time her temple met her father's collarbone, and she breathed in his familiar orange-patchouli scent, she had let go entirely. Tears spilled onto his shoulder. "Dad," she whispered into his chest. "Ingrid. I missed you."

"We missed you, too, big sister," Ingrid said.

When they released each other, Effie tasted guilt in the back of her throat, pungent and sharp. "I'm sorry I stayed away so long," she said. "I know we talked on the phone, and that I visited a few times. But I should have made more of an effort. It was very . . . Mom of me."

"Eh," said Ingrid. "I get it. I have tons of friends here. And Sixto. But Alder Isle can be rough if you're . . ." She trailed off and blushed, her Olsen-blond hairline giving way to a pinkish red. *Single*, was the word Ingrid had swallowed.

Effie laughed. "You can say it. I was never exactly Miss Popular."

"But you had Ernie," her father said.

"Yeah," Effie agreed. "I sure did."

No one spoke for the next handful of minutes as they started on a heavy steamer trunk, this one full of books. Samuel broke the silence. "It may not be perfect, but you'll always have a home here, kiddo."

Effie reached into the trunk and flipped through a paperback romance. She wasn't sure how to respond, but she was saved by the sound of knocking on the back door. She dropped the book and ran to the attic window. Ernie and Mick were unloading cardboard boxes from the bed of Ernie's truck. She stuck her head out and shouted. "Hey! We'll be right down." Ducking back inside, she grabbed one handle of the trunk and motioned for Ingrid to help with the other. "Saved by the Callahans," Effie joked. "Let's do the rest of this outside."

Effie Olsen!" Mick dropped the old camping chairs he'd been holding and scooped Effie up in a hug. She'd been home for just about two months, but this was the first time she'd spoken to Ernie's dad. She felt a flash of guilt but shook it off by telling herself she'd been busy. Busy with, uh, Ernie. Samuel and Mick exchanged handshakes and surveyed the mountain of boxes, bags, and old furniture. There was a lot, and it seemed overwhelming, stacked in the driveway like that. Mick broke the silence. "Memories sure do have a way of piling up over the decades, don't they?"

Ernie clapped his father on the back and caught Effie's eye. "Sure do, Dad," he said.

The five of them worked for hours, breaking at 1:00 for iced-tea-lemonades and a platter of peanut butter sandwiches. Ingrid, Samuel, Mick, and Ernie put jelly on theirs, but Effie chose marshmallow spread. "It's nostalgic. Whatever! Leave me alone," she said, taking a big bite when Ingrid raised her eyebrows and asked if she could have the recipe.

"Fluffernutter probably doesn't pass the Brown Butter local test," Mick joked from across the table. "Better make sure Carina Shen doesn't find out about this."

"What does she have to do with Brown Butter?" Effie said, setting down her sandwich. Carina Shen was a reporter for the *New York Times* food section. She used to do the restaurant reviews, but had recently transitioned to investigative reporting. A few months ago, she published a damning exposé on some of the male chefs accused of sexual harassment since the #MeToo movement.

"Dad." Ernie was pulling the crust from his sandwich as color crept up his neck and into his cheeks. "I told you Effie wouldn't want to know about that."

"Is Brown Butter getting a review in the paper?" Samuel asked, helping himself to a handful of potato chips from the bag in the middle of the table.

"Highly doubtful," Effie said. "But elaborate."

"She's been calling around," Ernie said reluctantly. "Talked to Sixto the other day." Ingrid nodded in confirmation. "Nikki gave her an interview, too. There have been . . . allegations. Someone tipped off the paper that Jarrod's perfect restaurant isn't as Maine-y as it seems."

"Shitballs." Effie's stomach dropped. An exposé in the *Times* would put a screeching halt to business. Diners would cancel their reservations. Their reputations—the restaurant and all the cooks in it—would be tainted, possibly forever. "Did she call you, too?"

Ernie's blush had swallowed his face whole. "Yeah, but I told her I wasn't sure I wanted to talk. And I didn't want to tell you because I knew it'd stress you out. You're here to have a fun, light summer. Make some money. Not drown in restaurant drama."

"Oh geez," Mick said, looking between them. "I put my foot in it."

Ernie laid a hand on his father's shoulder to reassure him. "Eh. It was probably stupid to try and keep this a secret." To Effie, he said, "I thought it was possible Carina might not contact you. The PR team at Brown Butter hasn't even added your bio to the website's About page."

Effie took a deep breath, remembering the couple of calls from that 212 number. She'd rejected both. "It's okay. I think she has my number. Where she got it is a whole other mystery: I'm not listed anywhere. Thanks for telling me, though. I'm glad I know. If she calls again, I'm not going to answer."

"Then I won't talk to her, either," Ernie said.

"You sure about that?" Ingrid said. "Jarrod is a shady guy doing stupid stuff. People should know about it. He should be punished."

Effie forced a laugh. "Yeah. I'm sure. Too much is at stake here. We're talking about people's jobs. Ernie's job. My job. Your boyfriend's job! The entire island's economic infrastructure, at this point. Besides, I'm here for one summer and one summer only. I'm not going to get involved." She spoke the last sentence with conviction but directed the words to the half sandwich and pile of crumbs on her plate.

Nobody said anything for a few beats. Eventually Ingrid stood up and started clearing plates. "If you say so, big sis."

Effie pushed her chair back and collected their drinking glasses. She was positive. Brown Butter wasn't her problem. She and Ernie had agreed on that weeks ago. So why did this new development make her feel like she sat in the front seat on a roller coaster, and was about to reach the top of its steepest climb?

Chapter Twenty-Three

That week, Effie received another two calls from Carina. She let them go to voicemail, and the reporter left two vague messages with her contact information. Effie deleted each one immediately but copied Carina's number onto a sticky note that she plastered on her laptop. Just in case she changed her mind. Clearly Carina's reporting was kicking into high gear.

Unfortunately, whether she talked or not, bringing the problem into the light had had an unfortunate consequence: Effie could no longer turn a blind eye to Jarrod's many offenses. There was no way the packs of vacuum-sealed chicken breasts could have come from Alder Isle. Or the jug of red wine vinegar clearly labeled PRODUCT OF CALIFORNIA. The heirloom baby beets that garnished the plates? Sure. But the boxes of extra-large carrots they used for juice and stock? No way. The more Effie looked, the more she saw. And the more she saw, the guiltier she felt.

But still. Not her business. Not her responsibility! Even

though it took up an inordinate amount of her brain space. She was grateful for her daily walks with Dahlia, which were a happy distraction. On their Sunday walk, Dahlia invited Effie over. "You're off tomorrow, right? Have dinner with us. Kit and me. She makes a stupendous pesto zucchini lasagna thing."

"I . . ." It was Ernie's turn to plan a bucket list activity, but maybe he wouldn't mind if she canceled. They'd done it every week since she came home. And it wasn't like he owned her. She didn't *have* to hang out with him all the time. She chewed her lip.

"Excellent!" Dahlia barreled over Effie's pause. "Dinner it is. We're the last house on Lobster Cove Road. Very pretty oak tree next to the driveway. Come around six o'clock. Don't bring anything. You're not allergic to cats, are you?"

Effie ran down to the basement after her walk and asked Ernie if they could take a breather from the bucket list. He had been scrubbing scallop shells with a small brush, and covered the disappointment that flashed across his face with an understanding smile. Later that evening, he sent her a text:

Ernie

Hilarious plot twist: I ended up making plans for tomorrow. So I would've asked you to cancel, too.

Effie's heart felt tight as a flash of jealousy lit her up. She waited for it to pass, then texted back.

Look at you with so many friends. Enjoy the night off from me.

I will enjoy the night, but it'd for sure be better with you there.

Because you'll miss my snark and sass?

Because I will miss you.

Effie didn't respond. How she felt—*I'm going to miss you, too*—was too vulnerable. Too honest. Her thumbs hovered over the keyboard before she finally powered off the phone and set it facedown on her nightstand.

Dahlia's house was every bit as artsy and whimsical as she was. It sat at the northernmost tip of the island, on a secluded blob of land shaped like a lobster tail. Her property was on the right side of the tail. As she approached the house, Effie recognized the oak tree immediately—it was, as Dahlia said, very pretty, with stately limbs that shaded a single-story home. The house meandered over the landscape as if it couldn't quite make up its mind what shape it wanted to be, then stubbornly settled on all of them. The graying wood walkway was lined with a riot of wildflowers and buzzing with bees, and there were string lights hung across the wraparound front porch, emitting a pretty glow.

Effie knocked on the door, a bottle of fizzy rosé tucked under her arm. She was in her favorite off-duty outfit: trusty jean shorts, white T-shirt with thick sleeve cuffs, huaraches. No makeup, no jewelry, no perfume. Suddenly self-conscious at the thought of a grown-up dinner party, she tucked her hair behind her ears. She worried she hadn't fancified herself enough.

The top panel of the Dutch door swung out and the top half of Kit appeared, frowning. Realizing she hadn't entirely opened the door, she withdrew her hand and started jiggling the interior handle. "Shit, this is awkward," she said. "Sorry. One moment." The door closed, and Effie heard a click, then a turn. The bottom of the door popped open, and Effie jumped aside so it wouldn't hit her knees. She peered down and saw the lower half of Kit, wearing fuzzy moccasins and a pair of boot-cut jeans. "Still no. Really, really sorry about this. Hold on. DAHLIA!" The bottom door closed again. Effie heard footsteps, then Dahlia's laughter over a few more clicks. The door, finally in one piece, opened properly.

"Hurrah!" Dahlia said.

"Fuck this door," Kit said with a smidgen of grumpiness. She gathered Effie in a hug.

"You have a fantastic home," Effie commented, pointing at the paintings that hung all over the entryway. "Yours?" Kit nodded. Each one depicted Alder Isle wildlife and wildflowers in the same dreamy, muted palette. They were framed simply and tastefully. Muck boots and sandals sat on a metal tray, and a straw hat hung on a peg attached to the wall.

"Thank you. I think so, too. Minus the door," Kit said, taking the wine from Effie and leading her in.

"No, plus the door," Effie said, kicking off her shoes.

"You weren't supposed to bring anything! I love the door," Dahlia said from behind Kit.

Kit shrugged helplessly, although she was smiling. "She loves the door."

"Therefore, you have to love the door," Dahlia said, rocking back on her heels. She'd stood on her tiptoes so Kit could kiss her cheek.

"I say fuck the door," Kit repeated. "Thank you for the wine."

"We don't have to drink it," Effie said. She had assumed *Don't bring anything* was adult-speak for *Please bring a little something.* Now she was questioning. She didn't want Kit and Dahlia to think she was rude.

"We'll drink it," Kit said.

"We'll drink it!" Dahlia clapped her hands, then led them all into the kitchen, where an island was covered in the most impressive spread of food Effie had ever seen outside of a restaurant. Soft jazz played over a sound system. "Help yourself to everything," Dahlia encouraged, climbing on top of the counter to retrieve three glasses from a shelf. Kit returned to the cutting board where she'd been working before Effie's arrival, chopping a bunch of basil.

"Can I help?" Effie asked as she plucked a piece of bruschetta from a serving platter. She crunched into it. It was topped with halved cherry tomatoes and saucy with sweet, thick balsamic vinegar and a spoonful of olive tapenade. A teeny-tiny ball of mozzarella burst under her teeth and flooded her mouth with richness that tempered the saltiness from the olives. "Wow, Kit."

Dahlia popped the cork, and it made an exciting sound. "Ooh," she said and poured the wine.

"We're so glad you're here. Spoil your dinner with charcuterie. Drink too much. We have a spare bedroom. Wait—did you drive? I didn't hear a car."

"Biked," Effie said, then fanned herself. In the evenings, the air rolled into Alder Isle so insistent and wet that it felt like being in the sea itself.

"Well, guest room's yours if you want it. Whenever. Hey! A toast: to making new friends as adults, which is hard and admirable work," Dahlia said.

Effie lifted her glass and the bubbles burst like the lit end of a sparkler against her nose. She sipped. It tasted like strawberry Jolly Ranchers. Kit handed her a cracker topped with a fat wedge of Brie. Dahlia danced in a circle. "Well put," Effie said, meaning it.

"Oh, we did invite someone else." Dahlia stopped twirling and spoke in a tone so casual, it could only be forced. "We figured you wouldn't mind."

Kit smiled kindly. "Don't scare her; she's going to think it's a setup."

"It is a setup!" Dahlia said, taking a self-congratulatory sip of rosé.

"It is not a setup," Kit clarified to Effie.

The color drained from Effie's face. Maybe this was the real reason she avoided dinner parties: meddling couples who wanted to play matchmaker. She'd already gotten tangled up with two men on this island. She didn't need to add a third to the list.

"Who is it?" She almost didn't want to know.

A musical knock sounded at the door, and Effie instinctively began gathering her hair into a ponytail. Kit set down her knife and calmly made her way to the hall. "I'll just be half an hour, once I figure out this godforsaken door."

Dahlia grinned. "Yay," she assured Effie, and topped off her glass.

A male voice traveled from the entryway and into the hall. "Kit, I don't know if—" Ernie cut himself off as he stood still in the doorframe. From the look on his face, Effie gathered this was a surprise encounter for him, too. "Eff. Hi."

"Hi, Ern." Effie raised her rosé in his direction. "Sorry I had to cancel on you. I had plans."

Ernie chuckled. "We're such nerds. I think this actually counts toward our tally."

Kit glanced back and forth between the two of them. "Oh shoot. Your bucket list thing was today?"

"No worries," Ernie said. "We don't have to do it on Monday. It's just happened that way. A little recurring date."

"Not a date," Effie clarified.

"Of course. Definitely not a date," Dahlia said. "You're just childhood best friends who've reunited in your seaside hometown for the summer." She led Ernie into the kitchen and pulled out the chair next to Effie. "Bruschetta?"

Chapter Twenty-Four

Over a meal of Kit's excellent pesto zucchini lasagna, they talked about everything. They covered Kit's inspiration for her paintings; Dahlia's attempts to rewild their lawn with native wildflowers and grasses that attracted pollinators; and the pair's cryptocurrency investments, made with Ingrid's help. They talked about a book Ernie was reading and loved, and Effie's professional trajectory across the globe and then back again. Dahlia and Kit teased Ernie about his salsa class performance, and by the time they all had second helpings, everyone was feeling quite jovial.

Finished with dinner but still too full for dessert, the four new-old friends luxuriated around the dining table. They were all pink-cheek-level drunk, edging toward the cliffside of tipsy, feeling free and fine, and happy to stay right there. Once Effie and Ernie got Dahlia and Kit caught up on their history, the atmosphere relaxed even more. "Confessing your love on graduation night? So cinematic," Kit said, shaking her head.

"Oh yeah. I got thiiis close to buying a ring."

"I bet you both had a good laugh about it," Dahlia said.

"Not entirely," Ernie said at the same time Effie admitted, "Not exactly."

Kit raised her eyebrows. Effie clarified. "I went a little psycho. We didn't speak for years."

"Well, sometimes it's like that," Dahlia said. "I'm glad you're friends again."

"I am, too," Ernie said, giving Effie's bicep a light punch that made her laugh nervously. Despite their renewed commitment to friendship only, she couldn't shake the upside-down exciting feeling she had when his eyes locked on hers. She cursed Dahlia for trying to set them up. It was messing with her head.

"So." Kit divided the last of a bottle of chilled sauvignon blanc between their glasses. They had moved on from the rosé.

"Should we open another one?" Dahlia wondered.

"In a minute." Kit tenderly rubbed her wife's shoulder. "As a former front-of-house restaurant worker, I'm dying to know. What's the gossip at Brown Butter?"

"Let's open that wine," Effie joked.

"We've got something better and boozier than that. Amaro!" Dahlia jumped up and wandered into the kitchen to find the bottle of Italian herbal liqueur.

"Sorry," Kit said seriously. "I can tell this is not your idea of fun dinner party talk."

As Dahlia poured their digestifs, Effie and Ernie shared a look, debating without words whether to tell their new friends about Jarrod and his scam. Effie's eyes asked, *We can trust them, right?* and Ernie's said, *It's up to you.*

"Oh, it's just Jarrod being a shady motherfluffer," Effie said. She knocked her knee against Ernie's in acknowledgment of the borrowed word.

"Heheh," Dahlia said as she nosed the glass of amaro and gave a dreamy smile. It was a good bottle; smelled like anise and fresh tarragon.

"Wait, what'd he do?" Kit asked.

Ernie told them about the tomatoes and chicken and truffles and everything else. Effie added the part about the *Times* reporter and the Brown Butter staff's divided opinion on whether to spill the secrets.

Dahlia nodded gravely, but Kit arched an eyebrow. "I don't know. There are some weird details there. But do you have proof he's lying about ingredients? Have you seen a delivery truck? Where is he getting all these contraband ingredients? Is he keeping them stockpiled in his apartment or something?"

Effie pressed her lips together as the memory of being in Jarrod's apartment socked her in the teeth. "That would be dumb of him," she said. Eager to end the conversation, she added, "Anyway . . ." Maybe Kit and Dahlia wouldn't judge her for hooking up with Jarrod on day one. But that was too much to reveal to Ernie. Even if he was her best friend.

"I have proof," he said, stretching his arms overhead then

letting one fall across the back of Effie's chair. His fingertips grazed the sleeve of her T-shirt so quickly, it must have been an accident. "Every other crate of produce I prep is from Chile or Mexico."

Kit's gaze was focused on Ernie's fingers and the millimeter-width gap between them and Effie's bicep. "Mm-hmm," she asked. "So what happens now? Are you two going to confront him?"

"We shouldn't, right?" Ernie's words were spoken directly to Effie.

Effie shook her head and absentmindedly leaned into Ernie's touch. "I think it'd be a bad idea. This conversation doesn't leave the dinner table, okay?" Ernie nodded, and Effie continued. "Besides, it's not my place. I'm just here for the summer. It's not the way I'd run a restaurant, but . . . I don't run this one."

"You wouldn't want to?" Kit asked.

Effie opened her mouth, then closed it again.

Kit leaned in. "All I'm saying is if you wanted to be head chef at Brown Butter, there's an easy way to do so. Get rid of the dude currently in the role. You're his number two, right?"

"I don't have that kind of power," Effie said.

"No, you can't fire him," Kit agreed. "But you could probably *get* him fired. If people—if the media—found out about his deceit." Ernie was watching Kit closely, listening with an unreadable expression.

Dahlia cupped her glass with her palms and spoke. "Jarrod has got to go. I mean, even without the ingredient sourcing stuff. He's a predator. He makes women feel uncomfortable. Maybe worse, I don't know. That's reason enough. I heard him come on to Effie a few weeks ago in his office."

"What?" Ernie's voice was hard and low.

Effie dug her nails into her palms to ground herself. "It was nothing. Standard new-hire hazing. I'm fine. And nobody is going to the media about this. Nobody at this table, at least. I know Sixto already has."

"Got it," Kit said, leaning back in her chair with her hands raised. "It's your call."

Effie released her fists and reached for her glass. "That's the thing. It's *not* my call. I don't want to get tangled up in a place that's just a layover on my way to something better."

Ernie flinched at her last two words. He released her chair and let his hand settle on his own lap.

Dahlia said, "Let's talk about something fun again."

Kit's chair legs scraped against the floor. "Tiramisu?"

Another hour later, Effie was riding home in Ernie's truck, her bike stashed in the bed. He'd stopped drinking after the rosé, and offered to drive her back to the lower island. He turned on the high beams and spoke to the windshield. "Why didn't you tell me?"

"Tell you what?" Effie asked, even though she knew.

"About Jarrod. Did he . . . did he do anything?"

Effie sank down in the seat and pressed the soles of her sandals into the dashboard. "I can handle myself."

"I know you can. *And* I care about your safety. Is that okay?"

He'd just pulled into Effie's driveway. She unfurled her legs and unbuckled her seat belt and said, "Yes."

Ernie exited the car then came around to Effie's side. "For the record, I'm opening your door to be a gentleman. Not because I think you're one of those wildly beautiful but incapable women."

"Haha. Very funny." Effie hopped out and rubbed her arms to shake off the night air shiver. "I bet being wildly beautiful is a blast."

Ernie tried to hold in his laugh, but it came out rogue and genuine. "Come here, you dork." He held out his arms and she scooted in. He wrapped his arms around her in a bear hug. "Also, for the record: you're the prettiest."

"In current company, maybe."

He pulled her even closer, and time stood still. The night was full of sounds: cicadas and water lapping at the shore and Effie's small, soft breaths and Ernie's steady, deep ones.

"I really want to kiss you right now." His voice was quiet but confident.

Effie laughed nervously. She really wanted that, too. Even though she wasn't supposed to. "Haha, very funny. I believe you. I'm hot."

He ran his fingers up her shoulder and the side of her neck, where they buried themselves in her hair. He tugged a little and her toes tingled. His lips were at her temple, they were on her skin, his breath was warm and soft, and *oh God*, she needed this so badly. She closed her eyes and turned; offered him her mouth. His lips touched her own, featherlight and fleeting, and then they were gone.

"Hey," she said, her eyes still closed. "We shouldn't have done that."

She felt his forehead on hers. "I know. We can pretend it never happened." He squeezed the nape of her neck once more and, without looking back, got in his truck and drove the half mile home.

There was just one problem. After showering and lying awake in bed for an hour, Effie couldn't stop thinking about it. It was impossible to forget everything that had happened. Not that she was trying very hard. She rolled over and found her phone on the nightstand. She typed in her passcode and, before she could pull herself back down to earth, sent Ernie a message.

Ernie

Hi.

Hi yourself.

What if you had kissed me harder? What if you hadn't stopped?

Eff . . .

Is this a trick question? Are we playing some twisted version of Truth or Dare?

No. I don't even know what I should want anymore.

Forget about should for a second. If you can. Tell me what you do want.

I want you to kiss me harder and not stop.

What do YOU want?

We're going here? Really?

I'm already here. Are you coming with?

I want to kiss you. Hard. So hard it makes your barriers melt away. I want to coax your mouth open with mine as my fingers trail up your stomach, under your shirt. I want you to give in to the way you feel when my hands are on you. And I want us to stop pretending we don't both need this.

I want you. It took me years to get over you when you left. Years. And I was right back there when I saw you again.

So covering me in chocolate sauce like a maniac—that was just one big cover-up of your actual feelings?

Pretty much, yeah.

Are you going to let me kiss you the way you deserve or not?

I'll give you whatever you want.

I'm biting your lower lip and digging my nails into your back as your fingers reach the clasp of my bra.

Hilarious. I'm not wasting time with that. I've already pushed it up over your breasts. I'm holding you, teasing you. My thumbs are running over your skin. Is that enough, or do you want my tongue and my teeth?

What do you think?

Pull your shirt off. The bra too. Everything.

Everything?

Everything. I'm picturing you. Your coy smirk and the ridge of your collarbone. The scar on your bicep from when you were fifteen and got too close to the oven door. The curve of your hips and your strong legs. I'm going to let my hands wander. Lower. Do you want that?

I need it. But I'm taking off your belt and shorts first. You looked so fucking good tonight, by the way.

You're a goddess all the time. I can feel your hands at my stomach and I want this all so much.

You have it. Now touch me.

Imagine my hands on your inner thighs. Pushing your legs open. I'm not being gentle. Wider, Eff. Like that. That's good. Now imagine my first two fingers tracing you. Touching you. Taking my time.

Screw that, I need you inside me.

Then turn around and face the wall.

A rush of heat swirled then pooled between Effie's thighs. She closed her eyes and pictured Ernie's hands on her waist, pressing her up against the wood paneling in the boathouse.

Touch yourself. Touch yourself the way you do when you think about me.

Picture my hand under yours. I want you to guide me. I want to learn what you like. I want to learn everything about you. Everything I've missed in the last sixteen years.

Where is your mouth?

Against your ear, whispering all the dirty, sweet things I adore about you as I roll on a condom.

Effie read his words with her own palm over her mouth. She exhaled and brought her hand to herself.

I want all of you.

I love this. Being with you is the best thing I have ever done.

Never stop. Fuck me forever.

Is that a request? I think you should beg for it.

I don't beg. Never. Stop. Fucking. Me.

I'm close. Ern, I'm so close.

I am too. My lips are at your neck and I'm biting your skin. Enough that it hurts a little. Is that okay? Do you like that?

I can handle getting hurt. Come with me?

I'm here with you. I'm right here.

Their phones were quiet for a couple of minutes. When Effie's heart rate finally slowed, she picked up her phone and sent one last text.

Good night, Ernie.

Immediately, Ernie sent one back.

Sweet dreams, Effie.

Spent but no closer to sleep, Effie let memories and fantasies about Ernie mingle. Images of the boy who'd bared his soul to her at eighteen became intertwined with the confident, kind man he had become. The man who made her laugh and made her feel safe and, apparently, could make her come through a phone screen. Ernie Callahan would have been her perfect match—if only she wanted to stay on Alder Isle. If only he wasn't already her perfect best friend. *If only.* Effie tossed and turned as the sensation of his lips on her own haunted her.

Chapter Twenty-Five

A few mornings later, Effie was lacing her sneakers for a jog when her phone rang. She hadn't seen Ernie since Monday's dinner. Since the kiss. Since everything that happened after the kiss. They had both taken care to avoid the other at work, and she hadn't texted him. She was equal parts relieved and hurt that he hadn't texted her.

She tightened her laces, grabbed a banana from the counter, and absentmindedly hit the ACCEPT CALL button on her way out the door. "Effie here," she said.

"Euphemia, hi. It's Effie, though? Carina Shen," the caller answered. "I've been trying to reach you."

"Oh shit . . . sorry," Effie said, not sure if she could offer a valid excuse. "I was busy."

"I get it. Your time is valuable. I'll be quick. If you have a few minutes now?"

Effie rubbed her calf with the toe of her sneaker and glanced down the road. Sixto was crossing the street, on his way to work early. She waved and felt a pang of guilt. There was no reason for her to talk with Carina Shen. She should say she was busy, should apologize and hang up.

"Now's good," Effie said.

Five minutes later, she ended the call with her hands shaking.

Carina gave her a succinct version of the backstory: earlier in the summer someone had emailed an anonymous tip about Brown Butter. Head chef Jarrod Levi, the tipster had said, was falsifying dozens of ingredients and substituting conventional grocery store produce in at least a third of the restaurant's dishes. The newspaper had written about Brown Butter a few times because it was such a hot spot for the city's vacationing elite, and now it was taking the allegations seriously. Carina had spoken to what she described as a handful of Brown Butter staff about the rumor, and learned the restaurant's problems went far deeper than just Costco carrots. She also had waitstaff on record detailing Jarrod's unwanted advances. There was one instance of him threatening to "make a server's life miserable" when she ended a fling they'd had. Carina had plenty of anecdotal evidence from the front-of-house about Jarrod's monstrosities, but she was having a harder time getting the back-of-house to talk.

"So is it true?" Effie asked, trying to sound casual. "About the ingredients? And his . . . behavior?"

"I'm still trying to figure that out," Carina answered. "I'm wondering foremost if you might be them—the whistleblower," she said after a pause. "The timing lines up with your hire—you came on board in late May? I got the email in early June."

"I did, but . . . I'm not," Effie said. "Maybe it was a customer?"

"It's possible." Carina's voice was coated lightly in skepticism. "Well, would you be willing to talk about all this? I'd value your take, as someone relatively fresh to the environment."

Effie opened her mouth before she realized she didn't know what to say.

"On or off the record," Carina prompted.

"What exactly does 'on the record' mean?"

"If we speak on the record, you consent to being quoted, or to having information specifically attributed to you. Off the record, I'll use your information as a jumping-off point and do further research, or attribute it in the piece to an anonymous source. I'm sure you understand I'd prefer we speak on the record."

"I don't know." This all felt too fast. Effie wished she hadn't answered her stupid phone; she needed time to figure out how she felt about this before committing herself to anything.

"Tell you what, Effie. I'm coming to Alder Isle myself early next week to conduct a few follow-up interviews. Why don't we schedule a meeting for then?"

Why don't we schedule a meeting? Effie's mind careened over a track full of hurdles. If she spoke with Carina, she'd be forever linked with the takedown of a decorated restaurant. It would make getting her next job a lot harder: Who would ever hire a sous chef who'd squealed on the boss? Who would hire her for any position? Once you've been in the trenches with someone, your loyalties were supposed to be with each other, through and through. She'd look like a traitor. She would *be* a traitor.

On the other hand, it was like Kit had said: kick Jarrod out, and the job was basically hers. Her goal had always been the head chef position, and the opportunity was here—for the second and possibly last time—silver platter and everything. But taking this shot meant settling down here. In Alder Isle. Forever. Or at least for a while. She hated the way she almost wanted to. It wasn't like she'd been proactive in her job search. After sending her resume to exactly one restaurant in Copenhagen, she'd completely abandoned her email.

There was one more thing. Just a tiny possibility that had been nagging at her since Mick let it slip that Carina was researching the story in the first place. What if she spoke and the story ended up shutting Brown Butter down? Could it survive a scandal like this? Restaurants had closed for far less over the last few years.

It wasn't just Effie who would be out of a job.

It'd be everyone. Sixto, and Chad, and Jean-Claude, and B.J. . . .

Ernie.

Ernie, who only had this job because he'd lost his dream one.

Ernie, who needed this job to pay off his father's medical bills.

No. There was no way she could talk to Carina Shen about this story. She was certain.

Which was why, when Carina suggested they meet for coffee the next Tuesday at 1:00, Effie was so surprised to hear herself say, "Yes."

Maybe it was her subconscious. Maybe it was a force bigger than her. But either way, when the *New York Times* reporter came to town, one of her first stops would be Effie Olsen's kitchen. After confirming the address and ending the call, Effie ate the banana, stretched, and ran two miles at an uncomfortably fast pace, which didn't help to clear her head at all. As her sneakers pounded the pavement, all she could think about was running behind Ernie, trying to keep up as he effortlessly led her around and around the mountain.

As the week passed, summer arched its back and hinted at fall. Effie did exactly what she told Kit she would during their dinner: she worked hard, turned a blind eye to Jarrod's overtures and outbursts, and tried not to think about lobster ravioli. Or out-of-season tomatoes. Or Italian truffles. And in truth, forgetting about Brown Butter's sins—and the reporter who was investigating them—got very easy once she focused on the people who made it work.

She also tried not to think about Ernie. For the last month, she'd been coming in early two days a week to coach Chad before his shift in the dish pit began. During their first lesson, he confessed he wanted to attend culinary school, but didn't have the money. Effie had listened, then told him one of the restaurant industry's biggest secrets: he didn't need to go to school to become a professional cook. In fact, a lot of line cooks considered culinary school to be a waste of time and finances. She had done it, but looking back now . . . would she? She admitted to Chad she wasn't sure. "I think if you work hard, watch closely, and have a good teacher or two, you can learn everything you need to know simply by being in a kitchen."

And just like that, without realizing she had signed herself up for the job, Effie had become Chad's instructor. Their first few lessons were spent on basic skills. She taught him how to sharpen his knives before anything else. Then she taught him how to hold a chef's knife correctly, choking up on the blade with confidence rather than gripping it by the handle. She showed him how to cut carrots into a macédoine, a chunky, uniform square shape; and a brunoise, a tiny, neat dice. She critiqued his work and encouraged him to try again and again until he got it right. Late at night, Effie read through her old culinary school notebooks, formulating a curriculum for Chad's lessons.

That week especially, she was grateful for the distraction. Instead of her sexting session with Ernie and her phone call with Carina, she focused on lessons about the common French sauces: how to make them and when to use them. If he learned quickly enough, they could get into cooking techniques before summer was over. By teaching him how to braise, roast, sauté, and steam, she could open a world of possibilities for the young cook. It all flowed from there.

Teaching Chad and encouraging the interns made her feel useful and proud, like she had an impact not just on the people who ate at Brown Butter but on the ones who worked there, too. She didn't just feel an obligation to them. She was invested in their success.

It was the very thing she'd tried, and failed, to do at Cowboy Bean.

It was exactly what she'd promised herself she wouldn't do here.

Whether the staff at Brown Butter had been on edge since Carina began her reporting, Effie couldn't have said. She hadn't known to look for signs. But by Sunday, after almost a week of marinating in her own anxiety, she was positive she wasn't the only one looking around nervously.

That afternoon, she heard Nikki, the lead server, and Brent, a new hire, discussing Carina's story in hushed tones when she interrupted their glass-polishing time to go over the menu updates. ". . . Maria . . . off the record though . . . it's gonna be bad." Effie coughed as she approached, and they both clammed up.

She eyed Sixto as they ran through their prep lists, and she was certain she saw a change in his demeanor. He seemed jumpy and clumsy; he had dropped his Sharpie three times while labeling items for the walk-in cooler. Jean-Claude was huffier than usual, making constant annoyed little harrumphs. B.J. kept looking over his shoulder like he'd snatched a purse and was waiting for the owner to notice. Even the interns seemed on edge.

The only person who didn't seem perturbed was Jarrod.

There was no way he knew. The man was acting way too arrogant for a villain at the center of a major exposé. And that made sense. Carina probably wouldn't reach out for comment until she'd gathered all her sources. Sources like Effie.

It had been a slow build all week, but by 3:30, when the staff ate the family meal, the air felt poisoned and sickly, like a slow gas leak had just ruptured.

Family meal was a mainstay in most restaurants: everyone in the kitchen contributed an element to their pre-service dinner. At Brown Butter, they all ate together—front- and back-of-house—in the dining room, while Jarrod read through menu notes and addressed any issues. It was Effie's job to coordinate the staff dinner, and she usually themed it. Eating a cohesive meal was a nicer way to start their shift than just shoveling a bunch of old prep items into their mouths. It was also fun to watch her coworkers' creativity flourish. They'd done Tex-Mex, "all green everything," old-school pizza parlor, and breakfast-for-dinner, plus a rotating handful of other cuisines.

Her instructions for Sunday had been to re-create a dish or recipe that inspired them to become cooks. "It doesn't have to be fancy. In fact, the more nostalgic, the better," she'd said the day before. "Think of it as a potluck. No rules: just cook something that has special meaning to you."

Effie wondered if Ernie would show. He hadn't come to any of their family meals that week. It was possible he was just enjoying his adult Lunchables at the boathouse, but more likely, he was still avoiding her. Despite the bath of regret and embarrassment she'd been soaking in, she hoped he'd be there. She'd made tuna noodle casserole the way she remembered it at Ernie's house when they were kids. Mick had always topped it with homemade breadcrumbs, not the kind from a tin. She was just browning the crust under the broiler when Jarrod called out, "Family meal, yo! Dining room in five."

Effie placed the casserole next to Sixto's crock of pozole and smiled. Despite their buzzy anxiety, the kitchen staff had turned up for this. There was bouillabaisse with mussels and prawns, and a platter of crusty bread for dipping. There was focaccia pizza with caramelized onions and big gobs of melted mozzarella stuck in its dimpled surface. There were just-fried samosas, alluringly golden brown and still crackling, stuffed with mashed green peas and homemade masala blend. There was so much food, Effie almost didn't notice that Jarrod hadn't dropped off a tray or bowl.

"Hey, Chef, what's your dish?" Chad asked, pointing at his own: a pan of perfectly cubed carrots, glazed in butter and honey.

"Fuck that, I didn't have time," Jarrod said, riffling through a few papers covered in near-illegible scrawl.

"Neither did I," grumbled Sixto. "Still did it."

Jarrod shot him a look and started on his notes.

"Sorry I'm late!" Ernie's voice tumbled into the dining room before he did. "I was just finishing my . . . Oh. Sorry." Realizing he'd interrupted, he ducked beneath Jarrod's visual barbs and set a zippered cooler on the edge of the pass. *Hi*, he mouthed silently to Effie as he sank into the booth next to her. Her heart felt warm and wild, and she gave a little wave from her lap.

Once Jarrod was deep in his notes—around minute three, he'd started on a diatribe about not wiping the edges of soup bowls after plating them—Effie leaned in and brought her lips to Ernie's ear.

"What'd you make?"

She felt his heat immediately; the brush of her mouth on his skin had fired up a blush. "Ice cream sandwiches with gummy bears," he said, looking straight ahead.

She tried to hold in a laugh that came out as a snort, interrupting Jarrod once more.

"Olsen. Shut it." He snapped his fingers. Sixto made a face at her behind Jarrod's back. She returned the look and made a mental note to chat with him before her meeting on Tuesday. If he'd already talked with Carina, she wanted to know what they'd covered. They should align their stories to make sure the staff was a united front.

After another few minutes, Jarrod had gotten through the last of his notes. "See you fuckers at 5:00," he said, crossing the room toward his office. "I got shit to do."

His silence hung thick and thrilling in the air. Everyone, from servers to bar staff to Effie and her team, tried not to look at one another. How many of them had spoken to Carina? How many more knew about it? And what would happen when Jarrod found out? Effie let it be awkward for a second, then stood and clapped her hands. "Let's eat."

Once she'd filled her plate, she slid into one of the upholstered booths. She'd just lifted her fork when Ernie appeared at the table. "I know you don't *need* company," he said, a dangerous smile pulling at the corners of his mouth, "but if you want some, I'm your guy."

Her heart burst into a trillion rainbow sprinkles, and she moved over. "Normally, I don't dine with people who ghost me, but sure," she said, patting the booth.

"Who's ghosting? I've been busy. Very busy. Planning an

eating adventure through the city of Portland." Effie's eyebrow lifted. She'd been wondering about that. Their next bucket list activity was supposed to be tomorrow.

"A likely story," she said. "Hey. We should—"

Her hand was still resting on the bench seat between them, under the table. He placed his over hers and cut in before she could go further. "We shouldn't." She looked up at him, questioningly. Around them, the dining room hummed with chatter and laughter. His palm was cool and his hand steady. It felt comforting. Not urgent and sensual in the way his touch had been the other night. He dropped his voice and said, "I will never regret you, but I'm also not reckless enough to go any further."

"I don't regret it, either," Effie said to their hands. She couldn't bring herself to look at him.

"Monday night was special. More to the point, it was hot and you were perfect. I'm going to be thinking about it for a long, long time." She nodded, angry at the tears that were pricking at her eyelids. "But our intuition has been right all along. We're not supposed to do this. Not with you leaving. I'm going to pull us back. And we don't have to spend another second feeling bad or weird or guilty about it. I needed a few days to get my head on right, but I'm here and you're my best friend and it's all good."

"Okay." Effie's mouth felt dry. She knew he was saying all the right things, but it was the opposite of everything she wanted to hear. She finally brought her gaze to meet his eyes. There he was. Ernie. He just got her, and she understood him completely. This wasn't scary and it was only a little awful. If he could move past this, she could, too. "What time are we meeting tomorrow?"

"You tell me. I want you to be rested up and ready for the adventure of a lifetime." She rolled her eyes. "Okay, the adventure of a summer."

She thought for a moment. A slower morning would be nice, but she knew they had a ferry ride and a drive to get to Portland. "Is eight o'clock too late?"

He slipped his other palm under hers, creating an Effie-hand sandwich. He squeezed tightly and then let her go. "No, Eff. It's not too late."

Chapter Twenty-Six

"Wait—can I drive?" Effie asked, her hand on the passenger door handle of Ernie's truck.

Ernie had been loading a bundle of sleeping bags and foam pads into the bed of his truck when she arrived at the boathouse, hopping off her bike and letting it fall onto the neatly trimmed grass. It was five minutes before 8:00.

"Keys, please?" she asked again, holding out her hand to collect them. The sky was a brilliant blue and the air was still relatively cool, coming in off the sea. The cocktail of nice weather and a whole day off made her intensely miss driving through Maine in the summer. It was early; maybe traffic wouldn't be so bad.

Ernie's reaction was one of surprise and terror, and although it only lasted a second before he smoothed it into something more neutral, Effie caught it.

"Fuck you, I'm a great driver!"

"Effie, even if that was true—and I don't think it's a stretch to say *it is decidedly not true*—when was the last time you were behind the wheel of a car on a highway?"

Fair enough. Since graduation, she'd either relied on public transportation or lived in a village so small, all you needed was your legs and some good walking shoes. She came around to the driver's side and teasingly pushed him out of the way. "Twenty fifteen. Twenty fourteen? But relax. This isn't a car. It's a truck."

As he buckled into the passenger's seat, Ernie's face changed again, this time to an expression of horror and offense. "Okay, now that's just insulting. It's a *Tacoma*."

"Which is quantifiably a truck, no?"

"It's not. Trucks are F-350s with ball sacs hanging from the hitch."

"Truck nuts."

"Yeah, I don't want to be associated with that."

"Fine. Whatever. Can I drive your Tacoma?" The question was rhetorical; she'd already adjusted the mirrors. "Don't you think it's pathological how many people on this island own the same kind of truck? I mean, non-truck?" She turned the key and the engine coughed and wheezed like it was attending its first Phish concert. Ernie tenderly patted the dash.

"I guess I'd never noticed," he said.

Effie couldn't believe that. Practically everyone she knew on Alder Isle drove a Tacoma. "Did this place get Toyota spon since I left or something?" She reversed out of the driveway and started toward town.

"Ha. Yeah, it's like that movie with Jim Carrey," he said.

"*Ace Ventura: Pet Detective.*" She was quick with her banter as she rolled down Main Street to the ferry terminal.

He gave her a pained look. "Don't be smart. The other one."

"*Ace Ventura: When Nature Calls*?"

"Nooooo."

"The one where he mind-erases Kate Winslet?" She knew she was riling him up now.

"*The Truman Show*," he said, gripping the edge of his seat as she narrowly missed a hedgerow.

"I think it was called *Eternal Sunshine of the Spotless Mind*."

"No, *I'm* talking about *The Truman Show*."

Ernie flashed their tickets to the attendant at the ferry, and she steered them into the line. "Never saw it," she said with a shrug.

"Basically, he realizes that his entire town is a TV set with hidden cameras, and everyone knows it except him. So he's been manipulated his whole life to entertain other people. His entire existence has been a lie, thanks to this tiny . . . quaint . . . town."

"Oh no, don't even joke about that."

"And at certain points his wife would awkwardly look into the distance and be like, 'I love Sunshine dish detergent because it's the best around. Sunshine dish detergent, for your family's needs!'"

"When this ferry docks, I'm going to drive the car over the ramp and straight into the ocean," Effie said.

"It's a Tacoma," Ernie reminded her.

Effie grinned and turned off the ignition. "Alrighty, then."

. . .

The morning's gentle coolness soon turned brutal. Sun poured in through the windows, baking their shoulders. They stopped at a fast-food restaurant and ordered a large Coke and split it, then passed the cup back and forth, shaking ice cubes into their mouths. Ernie asked if Effie wanted to plug her phone into the aux cord so she could play David Guetta and Effie told him to go to hell and he laughed to himself and turned the radio to a Top 40 new country station.

As they neared Portland a few hours later, Effie realized she had no idea where to go. She had, once upon a time.

"Where to?" she said, pointing at the sign for the next exit.

"Pull into the next gas station. I'll take over from here." She started to protest, and he playfully covered her mouth with his hand. She licked his palm and turned into a Sunoco.

"Ew." He blushed and unbuckled, grabbing his wallet to fuel up.

As the Tacoma drank gasoline, Effie ran inside, returning with a pack of Wint-O-Green Life Savers. She tore it open and tossed one to Ernie.

"Nice! You remembered."

It was Effie's turn to color crimson. Of course she had remembered. "Wouldn't be an Ernie and Effie road trip without 'em." She bit into the candy, and it sparked between her molars. "So. We're here. Where should we eat? What's good in Portland these days?"

Ernie capped the gas tank and climbed into the driver's seat.

"Here. Read this." As he adjusted his mirrors, Effie scanned the piece of paper he'd handed over. It was written in his messy, boyish penmanship, torn from a spiral notebook. She picked off all the little rough edges from the page and rolled them between her thumb and index finger as she read the list. There were six locations written down, with addresses and ETAs for each one. It started with a bakery in the West End and ended at an oyster bar downtown.

Ernie was watching her read, his brows knitted into nervous ropes. "Is this okay? I figured you wouldn't be in the mood to sit down for an overpriced four-hour meal. We'll just gorge ourselves at casual places all afternoon?"

"It is definitely okay," Effie said calmly, even though she really wanted to jump onto Ernie's lap and hug him. It was exactly the sort of day she wanted to have. But she purposefully tempered her reaction. The effort he had put into the itinerary made her feel self-conscious, like they were having the world's longest date instead of taking a friendly road trip.

And they were not on a date.

It was the friendly thing.

Just like they'd promised.

A million bajillion times since they swore they'd keep things rated PG.

He relaxed. "Okay, good."

"Hey—Ernie?" Effie said.

He turned the key and the engine came to life, even more chaotically than the last time. He stroked the steering wheel. "Good girl, Chanterelle. What's up, Eff?"

"Thanks for doing all this."

"Naw. It's nothing."

"It's everything," she said, but her voice was drowned out by the cranking and coughing of Ernie's Tacoma.

By the time they made it to the oyster bar, it was dark.

They had started with an absurd amount of pastries at Ernie's favorite bakery in a converted old-timey gas station. He wanted sesame banana bread; Effie wanted a cheddar and kimchi biscuit. They got both, then split a salted chocolate chip cookie. After that, fancy lattes at a new café that was decorated with white subway tile and staffed by baristas who played records on a vintage turntable. After that, they ate dense and chewy potato doughnuts sprinkled with cinnamon sugar. And then a walk around the waterfront. And then fancy grilled cheese sandwiches made with brioche bread. Another walk, and a stop into a tea parlor for cups of lemon hibiscus and Darjeeling. More food. More walking.

All the while, they shared an easy rapport. She was truly, deeply relaxed. It had been just a ferry ride and a few hours, but the stress and responsibilities—Jarrod and Carina and whatever the heck she was going to do about it—felt like a thousand miles away.

As night closed in, Ernie led them to their last stop: an attractive, low-key raw bar that Effie knew by name; it had opened a decade earlier and racked up Best New Restaurant accolades early on. She studied the dining room as she reached underneath the marble bar for a hook to hang her leather cross-body bag. It had been a birthday present from Ernie during their junior year. By now, it was worn smooth and thin in places, and the strap was so frayed it threatened to snap. It was one of the only things she'd taken with her when she left Alder Isle so many years ago. She loved it then for its no-fuss practicality, and she loved it now for all it had been through with her. She wondered if he remembered he had been the one to give it to her, or if he'd blocked out the memory after her graduation-night tantrum. He hadn't commented on it all day, so maybe he didn't. Which was fine. It was just a bag, after all.

After spinning around on her stool to take a full survey of the restaurant, she realized it was the ideal place to end their night. Good on Ernie. He'd planned this well. The street-facing side of the restaurant was covered in floor-to-ceiling windows that would have been cheery in the daytime; now they washed the room in the gentle glow from a sidewalk lamppost. It wasn't a fancy restaurant, but it was thoughtfully decorated, with chunky wood shelves behind the bar and metal-legged stools. It had that curated, high-end beachy vibe she had always associated with mainland Maine. Alder Isle, on the other end of the spectrum, was neither curated nor high-end. She felt a defiant swell of affection for her hometown—it was the real deal—then pummeled it down into the back of her subconscious. Alder Isle was her hometown, but it wasn't her home. Even if it felt like that some days. Even if it was full of people she cared deeply about.

The bartender, who was wearing suspenders and had a handlebar mustache, looked up from the cutting board where he was slicing limes. "Howdy, folks. What can I do you for?"

"A vomitorium, please," Ernie said, leaning in and holding his stomach with both hands.

The bartender didn't miss a beat. "Tragically, ours is currently closed for renovation."

"Ha, no, I'm kidding. It's been a big day. We're just here to gild the lily."

"You're at the right place, then. You do oysters, I assume and hope?"

Ernie's smile was so big, his eyes squinted at the edges. "Sure thing. We are at your mercy."

Effie watched this exchange with a bemused smile playing at her lips.

"You'll want Alder Isle oysters on the half shell," Mustache said. Effie coughed. She could run, but she apparently could not escape home. "Half dozen or a full doz?" he asked.

Ernie didn't even pretend to think about it. "Oh, heck, let's do the whole thing. With cocktail sauce."

"And Tabasco ice," Effie said, scanning the menu.

"And Tabasco ice," Ernie confirmed.

"And a celery gimlet," Effie added.

"And an old-fashioned," Ernie said.

"Anything else?" Mustache took both their menus.

"And a partridge in a pear tree." Ernie looked jovial as he punctuated their order, volleying back and forth with the bartender. Effie sat on her hands.

"No, seriously. And a side of coleslaw," he finished. Mustache nodded and turned around to tap their orders into the POS.

. . .

"How do you do that?" Effie asked once their drinks arrived, dunking a slender celery stalk in and out of her gimlet.

"Do what?" Ernie ate the cherry from his glass.

"Make small talk with people. Enjoy it."

He clinked his glass to hers in a wordless cheers. He took a sip, then set his glass down and held her gaze. "What do you mean?"

"Am I supposed to eat this? I guess so." She crunched into the celery. It was ice cold, juicy, and surprisingly sweet. "What do I mean? Let me think." She chewed. "Okay. When I lived in San Francisco, I went on a couple dates with this guy—"

"Who was a jerk," Ernie editorialized for her.

"Who was a jerk, yes," Effie confirmed. "But relevant to this story, he had a Saint Bernard. Like Beethoven. The movie with the dog who—"

"No. No. Absolutely not. I refuse to take another stroll down a 1990s Blockbuster aisle with you."

"Fine. But this is a big dog, right? And in a city. He'd walk it around the Mission or wherever. Sometimes he'd take it to the dog park and throw tennis balls. God, that thing was so slobbery. But the point: everywhere he went with this dog," she swallowed more gin, "people would comment on how huge it was."

"In fairness, I probably would, too."

"Well, yeah. That's where I'm going here. They'd be like, 'Oh my God, what a big dog! How do you fit him in your apartment?'

No matter how many times he'd had the same interaction, or how tired or grumpy he was, he would be like, 'He's my roommate. Gotta do something about those big city rents, right?'"

Ernie laughed.

"And they would do *that*!" Effie pointed at him. "They would laugh, even though it was not funny at all."

"It's a little bit funny."

"It's not! But every time, every person involved would play their roles. They'd say the stuff, even though it was the most banal thing."

"And this bothered you?"

"It intrigued me. It would have exhausted me if *I* had to make the joke. Or laugh at the joke." She looked down at her lap as the bartender reappeared, setting the tray of shucked oysters between them. "I've thought about that a lot since I came back here. Alder Isle is full of interactions like that. It's full of small talk and chitchat."

Ernie brushed his palm across the back of his neck and Effie caught a whiff of his scent. She held her breath until she couldn't smell him anymore, then continued in a rush that made her chest tighten. "I feel like everyone here likes it. The banal stuff. And I don't. I feel like something is wrong with me."

Ernie reached forward and touched her knee with his fingertips. "Why do you feel like everyone else likes casual conversation?"

"Don't you?"

"I do, but I'm not everyone."

Effie swayed on her stool. The day's indulgences—sugar and

salt and carbs, her gimlet and his touch—had finally reached a tipping point. She felt satiated and just the right amount of tipsy. Ernie smiled, the outside edges of his eyes creasing and his teeth flashing a brilliant white. He was handsome. *Really* handsome. And nice. Ernie was a good person. A good friend. A good, nice, handsome . . . friend.

"Effie, it's okay not to like small talk. Lots of people don't."

"But they still *do* it. I am incapable. Capable only of active bitch face."

"At least your resting face is sweet."

Was he joking? She arranged her features into a scowl but couldn't hold on to it. He laughed as she shook her head and took another sip of her cocktail.

Ernie continued. "Here's what I think. You can hate small talk *and* be bad at it *and* refuse to do it, and still be a good person. A person who has always taken care of everyone around her. A person who patiently teaches others. Don't roll your eyes, Eff. Chad told me about your lessons, and I know how much Anika values your feedback. Heck, you taught me how to run, and look at me now! I never would have started if you hadn't pushed me to try track. Because of that, it's become one of the best parts of my life." Effie tilted her head and rested her chin in her hand. Ernie kept talking. "You may hate small talk with strangers, but you show up for your people. You don't need to be an expert at chatting about the weather." He took a deep breath and instead of exhaling, gulped from his glass. "You don't have to be anything but who you are. I've always just liked you because you're you."

"I sound cool when you talk about me like that."

Ernie pulled her off the stool and into his arms. Was he tipsy, too? Or maybe it was the change in scenery; the anonymity a new town afforded them. Effie wasn't sure, didn't care. She stood between his thighs, letting him bury his nose in her hair. His chest was warm, and his arms felt strong. "You are very cool," he murmured.

If she had hugged him first, she reasoned, it would have been a date. But she hadn't. She was just receiving the hug. So it was the friendly thing. The drink-cocktails-and-eat-doughnuts-and-kimchi-biscuits-and-oysters-together thing. The drive-hours-away-from-home-without-a-plan-for-where-they-were-going-to-sleep thing. The let-him-gently-touch-his-lips-to-her-forehead thing. That thing. And it felt so nice.

Effie pulled back a half inch and raised her eyes to meet Ernie's. She tilted her chin upward and let her bottom lip pout out.

His voice was thick and strong when he spoke. It was just like she imagined back in her bedroom when they texted. Just like she imagined almost every night since she returned to Alder Isle. "Effie Olsen, are you trying to kiss me?"

She leaned in and wrapped her arms around him, lacing her fingers together at his neck, half terrified he was going to stop her.

Instead, he kissed her. It was hard and deep and knee-bucklingly good. The kind of kiss that was worth waiting for.

With one hand, he held on to the back of her head, his fingers working to loosen her tight ponytail. His other did a slow slide from her lower back to the frayed hems of her jean shorts. As he urged her mouth open with his own, he tugged on the denim, his fingertips just hinting at more when they brushed the tops of her thighs.

They were in the middle of a crowded bar, but his grip on her was confident and impossible to ignore. He explored her with touches that left her both wanting to devour him whole and needing to stop and catch her breath. He was still reclined casually on the stool; she was melting deeper into his lap with each passing second.

He was such a confident kisser, so good at it.

Pleasure pumped from her center into her extremities at the realization her quiet, gentle best friend was not that kind of lover.

When he finally pulled away, he ran his palms down her arms and looked into her eyes. "I'm going to pay this bill, and then we're going to get out of here, okay?"

She was certain she wanted the same thing, but her response came out as a whisper. "Okay."

As they waited for the bartender to process Ernie's card, he brought his forehead to hers and murmured. "We're so done with small talk."

Chapter Twenty-Seven

They were both laughing into each other's mouths as they tumbled out onto the street. Ernie had settled their bill with the bartender and left a generous tip, then grabbed Effie's hand and tugged eagerly toward the door. "Wow," she said, looking up at the night sky, stars twinkling through the mist.

"Wow," he said back, turning the corner down an alley and walking her backward so her shoulder blades met a brick wall. He held both her hands in his and kissed his way down her neck. Her heart drummed extraordinarily fast as her mind ricocheted around the words they'd exchanged over text, and the taste of bourbon and cherries on his tongue.

"Take me somewhere private," she said, bucking her hips toward his and pressing her upper back further into the wall.

Ernie's teeth pulled at the tender skin between her shoulder and her neck. He released her hands and ran his own up and down her waist. His mouth trailed down her chest, over the buttons of her blouse. By the time he got to her lower belly, he was kneeling in front of her, the backs of her thighs in his palms. "I thought you'd never ask," he said, giving her hip bone a sensual, slow kiss before rising and pulling her toward the street they'd parked on.

They were quiet on the drive. He held the wheel with one hand and rubbed her leg with his other. The electric current that had sparked and popped between them in the bar gradually dissipated into something gentler and sleepier. The trip took just five minutes, but by the time they reached the beach, Effie's head was resting on the seat back, her eyelids feeling heavy. She was slipping in and out of dreams.

Ernie parked the truck and unbuckled. "Hey." He brushed a few blonde flyaways from her temple.

"Hey," she said through her lashes. "I'm sorry I got so tired."

He rubbed her cheekbone with his knuckle. "No sorrys. It's been a big day, and I'm just happy to be here with you." She nodded. "I'm going to make up the bed. Don't go anywhere." She gave him a silly, half-dreaming smile.

Within minutes, they had bedded down in the back of the truck. Ernie had unrolled two sleeping pads and created a cozy sort of nest out of a sleeping bag and his Pendleton blanket. He was lying on his back, and she had curled into him, her head on his chest. He was stroking her hair and gently scritching her scalp.

The last thing she remembered before finally drifting off was murmuring into his skin. "Ernie," she whispered. "I'm yours."

. . .

Ernie stirred in his sleep, angling his body closer and squeezing her waist with his fingertips. His eyes moved back and forth underneath his lids, lashes fluttering. Still asleep. She envied him. Effie burrowed her nose into his shoulder as she marinated in the memories of the night before. Most of their day together had been filled with very normal, very friendly things. Nothing messy about them at all.

Unfortunately, she'd woken up with two words on the tip of her tongue. *I'm yours.* She wanted to own them and reject them at the same time. But it was true: she had been his from the moment she saw him on the beach. And perhaps for much longer. There was no way this could end well. Effie was in such deep trouble. She sighed quietly into his chest. "Oh, Ernie. Holy shitballs."

"I don't know a *ton* about Portland culture but I'm pretty sure that's not how they say good morning here."

She pressed her forearms into his chest, steadying herself as she lifted her torso up. She studied him. His nose had turned pink over the course of yesterday. His freckles had darkened, too, refusing to be ignored. "No, that was Italian," she said. "I thought you were asleep."

"I was. Until you started tickling my armpit."

"I was not ti—"

"I'm not complaining," he said, pulling her down into the tangle of nylon and wool. With one swift motion, he turned her onto her back and situated his upper body over hers. "Ouch." In the process, he'd hit his head on the roof. A small laugh escaped her. She felt wild and reckless. Probably looked that way, too. She'd left her hair down all night, and it was knotted now. Ernie tucked a strand of it behind her ear as he brought his lips to the blade of her cheekbone. "What is it, again? 'Good morning' in Italian? Bon Jovi?"

Her chest rose and fell once as his mouth crested up to her temple. "Buongiorno," she whispered.

"Buongiorno, Effie."

"Buongiorno, Ernie."

He brushed aside the wispy bits at her forehead and softly kissed her hairline. He seemed so sure of himself, so sure of what they were doing. The fire that had raged in Effie's belly the night before started smoldering again. She wasn't thinking. Just meeting an animalistic need. She gave him her mouth, and he took it. Ernie tugged at her bottom lip with his teeth, then released it and kissed away the memory of the pain.

She had slept in her clothes, her old denim shorts and a cream-colored peasant blouse with orange stitching around the hems. He'd taken off his gray T-shirt but had kept his shorts on. Although nothing had happened after their kisses last night, something was happening now.

Maybe it had been supposed to happen all along. Maybe she was just sixteen years late.

Ernie's palm danced over the waistband of her shorts and upward, underneath her shirt. His skin felt cool and refreshing against hers. He traced his fingers across her belly and ribs, lifting the fabric as he explored. The space at the top of her thighs pulsed hot and pleading, and she arched her back to meet his hips with hers. He was hard.

Of course he was hard.

He was hard and she was throbbing with need.

This was *definitely* supposed to happen.

She shook her head, trying to clear the cobwebs, grasping at rationality but getting caught in the sticky fibers of desire.

He whispered into her ear, "I am going to worship every inch of you."

She closed her eyes and let his words wash over her. She had stopped fighting it. Finally, she knew.

Seventeen-year-old Effie never would have gotten here. Never would have even entertained the idea. But eighteen-year-old Ernie had never held her like this. He'd never made her melt with just one single kiss and the promise of more. He'd never made her laugh like—wait. That was not true. He had always made her laugh. Always made her feel safe. He'd always been her friend. Her best friend. That was why she couldn't . . . why *they* couldn't . . .

"Ernie, we—"

"SHE GULLS!!!" A high-pitched toddler's voice pierced through the salty air as the sound of small footsteps thundered past the truck. A flock of gulls scattered, shrieking and circling the parking lot. Both Effie and Ernie froze. They were at East End Beach, their old camping spot. It was usually deserted by sunset, and rarely busy until midmorning, after the fog had lifted. Some young family had apparently not gotten the memo and started their beach day early.

The truck was covered by the topper, but Effie could see from the open window that the child was running in circles after a gull, who was running around with a French fry in its mouth, right next to the truck. The night before, they had parked at the edge of the lot, where gravel petered out into stones worn smooth from foot traffic and high tides.

"Maeve, wait for Mama," a woman's voice called. "This looks like a good spot," she said to the man next to her. "Not too close to the water." From her horizontal position, Effie could see two beach chairs strapped to his back, and a cooler in one hand. He dumped it on the ground, ten awkwardly close feet from the truck.

Seriously?

Effie squeezed her eyes shut, pulling Ernie closer against her body, trying to make them both invisible. Or at least as small as possible. If she could see them, they could probably see her. And Ernie. And his hard-on? Okay, probably not. She was being paranoid. But this was highly mortifying. The little girl and her parents had stopped them from doing the thing they'd sworn not to. They had almost—*don't even go there.* Her arms dropped to her sides, and she let him go like she was a rainstorm and he was made of sugar. If they'd gone all the way, it would have been electric and intense and incredible. And then what? Then she would leave Alder Isle and would try, for the rest of her life, to forget him.

"We have to go. Now," Effie hissed.

"But, Effie. The she-gulls." Ernie was shaking softly with laughter.

"Screw the she-gulls, we have to get out of here before someone calls the cops on us."

His laughter trickled off as he caught up with her tone. "For sitting in the back of our truck on a public beach?"

"That is not—was not—what was happening."

"What was happening, Eff?"

Oh for fuck's sake. He was going to make her say it.

"We were about to make a huge mistake. You have to know that."

His body, seconds ago so inviting against hers, felt corpse-like. He rolled off her and scraped his hand down his jaw and chin. "Got it. Well, thank goodness for Maeve."

She turned onto her side and propped her head up with her fist. "Ernie, I . . . I didn't mean to lead you on. At all. It was such a great night. I got caught up. We got caught up. I think that gimlet was stronger than I realized. We didn't actually want things to go so far. Right?"

"Right." He unlatched the gate and pushed his feet through the opening, then slithered his body out of the bed, landing in a jumble on the ground. *Relationships and truck beds*, she thought. *Hard to get out of gracefully.* That was why they had to stop! Before things got any more complicated. The little girl's mother shot a surprised look their way as Ernie stood up, then returned to her task of setting up a lime-green umbrella. "We should get going. Long drive back, and traffic will be bad," he said, then walked around to the driver's side door without looking at her.

"Wait." He'd never been cold and short like this with her. Well. Not never-never. The last time was . . . graduation night. She hadn't wanted to lose him as a friend, which was why she'd denied him so many years ago. But now? She didn't want to lose him, period. Why couldn't he see that they had to sacrifice whatever this was to make sure their friendship stayed safe?

"Ern. Please." She knocked at the window partition as he keyed into the ignition. She was still in the back. They could recover from this. They were more mature. Allegedly. It wasn't too late to take back everything that had happened over the last twentysomething hours. To go back to the way it was. If she could just make him laugh . . . She grasped at a straw: "Ernie. Can I drive?"

He sat back, arms crossed and jaw set, waiting for her to get into the passenger's seat.

"No."

Despite the broken air conditioner in the truck, the first two hours of the drive felt chilly. Effie stared out the passenger window and Ernie stared straight ahead. She really had to pee but was afraid to be the first to speak. Afraid she would make things worse, if that was even possible. What *was* it about Maine? She'd always thought it was Alder Isle that triggered her dumb and reckless side. Apparently, it was the entire state. She was acting crazy. Everything was out of her control.

Around 10:30, Ernie pulled into a Stewart's gas station. Wordlessly, he fueled up, and Effie slipped into the mini mart. After relieving herself, she paid for two coffees. She wondered if he still adhered to their old rule about gas station coffee: when the coffee is questionable (see: scaldingly hot warming plate and weak brew), load it up with cream and sugar. It disguised the burned-bland taste. She filled the cups halfway from the carafes, then topped them off with French vanilla cappuccino from a self-serve machine. She added a packet of real sugar to each one, then popped on the lids and walked back out to the pumps.

"I made it sweet," she said as she handed one over and buckled her seat belt. "Sugar and spice, just like I promised at the beginning of the summer."

He raised an eyebrow, letting the joke shrivel on the floor between them. But he did take the coffee. A whisper of a smile tugged at his lips after his first sip, and she allowed herself to celebrate the win. She'd chosen right.

"Hey, best friend," she said, kicking off her sandals and resting her feet on the dash. "We should talk about what happened this morning. What I said last night."

He situated his coffee in the cup holder and let out the most enormous sigh. "Hey, Effie. I really don't feel up for that."

She frowned. It's not like she was looking forward to the conversation, but . . . not discuss it? At all? She'd told him she belonged to him. And she did. Truly. She always had. She knew that now. She just couldn't do a damn thing about it. Unless she was willing to move to Alder Isle forever.

Maybe he had been tipsy enough not to remember.

"We can just forget about all of it," he said. "Obviously you don't actually believe you're mine and I'm yours or whatever."

And maybe not.

"It's just so complicated," she said.

"Yeah, well." He kept driving. After a few minutes of silence, he had worked something out. "You know what? I *am* glad for Maeve and the she-gulls. Forget all our history and baggage. We work together: that's reason enough not to go there with you. It's not right. If people found out . . . it wouldn't look good. I mean, I don't care about myself. But for you. I wouldn't want to jeopardize your reputation. For wherever you go next."

She frowned deeper. They didn't *really* work together. Not like her and Jarrod.

Not like that argument made her feel any better.

As if he had been reading her mind, he added, "Last thing I want is to be like Jarrod."

"What does that mean?" Effie worked hard to keep her voice level. Ernie couldn't have found out about her almost-one-night stand with him. Could he?

Ernie shot her a *Duh* look. "He's a creep who's slept with 85 percent of the waitstaff."

Duh.

"Oh," Effie said. "Is that it?"

He looked at her incredulously before turning his attention back to the highway, and Effie suddenly remembered he'd never worked in a restaurant before. Eighty-five percent sounded like a lot when you said it out loud, but she hated how the number sounded like a fair, unsurprising estimate for the circumstances.

"He's just a jerk, okay?" Ernie huffed.

No one liked Jarrod, but Ernie seemed to be dripping in vitriol.

"You could never be like Jarrod," she said quietly.

"Thanks," Ernie said.

"I'm sorry," Effie said, hoping that the two words held so much more.

"It's okay." Ernie's response was just as complicated, but when he said it, he reached over the center console and squeezed her knee. They were on shaky ground, but they would be okay. Eventually. Probably.

"Music?" she asked.

He nodded once. "Hit the CD player, actually."

She pressed play and "Are You Gonna Be My Girl" by Jet started. She fist-pumped the air. "Yes! This isn't our high school road trip mix, is it?"

"It very much is," confirmed Ernie, a stubborn smile making an appearance.

They listened in silence for a few tracks, and soon Effie felt reassured and calmed by the memories. "I do want to add just one thing," she said, turning the volume down a few notches. Ernie's nod let her know he was listening. "What I loved best about our friendship when we were younger was how few inhibitions we had. We just crashed through life like consequences didn't exist. Both of us! That attitude brought us to some pretty exciting places, but it's also what tore us apart. We've been round and round in circles about this, but I finally understand it. In a real way. Every time we almost go there, it's because we're acting impulsively. When we pull it back, it's because we've put on our adult pants and thought about the bigger picture. I don't want to act like a teenager for the rest of my life. I want to grow up and be mature and learn how to trust myself. So this"—she gulped in air and raced toward the finish of her speech—"this stepping back and making the hard but sustainable decision . . . it feels like growth."

"Well, shoot," Ernie said.

"Does that make sense?" Effie was working out the tangles in her hair and looking at him out of the corner of her eye.

"It does, and it's beautiful. And you have grown. A lot. It's one of the things . . ." His voice trailed off.

"One of the things what?"

They'd reached the ferry station in Rockland. He queued up in the line and turned off the engine before answering her. "I was going to say, 'It's one of the things I find most attractive about you.' But I probably shouldn't say it."

"Haha. Too late."

"Yeah." He gave her a tender smile that landed like a meteor in her chest. "I guess this time it really is."

Chapter Twenty-Eight

They spent the rest of the trip laughing and singing along to early aughts pop hits, but the air between them still felt charged and regretful. And Effie felt uneasy about it, despite her conviction that she'd made the right choice. That said, it could have also been her lie-by-omission about her meeting with Carina Shen and history with Jarrod. She'd almost told Ernie about Carina yesterday, on the drive to Portland. But then he had shared the latest on his and Mick's finances. They were currently fighting a big bill for one of his follow-up appointments, which made Effie swallow hard. She realized there was no point in admitting she'd booked a meeting with Carina, because she was going to cancel it. The reporter had been so persuasive on the call, but sitting next to Ernie, who might lose his job if she talked, was enough to right her ship. She didn't want to worry him. And more than that, she didn't want him to know she had waffled about their pact at Dahlia's dinner party in the first place.

But then the whole day had happened. And the whole night. Sometime between the chocolate chip cookie and his lips on her neck, she'd forgotten. It wasn't until they boarded the ferry that the coffee date reentered her consciousness. "Motherfluffer," she whispered under her breath, then waved away Ernie's questioning look. Once he parked the truck and the ferry left the dock, Effie excused herself to take a walk around the boat and get some fresh air. She dialed Carina's number but got her voicemail. She left a message explaining she no longer wanted to meet. She apologized, hung up, and hoped the message went through in time.

By the time the ferry docked on Alder Isle, it was a quarter after one.

"Hey, new car?" Ernie said, pulling into the driveway. "Or visitor? I somehow don't remember you having a relative from New York." There was a white sedan with New York plates parked behind Samuel's truck. *Carina.* Effie momentarily froze. "Eff?"

"Traveling salesman?" she joked, shaking off the shock and shrugging casually. "Weird."

"Text me later and tell me who it is," Ernie said, laughing. "This is the Alder Isle gossip I crave."

"Will do," she dodged, and hoisted her bag over her shoulder. "See you at work on Wednesday?"

"Wouldn't miss it for the world," Ernie said. "Or more realistically, wouldn't miss it because of the paycheck."

"Haha. Bye."

"Oh. One more thing," he said. "Thank you."

Effie looked nervously toward the kitchen. "For what?"

Ernie reached out through the open window and squeezed

her hand. "For helping me grow up a little. I'm glad we can be honest. And go through hard stuff together."

"Oh. You're welcome." Effie pulled her ponytail tighter. If she turned around now, he wouldn't notice the red blush around her hairline and temples. "Bye for real," she said, heading for the back door.

"Bye for now," Ernie called out over the rumble of his truck.

Breathe," she said under her breath as she opened the door and began kicking off her sandals in the mudroom. Immediately, she froze. From the kitchen, she heard her father's cheerful laugh. He paused, and a second voice—Carina's—answered. *Did she receive the voicemail? Or just not care?* Either way, she was here now. Effie walked calmly into the kitchen.

"Effie Pants," Samuel said, then realizing his gaffe, "Effie. This is Carina Shen. She's a reporter." In a dramatic aside, he whispered, "She's from the *Times.* And she's here to chat with you! Isn't that fantastic?"

"Fantastic," Effie said, letting her eyes take in the woman sitting on one of the cane-backed dining chairs. She looked normal in every way: Straight-legged jeans and nondescript brown boots with a low heel. Silk blouse, large bag resting at her feet. Her black hair was cut in a blunt bob. She smiled at Effie; it was a vanilla smile, mild and non-threatening. And yet, Effie couldn't shake the feeling of cold, murky dread that was slowly filling her toes and moving up toward her calves.

"Euphemia, hi," Carina said, standing and extending her hand.

Effie took it, and shook. "Effie," she corrected.

"Right, sorry. Thank you for making the time. I know days off are valuable for someone in your position." Taking his cue, Samuel shuffled out of the kitchen, most likely headed to the attic to continue sorting through Susan's possessions. He'd been working away at it every day, often with Ingrid's help. Effie and Carina stood awkwardly across the table from each other.

"I did receive your message, but I was already on my way here. I thought it wouldn't hurt to meet and see how you're feeling. Shall we sit?" Carina asked and Effie hedged. "I realize it can be stressful, chatting about all this. Are you okay with on the record?"

"Yeah, you said that on the phone. Hold on." Effie pulled out a chair and eased onto it. She felt dizzy. The smell of powdered turmeric wafted out of the teapot in the middle of the table. "Sorry he got to you with the turmeric tea," she said. "I keep telling him it's not good. Or it would be if he used fresh turmeric, and added some ginger, maybe cloves. Sugar would not be bad." Carina nodded. Effie chewed at her bottom lip and twisted her fingers together under the table. "Is it better to be on or off the record?"

"On," Carina said immediately. "My editor's pushing hard on this point because it's entirely possible we could get scooped by another publication. We need to tell the most complete story."

Effie thought about Ernie and his father's old boat. She

thought of him alone in the basement with a mountain of Chilean onions. She thought of Jarrod, surrounded by the world's best seafood and filling his menu with bland chicken. She thought of his hand on her back in his office. She thought of all the other men who had made her career difficult. All the men who had stolen opportunities from her; all the ones who lied to customers and terrorized their employees. It was so simple. They were bad guys. Jarrod was a bad guy. Bad guys were not supposed to win. She had to talk. She could figure the rest out later. "Okay," she said, lifting her chin with growing confidence. "On the record."

At the heart of the article, Carina explained, was a chef in way over his head. Jarrod Levi had an impeccable resume, but he had taken extreme measures to tell a story about a hyper-local, sustainable restaurant in a quaint Maine town. The story being, Brown Butter was a special place, with a kitchen that did everything "the right way." It went further than any restaurant had before in supporting local agriculture and aquaculture. It was the true future of dining in America, all thanks to a strong, visionary leader at the helm. There was just one problem: most of it was a lie. Jarrod Levi had been cheating guests at Brown Butter for the better part of three years with falsely represented ingredients. A handful of staff had gone on record saying they regularly cooked with vegetables and fruits from as far away as South America. Even the meat, which was said to be purchased by the whole animal and broken down in-house, regularly came from places like Costco.

Carina's reporting didn't stop there. She had also learned that Jarrod was an incompetent leader with a temper. He was a chef who created and perpetuated a hostile work environment. He routinely made rude remarks, and paid workers of color less than their white counterparts. His language bordered on emotionally abusive, and many female staffers felt unsafe being alone with him. One had described threats and bullying after she ended a romantic relationship with him.

When she finished speaking, Carina gave a small shrug, overly casual. "There is one more thing. The renowned lobster pasta dish may be fake. In Maine of all places! That one has stumped me. I can't find anyone who will confirm it, but it has the potential to blow the top off this story. If it's true, anyway."

Effie's heart stopped.

"What do you mean . . . fake?"

"Well, a source shared doubts that lobster is actually being used in the ravioli."

"Why? How?"

"Those are the questions I'd love for you to answer. If you can."

Effie frowned into her lap. The first part of the story had not been news to her. But hearing it in Carina's words made her realize it wasn't normal. It wasn't okay. Effie had become so numb to the stress and hostility of restaurant work, she had actually tried to convince herself that what was happening at Brown Butter was just business per usual. But just because it happened everywhere didn't make it okay.

And worse, she was suddenly confident she knew what was happening with the ravioli.

Carina let her process all this for a few heavy moments before clarifying: "I don't think you're a bad actor here. Many of my sources have named you as an ally to the staff, not an accomplice to Mr. Levi. What I'm looking for is just your story. You work closely with him. I'm interested in what you've observed."

"I don't know," Effie said, slowly testing the waters. "I've worked in a lot of kitchens, all over the world. Insults, angry male chefs, rude jokes, and secret relationships aren't that out of the ordinary. I've never worked in a restaurant that didn't feel toxic. At least a little."

"I'm sorry to hear that. But it sounds like Brown Butter is more than a little toxic. It sounds like the atmosphere has become unbearable. Would it be fair to say it's different than other places you've cooked?"

It hit Effie in that moment that maybe she had gotten too close, had been working too hard, to see clearly.

In all her travels, she had never worked with a chef who physically violated her personal space the way Jarrod had that morning in his office. But until now, until Carina had brought it into context, Effie had thought his behavior was her fault. Because she had hooked up with him, she felt like his attention was a punishment. Like she had invited it. Like she somehow deserved it. She hadn't been surprised to hear he'd slept with members of the waitstaff, but she hadn't considered that those relationships might not have been completely consensual, either. That those women could feel like she did.

Tears pricked at the outside corners of her eyes. A fat one escaped and rolled down her cheek onto her lip. It tasted salty. Effie closed her eyes slowly, willing no more to fall. Because she had just realized one other way in which Brown Butter was different. It was the first restaurant where she truly, deeply cared about her coworkers. Every single one of them. She didn't know who had sent in the tip to Carina, or which team members had given interviews. But she was sure of one thing: each of them deserved to work in a better environment than the one she had implicitly been a part of.

She couldn't deny that a tell-all of this magnitude, detailing the full scope of the ingredient fraud, may mean closure. A restaurant fallen this far from grace was as good as dead. Her mind careened around the corners of logic, calculating how many cooks, servers, bartenders, janitors—how many *people*—would be out of work if Brown Butter closed. It was the whole staff, and everyone the restaurant touched. It was Dahlia and her floral business. Kit and the lucrative commissioned pieces she earned when diners saw her art on the walls. Anika and her chance at a full-time position. Ernie, who had no other option, who didn't love the work but did it because he had to.

"Effie?" Carina's hand covered Effie's, which had been fiddling with the teapot handle. "What has your time at Brown Butter been like? Have you witnessed any of this?" she said, pushing a little harder.

"If I don't comment, what happens then?"

Carina sat back and pressed her lips together before speaking. "This story is happening, Effie. You can't stop it. But by sharing your experience, you can help create change, make things better for everyone."

"Have you spoken with Jarrod about all this?"

"Tonight," Carina said. "He knows I'm here; I called him this morning. I wanted to get a full scope of things before I reached out for comment. And I hoped that you, working so closely with him, would be able to help me see the entire picture."

"Got it," Effie said. Carina *didn't* get it. She didn't understand the interconnectedness, the fragility of a small community like the restaurant or even this island. How could she? She wasn't from Alder Isle. But, Effie thought, the reporter was right about one thing: Jarrod's time was up.

Effie nodded. "Okay. On the record." Carina produced a voice recorder from her pocket and set it on the table. She pressed the button, and Effie began.

Chapter Twenty-Nine

By the time Effie and Carina had finished speaking, it was close to 2:30. She had started small, with the story about Jarrod's truffles and her objection to them.

"So you refused to put them on the menu?" Carina asked.

Effie lowered her eyes to her lap. "No. I made a braised chicken special that featured freshly shaved truffles." Carina lifted an eyebrow but didn't speak. "At that point, I wasn't invested because I was just here for the summer—" Effie's sentence hurtled itself off a cliff.

"Just here for the summer?" Carina jotted something down in a notebook.

Too late to lie now. "Yeah," Effie said. "This is where I grew up. I only came back for a temporary job."

Carina nodded. "And Jarrod didn't want to hear your opinion, because you were just a seasonal worker?"

"No, he thinks I'm here for good."

Carina kept writing in her book, faster now.

"Which is why, I guess, I decided to kiss him on my first night back."

Carina's expression stayed neutral. "Go on."

"It was a mistake, but it was mutual. I should be clear about that. Jarrod's not my favorite person, and he's terrible at managing restaurants. But when we got together . . . he didn't force me. That was my choice."

"I understand. So what happened that night?"

"I don't remember." Effie rushed to correct herself. "I know how that sounds. But we were both pretty drunk, and we ended up just falling asleep. God, this is embarrassing. But I definitely woke up in his apartment, which is . . ." Effie pointed her index finger toward the sky.

"Above the restaurant." Carina flipped back a few pages to confirm her own notes.

"Yeah. And that's when I saw it."

"Um, saw . . . what?"

Effie's face got hot. "His freezer, I mean." Carina waited for her to continue. "He has a big chest freezer full of prepped monkfish."

"What did you think about that?"

"What did I think about it? I thought it was fucking weird."

"Did you ask him about it?"

"I did. He deflected. Tried to kiss me, and I dropped it. I just wanted to get out of there."

"Okay. So get me up to speed. Why is this freezer important?"

"Well. Monkfish looks and tastes a lot like lobster. It didn't make any sense to me then, but now it seems obvious he's using monkfish instead of lobster in the ravioli. It's a pretty smart trick, actually. There's no way you could tell the difference with all that cheese and filling."

"Hmm." Carina quickly flipped back to the beginning of her notebook and made several circles, pressing down hard with the tip of her pen. "Go on."

"Oh. And Ernie—he's the prep cook—he said that he used to clean the lobster and now Jarrod won't let him."

"Mmm," Carina said, making a few more circles.

"Oh . . ." The image of a manila folder flashed behind Effie's eyes as she blinked. "In his office. With his invoice files. He has one labeled 'Monk.' I didn't look inside; didn't think I needed to. But, right . . . ? There it is. Plain as day." She waited for Carina to respond, but Carina was waiting for Effie to say more. "It's all so stupid. I can't imagine he's saving that much money by skimping on the lobster, but then . . ." Memories of her time as Cowboy Bean's head chef hit her like a wave. Hadn't she been a walking ball of anxiety over her food costs and responsibilities? Didn't she feel desperate, and like she was drowning at times? She didn't agree with Jarrod's choices, but she could understand why he made them.

But still. Not a good guy.

Effie spoke more, about the way he berated the interns, how he never took responsibility when service got busy or stressful. She told Carina about the way he'd threatened her in his office, and how, even though she'd stood up to him, she felt defeated. "I hate having to say this, but I let him get away with a lot. With all of it. At first, I thought it was because I didn't care and because I was normalized to it. I'm only just realizing that maybe I was scared. A little bit, anyway."

Carina stopped writing. "Lots of women have felt this way," she said. "In every restaurant, in every industry. You're not alone there."

"It feels lonely though."

"As a woman in a male-dominated profession, I imagine it must."

Neither one spoke for a few seconds. Eventually, Carina asked Effie if there was anything else.

Effie shook her head. "When did you say this was going to be published?"

Carina closed her notebook and stopped the recorder. She was already on her feet when she spoke. "Online on Friday. In the paper the day after that."

Effie's heart sank, but there was a small corner of it that felt grateful. Grateful she wouldn't have to worry for much longer.

"I'll be on this all night," Carina said as Effie closed the screen door behind her. "I'm leaving in the morning, but you can call me if anything jogs your memory."

"I will," said Effie, knowing she wouldn't. She'd said all she could. "Oh. One more thing. If you have time while you're here, I recommend having breakfast at The Gull's Perch. It's a tiny little diner, on the road leading out to the ferry. Sit anywhere you like except at the third counter stool from the left; that's Dougie's spot and he'll get mad if he sees anyone in it. Order the sausage and cheese biscuit with a side of pancakes. Ask for Gertie, and tell her I sent you. Say hi to the locals, and listen to what they have to say."

"Noted." Carina snapped her bag shut. "Any particular reason?"

Effie smiled sadly from behind the door. "That's what I'd do, if my time on Alder Isle was running out."

Chapter Thirty

When Carina left, Effie sank back down onto her chair. Regret and fear pummeled her like high tide on a wild night. She knew she'd done the right thing, whatever that meant and however intangible it was. But a twisted feeling gripped her stomach as her understanding grew that everyone who read the *New York Times* was going to learn about her less-than-perfect past with Jarrod. Angry, dark thoughts crowded her mind as she berated herself for the choices she made back in late May. Just a few months, and yet impossibly long ago. Effie had felt like a different person then; lost and broken. She may not have figured everything out, but she knew now what was important to her. She only wished she could go back in time and erase that first night on Alder Isle.

When everyone finds out, you'll be knocked down a thousand pegs. Stripped of your coworkers' respect. Good luck fulfilling that dream of becoming a head chef.

And then, just as she was about to drown in the swampy waters of her own shame, her thoughts turned to Ernie.

Good luck explaining this to him.

That was the worst feeling of all, and she didn't know how to fix it, so she just sat with it.

I know I didn't owe him anything then, but reading about my night with Jarrod will still hurt him.

I shouldn't have shared what he told me about the lobster. That was his story, not mine.

And, loudest of all, *We agreed not to talk to Carina, and I did it anyway. After everything we've been through, I broke his trust.*

She sat at the kitchen table thinking about all this for a long time. Long enough for her father to come down the stairs, give her a kiss, and leave for a date with a beeswax candlemaker who had relocated to Alder Isle during the early days of the pandemic. She sat there long enough to ignore three calls and innumerable text messages from an unknown number that turned out to be Jarrod. She stopped reading the texts after the sixth, which called her a string of swear words too crass to linger over. She sat at the table long enough to let her phone die, and to watch the sun begin to set through the big window over the sink. She sat there long enough for Ingrid to come by with a covered casserole dish.

"Hey, big sis," Ingrid said, setting the dish on the stovetop. "I called, but got sent straight to voicemail."

Effie lifted her phone up, the blank screen explaining everything. "Hey, little sis." She let the phone fall on the table with a clatter. "Died a while ago."

"Mm-hmm." Ingrid turned the oven's knob and deposited the dish inside. "I made macaroni and cheese. Thought it might be nice to have dinner together, just sister-sister for once."

"You cook?" Effie asked.

"I do cook. Sixto's been teaching me. I'm actually not bad at it. Hard to believe, when you did all of it for us when we were little. For that I do thank you. Stuff got weird when you left and it was just Dad and his lentils."

"I think I feel guilty for not knowing that about you?"

Ingrid shrugged. "You don't need to feel guilty about anything, although you seem to, especially since you came home." She tossed two linen napkins at Effie, who caught them and set them on the place mats. "Wanna talk about it?"

Effie made a cradle out of her arms on the table and rested her head on top. "No. Yes," she said.

"Well, we've got a good fifteen minutes before that mac heats up. I'm all ears."

Effie told Ingrid everything she'd shared with Carina, and then kept talking. She told her about Ernie. About the dance they'd been doing all summer. About how she felt, and the ways in which she was scared. When she was finally done talking, she let out a low exhale and said, "Wait. Sixto. Has he told you all this? About the restaurant, I mean. Not Ernie and me. Was he the one who emailed Carina?"

Ingrid nodded, then shook her head no. "I get why you'd think that. He hates working for Jarrod. Once the reporter contacted him, he said he wished he'd thought of it first."

"Yeah. Oof. It should have been *me*, after everything I've

observed. And been a part of. I'm sorry. I was trying to protect everyone, but I let them all down instead."

"Effie, stop. You have to stop apologizing, and you have to stop trying to take care of everybody else to the detriment of your own emotional health."

"Do I do that?"

"You do. Here's my unsolicited take. You feel guilty and responsible for the fact Mom and Dad got a divorce. You shouldn't, because that was her own stuff. And thank frick she did. Could you imagine going through the rest of our lives with them fighting? Or, I guess, with them being mopey? But my point: ever since then, you've been doing this push-pull dance. One minute, you're trying to control everything, to protect everyone and be the stand-in mother they didn't ask for. The next minute, you're pushing us all away, afraid that if you let *anyone* get too close, they'll leave."

Truth bomb dropped and detonated; Effie let the shock waves wash over her.

"I think you're right," Effie finally said. "Wow." A recurring idea that had been increasingly insistent skipped to the front of her brain. "Have you had therapy?"

"Oh yes." Ingrid nodded. "Loads of therapy. Buckets."

"Who told you to get it?"

"The internet? I don't know. It wasn't something I talked about with Dad or a teacher or anything. It's just what my generation does. We reclaim decades-old fashion and we put ourselves into therapy to heal the traumas inflicted upon us by our families."

"Okay, but you have got to stop with the tube top and wide-leg jeans thing."

"Never," said Ingrid, laughing. "Really though. You've never done therapy?"

"No, I go running instead."

"I am sure that's excellent for your cardiovascular health. But don't knock talking to a professional about your problems. Mine helped me work out a lot of my own stuff."

"Like what?"

"Oh, you know. Feelings of abandonment, responsibility for taking care of Dad . . . guilt that my big sister resented me."

"Ingrid, I could never."

"I know that now. Thanks to therapy!"

Effie walked to the hutch and took out two plates and a serving spoon, while Ingrid laid out the silverware and filled two glasses with water from the tap. They ate the first few bites of macaroni and cheese in silence before Effie set down her fork and gave a little golf clap. "This is really good."

"I know," Ingrid said. "If you stick around Alder Isle for a minute, we could even cook a meal together once in a while." She looked at Effie with a smile flirting at the corners of her eyes. "You are sticking around, aren't you?"

"I hadn't planned on it."

Ingrid dabbed at her mouth with a napkin and knowingly asked where Effie was moving to next. Effie admitted she hadn't thought about it. She was saving all her paychecks. But planning the next step? It hadn't happened. "There's always the possibility of going back to New York, but . . ."

"But you've got the hots for your childhood best friend, and suddenly your dumpy little hometown is looking a lot brighter?" Effie gave her a righteous scowl. Ingrid smirked. She had always been good at playing the feisty younger sibling role. "So this review."

"Exposé," corrected Effie.

"Exposé. It's getting published at the end of the week?" Effie nodded at her sister's question, then ate another forkful of Gruyère cheese and elbow noodles. "And you told Ernie you weren't going to be a part of it?"

"Correct. And he told me he wouldn't, either."

Ingrid served herself another scoop and sighed audibly. "You two. Seriously. Should've come to Sixto. He is very fired up right now! But, sis. I don't want to be drearily obvious about this but isn't Ernie, like, the only one who would truly know what Jarrod was up to? You don't think the reporter would have talked to him *first*?"

Effie's fork froze in midair, halfway to her mouth. Was that even possible? That Ernie had decided to talk with Carina after all? What if the reporter had followed up with him and he'd cracked, too? "There's no way," Effie said. "If Ernie talked, he would've told me."

"I am not a relationship expert," Ingrid said, "But maybe *you two* should have a conversation before this article gets published."

"I am not in a relationship," Effie said defiantly.

"No." Her little sister grinned demurely. "But play your cards right and you could be."

Chapter Thirty-One

Dinner was over quickly after that. Ingrid had arrived at sunset, and now it was almost ten. She told Effie she'd do the dishes and clean up.

"Thank you!" Effie was almost out the door when Ingrid grabbed her by the wrist and spun her around.

"You are not wearing *that* to win over the love of your life." Effie glanced down at her clothes. She was wearing yesterday's denim shorts and top. She almost argued with Ingrid: she wasn't trying to win anyone over. She was going to have a conversation. She looked fine. Ernie wouldn't care how she looked. Ernie wasn't the love of—

Yes, he was.

Effie stood still and let the realization fill her. It started slowly, in the cavern of her heart, and flowed downward, flooding her chest with a warm, glowing feeling that spread into her belly. Every one of her fingers felt sparkly. Effie wasn't just imagining smashing her face against Ernie's. She was thinking about holding his hand. About smiling at him over cups of coffee on Sunday morning. About falling asleep next to him in her retainer. Waking him up when she had a bad dream. Effie was thinking about just *being* with him. Here. On this tiny, dumb island! Forever? Forever.

He didn't complete her. Effie didn't believe relationships worked that way. But he did help fill in her gaps. When she felt hot and flighty or angry and sharp, he helped her step back and see the bigger picture. His patience softened her edges. And hadn't she done the same for him, all those years ago? Drinking beers and planning adventures and going late-night swimming, just for the fun of it? When he felt shy or acted timid, she coaxed him out of his shell and into the world. Or at least, she had, once upon a time. When she relaxed into his company now, she was able to access that free feeling again. She hadn't felt it in a long time.

She ran up the stairs and into the bathroom, where she took a fast shower. Hair wrapped in a towel, she kneeled on the floor of her bedroom and tore through her dresser drawers, cursing herself for not folding things properly. Everything she owned was wrinkled, stained, or a pair of elastic-waist pants. She threw a balled-up bandana at the wall and huffed, allowing herself a mini tantrum: besides, Ernie had already seen her in everything she owned.

Everything except—

Mom's dress.

She crashed up the attic stairs. Ingrid had taken her clothes from the keep pile, but their mother's dress was still there, flung over the edge of the mirror. It looked sunny and bright, with the sherbet-orange bodice. Effie just hoped it fit her.

WOW!" Ingrid said as Effie descended the stairs. "Perfect." Effie spun around once, then felt self-conscious and held out the skirt for further approval. The bodice nipped in at her waist, and the open back showed off her best assets. Carrying around heavy pots and pans all day was a better workout than lifting barbells could ever be, and it showed in her strong shoulders and biceps.

"It's okay, you think?" Effie fussed at the ribbon, which she had knotted.

"Okay? His eyes are going to pop out of his head." Ingrid swooped in and untied the ribbon, then redid it in a flouncy bow.

Effie checked her reflection in the speckled, cloudy mirror by the front door. Her hair was halfway dry in beachy waves around her face. It fell to just below her shoulder blades, and swung when she moved. She gave herself a small, anxious smile.

"If he doesn't decide to stop speaking to me for the rest of his life, once he hears what I've done."

Ingrid flung the dish towel over her shoulder and gave Effie a hug. "Naw, you and Ernie are bigger than some dumb article. If you can come together after a sixteen-year grudge, this is nothing."

Effie slid into her huaraches. "I hope you're right."

. . .

She decided to walk to Ernie's rather than bike: her ensemble didn't inspire pedaling. She also needed the extra few minutes to figure out what she was going to say to him. For the first time since coming home, she was one hundred percent confident in how she felt about her childhood best friend. But how to express it to him after so many false starts? She wasn't even sure he felt the same. He had *thanked* her this morning for putting on the brakes. Anyway, it would be difficult to translate "You make my fingertips sparkle" into something that conveyed the real depths of her feelings for him.

As she approached the boathouse, she passed the main house and saw Mick in his favorite chair. He was illuminated by the soft glow of a banker's lamp. She knew the one; it sat on Ernie's old homework desk right next to the window. He waved, and she waved back. Her belly flipped, but this time out of comfort and contentedness. Walking to the Callahans' as night took the island was the most familiar, best thing in the world. And she was lucky enough to have gotten another chance. Ernie's truck was parked out front. She took a breath, then knocked.

Nothing.

She knocked again, louder.

Still nothing.

"Ernie Callahan, I know you're in there!" She yelled the words, then pounded on the door with her palm.

The latch gave and the door opened to reveal a half-asleep

Ernie. He was wearing blue-and-green-checkered flannel pajama pants and that was it. He scratched his head, and as he did, Effie let her gaze linger over his messy hair. She simply loved him, from start to finish. Ernie suppressed a yawn.

"Did I wake you?" Effie said, fully aware that she had, and feeling only the smidgiest bit guilty.

Ernie nodded and stepped aside as he opened the door wider. It wasn't until he closed it behind them and switched on a floor lamp that he noticed the dress. "Oh . . ." he said, the word dusted with surprise and desire. "That's really pretty, Eff."

"Is it?" She felt self-conscious, painfully aware that she'd leveled up her typical wardrobe for no reason. No reason beyond an overdue declaration of love. But he didn't know that. All he knew was that Effie was knocking at his door at an unreasonable hour. He probably thought she was having a breakdown.

"Sure is," Ernie confirmed, unapologetically drinking her in. They stood a generous foot apart, waiting for the other to begin. Effie realized the responsibility was hers.

"Are you free right now?" An amused nod. Of course he was free. "I guess I mean, are you up for chatting? About some stuff?"

"Ten p.m. stuff," Ernie clarified. "Should I be nervous?"

"No, I've got that part covered," Effie said.

"Couch?"

He shrugged into a soft old hoodie, which caused Effie a tinge of sadness (she'd miss looking at those abs) and a sigh of relief (she didn't have to look at those abs). They both sat. Effie bit at her bottom lip and smoothed her hair. It felt heavy and new after so long in its elastic prison.

Her anxiety was palpable. It must have been, because the next thing Ernie said was, "Drinks?"

"Oh thank fuck, yes."

After mixing them vodka lemonades in two of his handmade cups, he settled back onto the couch. She took a fortifying sip and shook the cup lightly, the ice agitating against the clay walls. She began by admitting, "I don't know where to begin. So this may be out of order. I talked to Carina Shen this afternoon, and I'm wondering if you did, too."

Ernie's swallow of vodka went down roughly as he coughed.

"So you did! I'm not mad, by the way. If you're not mad."

"I'm not mad. If you're not mad? It's not like we took a blood oath at Dahlia's."

"Exactly! It just seemed like the right thing to do. Even though it was hard." Effie explained how she'd agreed to the meeting, then canceled on account of nerves, but Carina had showed up anyway.

Ernie wanted to know why she hadn't mentioned it during their road trip. "The whole car ride—we were singing the Black Eyed Peas and you were just waiting for your meeting."

"I had honestly forgotten. A lot of other things happened over the last twenty-four hours! Why didn't *you* tell *me*?"

"She showed up at Dad's at about five thirty tonight, and I don't know what happened," he said. "I just started talking. I told her everything. Everything I knew, which I doubt was anything she hadn't already heard." Effie scrunched her nose. "I called you as soon as she left, but your phone was dead. And it didn't feel right to say all this in a voicemail. I was going to tell you tomorrow. Or the next day." He smoothed his hand over the leather seat back and said the next part in a hurry: "I'm sorry. We got so off course. All I wanted was to make your summer here feel light and sweet."

Effie stacked her palms over his knuckle. That part of Ernie hadn't changed in the entire time she'd known him. He was generous with everyone and with everything. Including and especially the intangible stuff. The way he took care of her in infinite hidden ways. The way she cherished him for it. Clearly she should have led with *that*, not the exposé.

"Thank you," Effie whispered.

Ernie turned his hand upside down so his palm was touching hers. "So this story really is going to be a thing?" he asked.

Effie said it was set to publish on Friday.

And then she said she had something else to tell him.

Ernie said he was listening.

It wasn't the most graceful or romantic transition. But it was an honest one. And Effie didn't want to be anything other than real with Ernie. She told him that the suspicious lobster ravioli wasn't lobster ravioli at all. She explained how she'd seen a chest freezer full of monkfish in his apartment on her first morning back in town. Because she had spent the night there. She spoke softly, hoping Ernie could hear her over the buzzy white noise of her shame. "I told that part to Carina. Because without it, it was just speculation. I had to be honest because I'm the only one with real proof. I spilled my guts while she recorded everything. Ernie, there's no way she's going to leave out that detail."

Ernie was quiet but she could feel his gaze on her. His other hand covered hers.

She continued. "So now I am telling you. Before the story

gets published and you read about it on the internet." Effie raised her head and finally made eye contact with Ernie. It was a hard journey to make, but it felt good to arrive. "I am telling you I was at Jarrod's apartment the first night I came home, and some stuff went down, but it hasn't happened since and won't ever again." The next words came in a rush. "And I'm sorry, and I'm embarrassed, and I just *hate* my—"

Ernie pulled his hand out of their pile and pressed his first two fingers to her lips, a serious expression on his face. "You have nothing to be sorry about. You don't owe me anything."

"That's not true," she said, clutching his hand in hers and lowering it down to rest on her heart. "Everything I have is for you. It always was."

A low, wild sound came from Ernie's throat, and he shifted on the cushion.

"And I'm scared because I keep fucking it up. We keep almost going there, and every time we're close I run away. And now you don't want anything to do with me."

His lips were on her forehead before she had finished speaking. He brushed them down the bridge of her nose as he murmured the next words. "I want the real Effie. The impulsive, fiery one as well as the brave, kind one. The one who's in front of me now, and the one who crash-landed on Alder Isle earlier this summer. She's perfect exactly the way she is."

Effie lifted her lips to meet his. Their kiss was tender and soft; gentler than they'd ever been together. After a few moments, during which Effie had nestled into Ernie's lap, he pulled away and pressed his forehead against hers. "But friendship."

"Forget friendship. I want all of you," Effie said, breathing quickly and surer of it than anything she'd ever desired.

He growled—actually growled—and Effie would have laughed if he didn't do it as he pulled away from her. The absence of his warmth felt like a devastating defeat. He hung his head between his legs, like he was seasick. Like he wanted to be alone; like he was rejecting her. She waited to see what would happen next.

"We've been drinking," he said.

"I've had half a vodka lemonade. Which is very light on the vodka, I might add. Not that I'm knocking your bartending skills."

He skated past her joke. "We've done this before. Almost. Then no. We did it this morning. You changed your mind."

"I'm sure this time."

"How can *I* be sure of that?"

Honestly, she didn't know. "You just have to trust me."

Ernie stood and walked in a circle around the boathouse. Effie set her cocktail on the side table.

"I need time to think about this," he finally said, leaning against his kitchen counter.

"If it's Jarrod, I promise, we're over. We never started. Not even that night, not really."

"It's not Jarrod. It's me. I need *time.* We had a pact not to do this. Effie, are you even planning on sticking around here?"

In her quiet moments, she had grown to appreciate the island in ways she hadn't been able to before. But she remembered how quickly a trattoria felt like a prison. If beautiful Italy had made her lose interest, what would happen in her little hometown? "I could," she said. "I could work at Brown Butter."

"Yeah, you could. If it doesn't close. Listen, Effie. When I spoke to Carina, I didn't realize this story was that big of a deal. It seemed like Jarrod would just get fired. Maybe there'd be a couple hundred words in some blog. But the story you're telling me about is bigger than that. If the only high-end restaurant on Alder Isle shuts down, you're honestly telling me you'll stay? For me?"

"I could."

"But it wouldn't be fair. To you. Or to me, in the long run."

"You don't know that." She was getting frustrated and took the feeling out on her hair, which she whipped back into a tight, high ponytail.

"I do. And I think you do, too."

Effie slumped on the couch. This was not how she envisioned the conversation going. She had felt powerful and full of promise on her way here. Nervous, but certain. Now, she hadn't even gotten to "I love you." *What can I do to make him trust me? To believe in the me he fell for?*

Effie stood, ruffled the bottom of her dress, and extended her arm, her hand pleading for his. He paused but eventually slid his palm against hers. "Gimme your keys," she said, tugging him toward the door. "Let's go to Dulse Cove."

Chapter Thirty-Two

They could have walked. It was close enough, and the moon was nearing fullness, giving off plenty of light. But driving through the winding island roads with the windows down was a tonic that revived them both. The air was so thick, she could taste brine when she breathed. The roads got darker and seemed wild. She could hear nighttime birds calling to one another and she stuck her head out the window as she took a corner sharply. "Hoooo!" she called back.

Beside her, Ernie chuckled. He leaned out the passenger window and shouted, too. "Hoo-hoo-hoo-hoooo!"

"I think you just did a mating call. Watch your back," Effie said, pulling onto a patchy bit of grass near the main beach. It felt easier to be with him like this, on their way to the water. No pressure. No complications. Just Ernie and an ocean of possibility.

Ernie smirked and unbuckled. "Race you," he said, pulling

off his hoodie as he ran toward the path without waiting for a fair start.

"RUDE," Effie shouted, scrambling after him as a huarache went flying through the brush. She kicked off its mate and pumped her arms, running as fast as she could. When she reached the end of the path that opened onto Dulse Cove, she slowed, seeing Ernie standing hesitantly at the water, shirtless in his pajama pants.

"It's gonna be cold as balls," he said.

"Yep," she said, turning her back to him and pointing to the bow across her back. "Untie me?"

The brush of his knuckle against her spine caused her to shudder, and she leaned into him as he worked the halter tie free. She stood still, waiting. Hoping to feel his lips against the nape of her neck. The sensation didn't come, but he was still close, his breath steady. Effie held the front of the dress against her chest and waded ankle-deep into the ocean. "It's not gonna get any easier, Ern." She looked over her shoulder with a smile, then pulled the dress over her head, threw it onto the rocks, and crashed into the water.

The waves were lazy and small, but the icy temperature felt like an assault. She gasped for breath as water touched her knees, her lace underpants, her waist, her breasts. A shower of curse words tumbled from her mouth as she dove in. When she surfaced, Ernie was still on the shore. "Get in here, chicken!" she called through cupped hands.

He jumped up and down a few times before sliding his flannel pants down.

"Boxers off, too," Effie shouted.

It was dark and he was far away, but she could make out the sharp cut of his waist rolling down to his narrow hips and toned thighs. Or maybe she was just imagining all that. Had been imagining it since they first met in this same spot three months ago. Ernie ran in but didn't go under.

"Dunk! Dunk! Dunk!" Effie said, hopping up and down in the water to stay warm. Her palms hit the surface and sent sparks of sea flying into the night.

He lifted his middle finger in her direction, and she shouted with childish glee.

She grabbed his hand with hers and counted. "Three . . . two . . . GO!" They let the water swallow them. Ernie squeezed Effie's wrist as they went under. It felt urgent and erotic to be held like that, tightly, confidently. When they surfaced, they were facing the deeper ocean, away from the shore, but they could still touch the floor. "What if we swim out forever?" Effie said.

"And live on an abnormally large piece of driftwood?" Ernie said. "Eat seagulls?"

"She-gulls," Effie corrected. A pause for laughter that didn't come. "I guess it wouldn't work. We should go back in."

"Oh thank God," Ernie said and yanked her back toward the rocky beach.

He didn't let go of her hand when they reached the shore. Didn't let go as he scooped up their clothes and jogged to the Tacoma. Didn't let go as he yanked open the door with his other hand and grabbed a towel. Only once Effie was swaddled in plush terry cloth did he leave her side, keying into the ignition and fiddling with the heater knobs so the cab would be warm when they got in. She dried off and handed the towel to him. He was still entirely naked, and in her peripheral vision all she could see were freckles. Freckles and muscles and her best friend in the whole world.

They both dressed and climbed in.

"Here we are again," she said, thinking back to the rainstorm and their failed berry-picking session. Trying to warm up together. They'd never finished their summer bucket list. What if it was over? What if the restaurant really did close? What if she had killed everything by speaking up? "You think it'll shut down? Brown Butter?" she asked, biting the tip of her thumb.

"Who can say? Jarrod will get fired, for sure. Right?"

Effie nodded. Bad guys got fewer chances since the #MeToo movement. "But this isn't a career-ender for a dude like him."

"Right. Sufficient period of fading into the background and a well-timed apology crafted by a PR agency. He'll be fine. He'll probably resurface as a judge on a reality cooking show."

Effie snorted. "Shitty men have come back from worse. But what happens to the rest of you?"

"The rest of us shitty men?"

"Haha. No. The rest of the staff."

"Including or minus you?"

"The rest of *us*. I knew talking to Carina was a risk. I knew people could lose their jobs. That we all could. But I thought if there was a chance Brown Butter makes it and I can help change things, I should. I guess we have to wait and see what those changes actually look like." She leaned over and placed her palm against Ernie's cheek, trying to hold him with the same patient tenderness he'd shown her these last two months. "What are you going to do if it closes? Your dad's bills . . ."

He shook his head. "What are you going to do? Your career . . . your plan. Have you saved enough money for the next adventure?"

Effie slid her hand down to his chest, letting it rest there. It had all seemed so simple an hour ago. She wanted him. There was nothing else she needed to know. Romantic, maybe. But foolish. "I don't know. I haven't thought about where I want to go."

He brought her hand to his lips and kissed her fingers. "I don't know, either. For now, I should take you home."

Ernie drove them back into town, taking the corners and curves slower than Effie had. When they reached her house, he came around to the passenger door, and she stepped out. "I'll see you later?" he asked.

There was so much uncertainty lingering between them. Effie hated the way it gripped at her. She didn't want to be away from Ernie, not until they figured it all out and she felt sure again. "I'm still cold," she said. A non-answer and a question at the same time.

He motioned for her to come closer, and when she did, he held her tightly, pressing her cheek against his chest. "We can't have that."

No, we can't. Effie nuzzled her nose into him, letting his sweet almond scent comfort her. "Can I stay over?"

He nodded. She smiled into his hoodie. He helped her back

into the truck, then drove them both to the boathouse. And then, through her laughter and halfhearted protests, he lifted her off the passenger seat and carried her all the way back inside. Back to the warm, quiet peace that had been waiting while they swam. Waiting for them both, all along.

Chapter Thirty-Three

As she squinted from one eye, she took in her surroundings. Ernie's boathouse. She was wearing a loaned T-shirt and gym shorts, lying on the leather couch with the deep-set cushions. The details filled themselves in quickly and clearly. *Right. Last night. The talk with Carina. Mom's dress. Walked here. Vodka lemonades. The swim.* After they arrived home from Dulse Cove, he made them tea and said he was tired. He offered his bedroom, but she threw herself over the couch and kicked his thigh with her foot, trying to push him toward the pocket doors. "It's yours," she had insisted, draping her body stubbornly across the cushions until he relented and brought out extra bedding for her.

Effie opened her other eye.

The floating shelves in the kitchen were stacked neatly with plates and mugs; the countertops were clear except for a large chopping block and a quart of cherry tomatoes. There was a plant by the front door. She didn't know what kind. It didn't matter.

Umbrella bin, coatrack, boot tray. The wood floor planks shone like they'd just been polished. The windows were hidden behind cream-colored pull-down shades. The air smelled like clean laundry. Her dress had been folded neatly, set on the ottoman. There was a new toothbrush standing in a pottery cup on the coffee table.

It looked like a home.

She felt peaceful.

No matter what happened, she knew she was safe.

She sat up. Through the frosted glass doors, she could make out the shape of Ernie's bed. The feelings she'd welcomed in the night before rolled over her in gentle, lapping waves. Ernie wasn't a crashing kind of love. He was a quiet cove in a wild ocean.

No matter what, she wanted to tell him that.

Effie stepped off the couch and onto the jute rug. Simple, attractive, clean. She loved it. She needed to tell him that, too. Tiptoeing to the other side of the room, she ran her hand through her hair. Nervous, again. Just a little. She stopped with her fingers in the groove of the door pull. She closed her eyes. Anxiety floated away like driftwood back to sea. *Ernie.* She was safe.

The door squeaked on its track, but Ernie didn't stir. She stood in the doorway, drinking in the room. Knotty wood walls, one large window at the head of the bed; arched top, bright white sill. Oak dresser, matching trunk at the bottom of the bed. Framed photos on a shelf. There were pictures of childhood Ernie and his dad; teenage Ernie holding a large lobster.

Ernie slept shirtless in his pajama pants, in the middle of the mattress, on his left side. Blue jersey sheets, Pendleton blanket folded at the bottom. Two fluffy pillows. The bed beckoned. He shifted in his sleep. Her heart skipped.

She walked across the floor and, as softly as she could, slid into bed with him. Still dreaming, he lifted his arm to make room. She burrowed in, facing him. Their noses were almost touching. "Ernie," she whispered.

"Mm?" He pulled her body closer, eyes closed.

"You are a quiet cove in a wild ocean."

His eyes opened.

"And I love your rug."

"You woke me up to tell me that?"

She ran the pads of her fingers over his scalp. He groaned a little. "I woke you up because I want to be with you."

Ernie's arms were relaxed, and his hands wandered her back confidently. "I'm right here."

A stubborn tear trailed down her cheek. He caught it with his thumb and touched it to her nose.

"Effie, I can't be doing this if you don't mean it."

"I mean it," she whispered, and parted her lips. He rolled the tip of his thumb down and onto her tongue. She licked him, slowly, then took his hand in hers. Lacing their fingers together, she shifted so his leg was close to her center. "I mean it all the way."

And she did. If it required staying on Alder Isle and working at Brown Butter or helping her dad at Meadowsweet Scoops, she meant it. If it invited the possibility of going somewhere new together, she meant it. Details were inconsequential. What mattered was them. She could figure out the rest of it.

Ernie gripped her waist and hesitantly slid his palms upward, guiding the T-shirt over her breasts. He kissed the skin just below each one, then grazed his tongue upward. "Yes," Effie said, and her whole body rushed with warmth. He moved to her other breast, teasing her gently.

"Ernie," she said, again desperate to tell him something.

"Effie." He grew harder as he murmured her name; she felt him fill the space between her thighs. He brought his face back up to hers.

She wanted him, but was embarrassed about all the missteps they'd taken along the way. Needed to feel him, but staggered under the weight of their history. So she pressed her hands to his smooth, warm chest and spoke the next words into his mouth: "I want you to fuck me like we're meeting for the first time."

"Effie." He cupped her breasts and kissed her mouth, cautious and curious. "We are."

Desire roared through her, and she reached for him under the sheet. He caught her wrist and pushed her away. "No."

"No?" Her eyes were questioning, her body pleading.

"No. If we're going to do this, we're going to do it my way." He lifted her up to remove the shirt, then lowered her down again, on her back. He pulled off the shorts and kissed the side of her ribs; trailed his lips over her navel. She squirmed, feeling ticklish and hungry for everything. "It starts with making you ache for me as much as I've wanted you for the last two decades," he said and pushed her legs farther apart. He nodded as she instinctively bent her knees toward the ceiling. "And I'm just getting started."

"You're the boss," Effie said as his breath met her skin.

"Do you really believe that though?" His face and his hands were close. Everything was close but not close enough. He stroked her, then took his hand away.

"Come back." She pedaled her heels on the mattress in frustration. Urgency pooled inside her.

"Manners," he said, a teasing laugh unfurling from a hidden place deep inside him.

"Come back, please." She tilted her hips upward.

He didn't. Instead he replaced the touch with his tongue and traced the edges of her entry with an impossibly light pressure. She held her breath as he teased and tasted her, and only when he felt her exhale did he return a finger to her most sensitive spot. He explored the same way he did everything: Patiently. Unhurried. She shuddered against his touch, begging him to give her more, press harder, push deeper. He wouldn't, and her buildup was slow but intense. When she came, she did so ferociously and with her whole body. Afterward, he kissed her inner thighs and worked his way back up to her neck, meandering over her torso and her shoulder blades. She felt him, stiff and thick, against her hip bone and gave an indignant huff. He had been in charge for much too long.

"Let me get on top," she said, pawing at his pajamas.

He laughed and let her yank them to his ankles. "I was going to make you beg for it, but I want you just as much, baby."

She stopped, softened, melted at the word. "Baby," she repeated, raking her nails down his biceps.

"Is that all right?"

Yes, she thought. The word wrapped itself around her tenderly, arousing her in a way she hadn't known was possible. "Yes," she said, and straddled his waist, sitting on top of him and bringing her mouth down to his ear. She kissed the top ridge of it and crushed their bodies together.

He pushed himself up against her wetness and stroked her jawline. "I want to disappear inside you."

Effie wanted that, too.

"Condom?" she asked, eyes frantically searching the room. He reached for the nightstand drawer, but she got there quicker and tore off the wrapper, rolled it onto him. She squeezed at his base and lowered herself down in a hurry. "Oh fuck, Ernie." He filled her completely, and she strained against the sensation of him hitting her limit. Neither of them was perfect, but he was perfect for her. They were a perfect fit. Had they always been, or was it only right after waiting for so long? Rocking her hips forward, she tightened around him. He held on to her waist and moved her to his rhythm. She let him guide her for a few moments, then tore his hands away and pinned them to the pillow. She grinned and he grinned back. There was room for both of them to lead, and now it was her turn. Satisfied she had him where she wanted him, she closed her eyes and waited just long enough to drive him wild before grinding herself down against his body. She took him in entirely.

"Hey." His voice was strained and heavy. "I'm supposed to be the one in charge. You're not playing by the rules."

She bent down as if to kiss his neck, but pulled at it with her teeth instead. She was fully in control now. "I'll bet you like that."

He answered with an affirmative groan and wrested himself free, grabbing the place where her hips met her thighs. He moved her onto her belly without missing a beat. "Not so fast. I don't want to—"

". . . not yet." Effie finished his sentence with her face pressed into the pillow. He stroked the very top of her spine with the pad of his thumb. She moaned in pleasure. He responded by going deeper. They continued like that, her prone on the mattress, his hips rolling against her until they were both nearly there.

"Look at me," he said, and she rolled over onto her back.

"Oh, I love you," she said, the words tumbling out of her before she could taste them.

"I love you so much." His toes flexed on the mattress as he leveraged himself up on one elbow. His other arm curled around her, his hand cradling the back of her head. Effie closed her eyes and let pleasure flood her. She could have stayed like that forever.

Except that Ernie was close—she knew it, she could feel it—and she was, too. She pulled him in, then held on to his rear. She caught his heaving groan with a kiss and didn't let go until his body tensed a final time and they collapsed together.

An hour later, they were still in bed, falling in and out of sleep, tangled in each other. Effie's head was resting on Ernie's bare chest, and he was making slow, soft circles on her shoulder with the tips of his fingers. Her heart felt full, like she had come home in a way that was bigger than any island, bigger than any job. She turned to press her lips softly into his skin. "I liked that a lot," she said.

He shifted in bed so he could look at her adoringly. "Me too.

You know what? If I'm a cove in the ocean, you are the whole ocean in one woman." She swallowed the compliment whole. Her lashes fluttered a few times, and she succumbed to the heavy, pleasant feeling.

As she slipped back into the hazy edges of sleep, she heard his voice in a faraway whisper: "I can't believe we almost missed out on this. I can't believe how much better it is than I could have imagined." She burrowed in extra close and nodded as he added, "Waiting for each other was worth every second of every year."

Chapter Thirty-Four

The next few days were weird. Jarrod didn't show up to work on Wednesday or Thursday, and no one knew why. Well, everyone knew why, but their suspicions hadn't been confirmed. Effie, Sixto, and Jean-Claude all sent emails to Geoffrey Goldman, Brown Butter's owner, who had yet to respond. Despite the impending article, the atmosphere at Brown Butter was largely free of tension. Effie worked the pass while Sixto jumped in on Jarrod's grill station. Jean-Claude let Chad help him out with sauces, and Ernie joined everyone in the kitchen upstairs, working through his mountain of mise en place at the interns' station. There were still miniature crises—a steak that wasn't done to a diner's liking, a couple mixed-up appetizer orders—but for the first time, the staff at Brown Butter worked like a team.

The next few days were also wonderful. Effie slept at the boathouse, getting tangled up in the sheets late into the night. When she woke up with worry on her mind, Ernie pulled her closer, and placed quiet, sweet kisses all over the bridge of her nose. It wasn't quite enough to make her forget about Carina or Jarrod or the *New York Times*, but it soothed her and helped her carry on until Friday morning. The day arrived without fanfare, and Effie woke wrapped in Ernie's arms. The sun was bright and hot, and they'd kicked the sheet down around their feet. Ernie was peppering the back of her neck with soft, light kisses, and he spoke into her skin. "My phone has been blowing up for the last half hour."

"Screw that thing," she said, but by the time she finished the sentence, a low dread had set in. She buried her face in her hands. "The story." She sat up and swung her feet over the side of the mattress. "Have you read it yet?"

Ernie laughed. "I've been in bed with you. And I'm not touching it until we have coffee and you're in my lap." He grabbed her and pulled her back into his arms. The herd of wild ponies that had begun galloping around Effie's chest slowed to a trot. She knew she was safe.

But she also wanted coffee.

Ernie filled an ancient-looking Mr. Coffee with grounds and water, and they waited, watching it drip into the carafe. "I'm sorry I don't know how to make fancy coffee," he had said at the exact moment she said, "I'm so glad you're not one of those snobby coffee people."

"Water heated to the tenth of a degree? Who has the time?" he said, reaching up to the shelves for two of his handmade mugs.

She nodded and accepted one with a dimple on the side. Her

thumb settled into the groove perfectly. "People who weigh their beans on miniature scales before crushing them in a hand-crank grinder? Questionably sane."

"Can I be honest?" he asked. She laughed. *Obviously.* "I like our gas station coffee moments. Would choose fake cappuccinos over sludgy black French press or espresso any day."

He poured a splash of milk and stirred a spoonful of sugar into each mug, then gave one to her.

"Can I be honest back?" she asked. "For the longest time I drank coffee like that—boring, unsweetened, black as my heart."

"Ha."

"But sweeter is better. I think I've always preferred it this way."

He touched the lip of his mug to hers in a quiet toast, then held her hand and guided her back to the warm serenity of bed. He turned on an iPad and navigated to the *Times* website. "It's not here," he said. Effie's heart stopped for a moment. "Hold on." He tapped to the Food section. "Oh heck."

"What?" Effie set her mug on the nightstand.

"There's pictures and everything," he said, and moved closer so they could look at the screen together. The headline read A SLEEPY MAINE TOWN SELLS AUTHENTICITY. THE MENU TELLS A DIFFERENT STORY.

"Who says we're sleepy?" Ernie frowned.

"Carina Shen." Effie used her fingers to zoom in on the lead photo. It was an artfully shot plate of ravioli, backlit by the evening sun in the dining room. You could see the ocean in the distance, through the windows. "But she's not wrong. Alder Isle *is* sleepy."

"Not anymore," Ernie reminded her. He bent his knees so the iPad could rest on his thighs. Effie snuggled in closer, and together they read.

> Brown Butter was not supposed to be a success. The fine dining restaurant opened on Maine's Alder Isle mere weeks after the first Covid-19 pandemic lockdowns began and spent much of its first year navigating a labyrinth of new health-and-safety rules. But despite the odds, Brown Butter, which is owned by New York restaurateur Geoffrey Goldman, has enjoyed a meteoric rise over the last three years. Now the holder of a coveted Michelin star, the restaurant's reservations are booked a year in advance, with diners crowding onto an unpredictable ferry and taxing the island's few inns and hotels—all for a taste of the most authentic, sustainable, and local cuisine the country has to offer.
>
> There's just one problem: very little, if any, of the restaurant's staggeringly expensive meals are actually made with the local ingredients it purports to champion.

"Yikes," said Ernie. "What an opener."

Effie bit the insides of her cheeks and closed her eyelids halfway. She nodded. "Let's keep going."

> Over the course of reporting, almost two dozen workers at Brown Butter, employed in both the dining room

> and kitchen, spoke about ingredient fraud, as well as what one described as a "dangerously toxic" work environment. Farmers and food artisans on the island also expressed bewilderment at the restaurant's decision to purchase ingredients and produce from farther afield, often from big-box stores. At the center of these allegations is Jarrod Levi, the head chef who opened Brown Butter in May 2020, amidst a global pandemic, and who runs operations for the famed Goldman.

Effie reached for her coffee and took a slow sip, trying to ignore the turbulent feeling in her heart. Ernie may have known her whole story, but the rest of Alder Isle didn't. And she was dreading finding out how much Carina Shen had told. Ernie's lips landed on the top of her head, and she relaxed into the sensation. Only one way to find out: they kept reading.

> In a surprising twist, Levi doesn't deny the allegations of ingredient fraud. In a joint statement released with Goldman, he cited the public's "maniacal demand" for local, seasonal cuisine "at all costs" as the catalyst that caused him to lose his North Star. "As a society of restaurant-goers, we have become so invested in the story of hyper-local cuisine that we demand a farmhouse fantasy even when it is untenable and unsustainable, agriculturally and otherwise," a separate statement from Goldman reads. It is this insatiable desire for kitchen gardens and low-carbon-footprint

> food that prompted Levi to find what he calls "creative" means for cutting costs.

"So *he's* the victim?" Ernie said, scrolling down then returning his hand to the back of her neck, where he rubbed gently. "He's annoyingly good at playing this game."

"He had help, I'm sure," Effie said, leaning into his touch. Her chest was pounding with each new word she read, but the rest of her body felt calm and relaxed against his. "This statement has urgent-call-to-their-PR-agency written all over it."

> Levi is right: adored restaurants across the country have undergone similar growing pains. It is difficult to feed diners at the volume required by their popularity without cutting corners. Brown Butter finds itself in a uniquely challenging position: as a state that shares a border with Canada, Maine's growing season is short, and its fallow-field winters long.

Effie couldn't believe it. Carina Shen was insinuating Jarrod had no choice but to lie. That *all* these expensive, fancy restaurants were suffering instead of lying to their customers. That they—what?—deserved pity? And hadn't Effie been a part of that culture for years? Her cheeks burned as she continued reading.

> But Maine also enjoys a unique privilege, owing to its coastal location: it has a storied history and rich culture as one of the best and most abundant lobstering

> communities in the country, if not the world. It is perhaps understandable Levi would choose to import tomatoes or tender salad greens in the brutal months, but perplexing is why he would use monkfish in the restaurant's signature dish, a plate of five well-sauced "lobster"-stuffed ravioli bearing his name.

"Shots fired," said Effie.

Ernie gave a little fist pump. "'Bout time she got there." The article went on to describe the dish—the ricotta and garlic, Jean-Claude's brown butter sauce, even the teardrop-shaped plate—then explained monkfish was less expensive than lobster; less labor intensive, too. There was a quote from Jarrod in which he claimed by buying monkfish, he wasn't just saving the restaurant thousands in food costs, but was supporting a local "upstart" seafood import company. "Probably more like 'sketchy man in a white van,'" Ernie said, and Effie snorted, but quieted herself when she got to the next line.

> Aware that this deception would not be accepted by the staff, Levi purchased the monkfish in bulk and stored it in a freezer in his own home—a secret that deceived customers paying an upcharge for the luxury of eating Maine lobster on an already-expensive tasting menu, and also one that violated restaurant health codes for safe food storage.

The next paragraph stung. In it, Carina briefly outlined

Jarrod and Effie's fling, and how it led to Effie's discovery. That was it. Then the tone shifted into a new paragraph. Although Olsen maintains that her romantic connection to Levi was mutual, other employees at Brown Butter felt taken advantage by and even violated by the head chef. They kept reading, and the article transitioned to Jarrod's workplace liaisons. Effie scanned over the words with a breath caught in her throat. She learned the youngest servers felt pressure to join Jarrod for drinks at Son of a Wharf after-hours. She learned a handful of female waitstaff said Jarrod had aggressively pursued them with gifts, special treatment, and declarations of love, only to lose interest when they were finally intimate with him. "I felt gaslit," read a quote from Nikki, the head server. "Like I was some crazy ex-girlfriend, not someone he'd spent months pursuing to the point of scaring me. Once, before I finally gave in, he cornered me in the wine room and felt me up over my shirt. 'Violation' doesn't even begin to cover it, but what could I do? He's the one in charge. The one who controlled our tip pool. He could get me fired like nothing at all." In fact, the article continued, every relationship Jarrod claimed to be consensual was not, with the exception of Olsen.

"No one's going to judge you for it," Ernie said as the groan left Effie's mouth. She gave him an *Oh, come on* look. "Well, I don't judge you for it," he said, and she squeezed his hand.

"Read the rest out loud to me?" she asked. She was suddenly too tired to keep going. He did, giving a squeaky, scratchy voice to Jarrod every time he was quoted. It made Effie giggle, and made her feel a little less ill about the entire situation. The article quoted Sixto and Jean-Claude and B.J., who all admitted to knowing about the ingredient fraud but feeling helpless to do anything about it. It quoted Chad, who said simply but rather effectively, "He's not right in the head." Ernie was quoted as saying, "Someone who disrespects Maine lobster should not be someone in charge of a Maine restaurant. That role would be better served by someone with roots here." The article went on and on, and covered the problematic nature of restaurant culture at large, revisited the #MeToo movement, and even gave voice to the residents of Alder Isle, who were less than pleased about the influx of tourism, a burden for which their small island's infrastructure was unprepared. The article finished with a short, tight paragraph:

> It is difficult to choose a side in this battle, as restaurant owners and workers often feel their alliances shifting like the marine wind. Who are they beholden to? Who is to blame? But one thing is certain, as evidenced through this regrettably familiar story, now acted out through the players at Brown Butter: the fine-dining restaurant economy is experiencing a reckoning. And it is time for a change.

Chapter Thirty-Five

Ernie set the iPad on the bed and pulled Effie fully into his lap. Neither spoke. They sipped their coffee, and he periodically kissed her temples, the top of her head, the crook of her neck. Her body softened with each touch of his lips, and with the realization that she hadn't been alone. Not through any of this. She'd spent so much time wringing her hands, worrying about the power her confession had to take down the restaurant, that she hadn't considered she was fighting this battle with her coworkers. With her friends beside her. Neither her quotes nor her actions were the whole story.

Eventually, Ernie got up to make a second pot of coffee, and Effie stretched out like a cat, arching her back then reaching her hands overhead, toward the sun. Both his devices dinged at the same time with a new alert. Effie padded out to the kitchen to deliver the phone to Ernie. He swiped up and said, "Oh." It was an email, sent to the whole staff from Geoffrey Goldman. He handed the phone back to Effie and she read aloud as he busied himself with the coffee maker.

> Dear colleagues and employees of Brown Butter:
>
> You have no doubt, by now, read an article published in the *New York Times* written by Carina Shen. While it reads like a sensational exposé, it is of the utmost importance you, the staff, know we are taking every allegation seriously. An internal investigation will begin immediately, and we appreciate your cooperation and honesty if contacted by a member of our HR team. We ask you to think thoroughly and with a clear head before speaking to any additional members of the press. As regards restaurant operations: Brown Butter will close immediately until further notice while we begin the difficult work of healing our community. All bookings within the upcoming week have received a $100 credit to be redeemed at one of our other restaurants. If you have any questions or concerns, please know I am only an email away.
>
> Sincerely,
>
> Geoffrey Goldman

"That's a lie. He won't answer any emails," Ernie said, handing over her mug. "But Jarrod's toast, right? That's what this is about; Carina said it in her article, it's time for a change." His features shifted into something like hope. "One man's sacking is another woman's promotion?"

"Whoa," said Effie, like she was trying to calm a runaway

horse. "That's not what this is about . . . Is it?" Ernie shrugged, his smile so big it peeked out from behind his mug. *Maybe it's like Kit predicted. Jarrod's out, I'm in.* The thought dangled tantalizingly. In some ways, it was perfect: she had committed to Alder Isle for better or worse because Ernie was here. And this made things so much simpler. She could keep her job. No, she'd get an even better job. The one she'd wanted for years. The one she fumbled at Cowboy Bean. This was it. Her second chance. Her happily ever after. So why was there such a heavy pit in her stomach? She didn't know, but she knew what would make her feel better.

"Hey," Effie said, abandoning her mug on the counter and standing on her toes to meet Ernie's lips. She gave him a soft kiss. He murmured "Hey" back into her mouth and the pit in her stomach got a little smaller.

Ernie hurried to set his own mug next to hers so he could use both hands to properly kiss her back. He was just getting to the good part—the part where those hands started getting bold—when a knock on the door broke them out of their spell. Ernie groaned and Effie gave a frustrated sigh, but she stepped aside and let him pass.

The knock sounded again. "Be right there," Ernie said, sliding into his hoodie. He opened the door to find Ingrid and Sixto on his porch. Ingrid had a beach bag and was holding a package of wavy potato chips and two tins of French onion dip. Sixto had a towel slung over his shoulder and a cheeky grin. "Good morning?" Ernie said. Effie appeared behind him and gave her sister a weird look.

"Figured you'd be here," Ingrid said, rummaging in her bag and tossing Effie her swimsuit. "Get changed! We're going to the quarry to celebrate."

I know you weirdos like to swim in freezing cold water, but the rest of us"—Ingrid motioned between herself and Sixto—"prefer this." They had taken the short hike through the trees and laid out their towels on a flat, wide rock on the far edge. She took off her sun hat and opened the chips, ate one, then handed the bag to Effie. Effie took a handful and passed the bag to Sixto. She arranged the chips neatly on her towel and leaned back, looking up at the sky. It was bright blue without a cloud in sight. A perfect seventy-seven degrees. *This.* This was what Effie loved about Maine. The summer days spent with people she'd love forever.

Friends who were acting, all things considered, rather odd.

"We have a lot to talk about!" Sixto said.

"Wait, first we need to put on sunscreen," Effie said. "You especially." She pointed at Ernie and his freckles. "Here, I'll do your back."

"You really don't have to take care of everyone all the time," Ingrid said, but she handed over the squeeze bottle of lotion anyway.

"Maybe not. But I do have to take care of my people." She thought about it, then amended her statement. "I *want* to take care of my people." Once everyone had properly lotioned up, Sixto produced a bottle of expensive vodka. "Oops," Ingrid said with a giggle. "We forgot cups."

Sixto took a swig, then handed the bottle to Effie with a

brimming smile. "Drink up, partner," he said. She gave him an inquisitive look and grabbed the bottle by its neck and drank, then set it on the rock.

"So, uh, what are we celebrating? The fact that our restaurant is going down in flames? That we're not working but don't know if we'll be getting paid? That my big mouth got us into trouble?" Effie asked.

"Hermana, we all talked with Carina," said Sixto. "You read the story. But there you go, trying to shoulder the burden by yourself. Let your teammates help you out a little, no?"

Ingrid took a turn with the liquor and handed it to Ernie. He set it on the rock next to him. "That article was brutal!" Ingrid said, seemingly unruffled about it.

"Yeah," Effie mumbled into her lap. "Some parts more than others."

"Oh, your 'consensual' thing? Nobody cares about that," Ingrid said. "At least no one who matters." Ernie gave her a look like, *See? I told you.*

"There's time to hash out every gritty detail of Carina's hatchet job, but right now, we've got to move fast on some important stuff," Sixto said, handing over his phone. Ingrid nodded and smacked Sixto's thighs with her palms like she was doing a drum roll. Effie had never seen her little sister so animated.

Effie took the phone and angled it so Ernie could see, too. It was a real-estate listing. For the old farmhouse where, for the last three years, Brown Butter restaurant had operated.

"What?" Effie's voice was a whisper, but her body felt like a scream. This didn't make any sense.

"I know. Goldman moves fast. The listing went up late last night," said Sixto.

"I have an alert for Alder Isle properties," explained Ingrid.

"Here's the timeline, best I can tell," Sixto continued. "Carina talked with Jarrod on Tuesday."

"Yeah, after she spoke with Ernie and me," Effie confirmed.

"After that, Jarrod goes to his boss in a panic. Can you picture it?! Oh, to have been there. Obviously Geoffrey starts doing whatever damage control he can. He calls around, calls his people, whatever. Realizes this isn't something you can talk your way out of. Or buy your way out of. He calls his lawyers because *obviously* he calls his lawyers. His lawyers are like, 'Hey, homeboy. You need to get out of there pronto.' He's like, 'Oh shit.' He calls his real-estate broker because *of course* he has a real-estate broker on speed dial. Homie hooks it up on Zillow real quick, doesn't matter that the photos are all shot on iPhone and most are outdated, from before the Brown Butter renovation. Boom. It's listed. The retreat has begun."

Ernie's eyes widened. "So you think 'Closed until further notice' means 'Closed forever'?"

"And EVER!" Ingrid said.

"Geoffrey Goldman was never on our side," Effie said quietly, the familiar realization settling in deep, heavy in her feet. Just like her bosses in New York. And California.

"You can't be surprised," Sixto said. "The big man is never on our side."

Effie's mind replayed fuzzy bits of her lost promotion in Paris, of her failed trial at Cowboy Bean. When had she ever felt supported by her restaurant bosses? The last time was . . . Gertie? At The Gull's Perch? *Tragic.* "I guess you're right."

Ernie fiddled around with the bottle cap. He looked frustrated. "I think we're missing something. At least Effie and I are. Why are we celebrating? Why are we drinking"—he tossed the cap to Sixto—"this?"

Ingrid and Sixto exchanged a conspiratorial grin. "Get ready to have your minds blown," Ingrid said, "because we've got a plan."

"We buy the building," Sixto said. "Open our own restaurant. It's basically turnkey. Bar, tables, chairs, kitchen equipment . . . all of it. I mean, even the frickin' *oven* is still there."

"The sexy one that you like, Effie," Ingrid added.

"You have the hots for the oven?" Sixto said to her, eyebrow inching upward.

"She has for years," Ernie confirmed.

"It's French," Effie said with a shrug.

"So we buy the building, right?" Sixto said, laughing, then launching into another monologue. "And we rename the restaurant, and we create a new menu. A menu that's honest; that reflects who we are and where we've been. A menu that doesn't try to be anything other than just dinner. We hire Ernie to make all new dinnerware for the restaurant. Plates, bowls, cups. It's a little thing that would differentiate us from Brown Butter. Wipe the slate clean. Big commission here, guy. Big jumping-off point for future work. Then we rehire what staff we can and get Carina Shen back here. Or get whoever back here, I don't know how these things work. But we get some new press. Good press. We get the rebirth story. We get ALL. THE. BUSINESS. We get on *Bon Appétit*'s Best New Restaurants list. We get famous! We get to do what we love; with people we respect." He finished, breath quick and eyes shining.

"What do you think?" Ingrid said, bouncing up and down and weaving her fingers into Sixto's. They smiled at each other.

"I mean . . . yeah," Ernie said, looking cautiously optimistic. "I would love to do a job like that. Especially now that I'm no longer a basement butcher troll. I'm sure Lake would let me use her wheel and studio. Until I saved up enough to buy my own."

"Effie?" Ingrid reached out with her other hand and squeezed her sister's forearm.

Effie frowned, unsure why it felt like she'd just swallowed a pile of crushed granite. "Who's the *we* in all these scenarios?"

"*We*"—Sixto circled his finger in the space between himself and Effie—"create a new restaurant as co-owners and co-chefs."

"And *I*," Ingrid said proudly, her hands on her hips like Wonder Woman, "buy the building!"

Chapter Thirty-Six

"Who *are* you—Daddy Warbucks?" Effie said. "There's no way you have the cash to buy a building right on Main Street. I don't even have enough money to rent an apartment."

Ingrid shrugged modestly. "I got lucky," she said.

"From Bitcoin?" Ernie's face was slowly lighting up in recognition as he looked from Ingrid to Effie to Sixto and back to Effie again, scrubbing his palm down his jaw.

"No way," Effie said.

Ingrid nodded. *Really*. "Not with my salary. I invested and I got lucky. I mean, I'm not Jeff-Bezos-rich. I can't buy the building outright. But there's definitely enough for a down payment and a mortgage with a decent interest rate."

"You . . . are rich," Effie said, piling her chips in a tall stack.

"Rich-ish."

"I guess this is where I confess I don't actually know how crypto works," Effie said.

"Wait, really?" Ingrid asked.

"Really," Effie said.

"So does the word *blockchain* mean anything to you?"

Effie howled with involuntary laughter.

"Okay, wow. This is going to take longer than I thought. Picture a spreadsheet. Like a Google Sheet."

Ernie nodded. Effie held up her hand. "You know what? I've already stopped listening. My brain refuses to process this information."

Sixto chuckled and rubbed Ingrid's back proudly.

Ingrid sighed dramatically and rolled her eyes toward the cloudless sky. "CliffsNotes version: I bought a bunch of Bitcoin back when I was a freshman in high school." She ignored Effie's jaw drop. "With the money I earned at Meadowsweet Scoops," she explained. "And I borrowed a little from Mom. But I cashed out in college." Ingrid had gone to RIT, majored in computer engineering. She lifted her shoulders and let them drop casually. "I got in before it got too expensive, and I got out before it got fucked."

"And you've just been sitting on this money?" Effie asked. "I would not have that kind of self-control."

"Well, no. I made more investments. So my money turned into more money." Ernie laughed. "Hey, you wanted the simple version. But that's where the funds for this purchase would come from."

"Invested in *what*?" Ernie said. Effie shook her head as if to say, *My brain can't handle it.*

Effie jumped in. "The actual important question here: you

want to spend years of invested cash—hundreds of thousands of dollars—on an old building? For real?"

"It's not just an old building," Ingrid said, pouting. Her exciting big reveal was losing momentum. "It's Sixto's and your future. A job you can grow into. A place for *you* to invest in. Big sis, it's a way for you to stay on Alder Isle without feeling miserable."

Effie flicked her eyes toward Ernie. His expression was neutral, but she could feel hot sparks of electricity jumping off his body.

"Can I think about it?" Effie asked. She reached for Ernie and her fingertips found his knee. She wanted him to know that even if she was not sure about starting a restaurant with Sixto and Ingrid, she was certain about him. His hand, large and cool, folded over hers.

"What's there to think about?" asked Ingrid.

Ernie squeezed her hand tighter.

"Yeah, that's cool," said Sixto, his hand settling on Ingrid's shoulder. "I get it. But I'm going to talk to the waitstaff, Jean-Claude, and B.J. soon. Try to get them on board before they get out. Oh. And Chad. I may offer him prep cook—unless you want to keep that job, Ernie?"

Ernie shook his head. "If I don't consider this a sign to try doing pottery full time, I'm not . . . very good at reading signs."

"Right on," said Sixto. He turned to Effie. "Is twenty-four hours enough time for you? I want to have a solid plan when I connect with the rest of the team." Effie nodded, feeling in a daze. It was time enough for her to make a very important call. One she never would have considered at the beginning of the summer. One she hadn't considered for almost twenty years.

"And you're *sure* Brown Butter is going to close?" Ernie said.

On cue, Sixto's, Ernie's, and Effie's phones beeped and chirped. They swiped up and scanned the email that had just landed in their inboxes.

"Ha," said Sixto.

"Here we go," said Ernie, handing the phone to Effie. "Guess we should go home and change."

They had exactly one hour before a staff-wide meeting at Brown Butter, led by Geoffrey Goldman.

Fifty-five minutes later, Effie was freshly showered and changed into a pair of high-waisted jeans and a peasant top. She pushed open the door to the dining room.

The bar area was crowded and buzzy, with cooks and servers perched on the barstools and upholstered chairs. Her eyes did a quick sweep of the room. Sixto and Jean-Claude were huddled together, arms across their chests and backs against the wall. Sixto tossed a nod in her direction, and she met it with her own. Nikki was crying into a napkin, surrounded by a small group of waiters. Effie heard snippets through her sniffles. "And it's . . . my fault . . . not fair . . . completely screwed . . ."

Ernie was seated on a stool at the bar, looking calm and handsome. Effie took in his dark denim, his soft T-shirt, his freckled forearms. He was such a good man. And so hot. He caught her looking and blushed, then waved her over.

"You look nice," he said, leaning toward her ear. "But then, you always do. I'm so lucky." She touched her fingertips to his behind their backs, then changed her mind and rested her palm in his, settling both their hands onto his lap. She still felt a low-grade residual shame over her tryst with Jarrod, but she was proud to be with Ernie. Proud he was hers; proud she was his. There was no reason for them to hide. *No secrets, no lies.*

But first things first. First, we get through this meeting. The doors opened again and in came Geoffrey Goldman, followed closely by Jarrod.

The room went silent in an instant, which caused Chad to laugh nervously, then blush violently. Geoffrey ignored it and cleared his throat. "Hey, quiet please," he said, as if you couldn't already hear a paring knife drop in the next room. The restaurant's owner had salt-and-pepper hair, curly and cut short. He was dressed very nicely, in Italian loafers and a bespoke graphite-gray blazer. He looked too sharp to be relatable, too rich to be trusted.

"Thank you all for coming," he started, while Jarrod stood next to him, hands pushed down into his jeans pockets. Although every eye on the room was on him, he refused to look up from a notch in the wood floor.

"We were already here, man," Sixto said a bit too loud to be considered an aside.

Geoffrey ignored him. "I'm sure you've all read the article, so we don't need to go over the details." Effie cocked her head. *We don't?*

"Unfortunately, we're not the first restaurant to suffer such . . . attacks." Geoffrey worked his tongue around in his mouth before adding the last word. "Fine dining restaurants across the globe are being painted as bad actors." His voice sounded scratchy, like he'd slept little the night before. He took a sip from a water bottle. "It's unfair, when all we've tried to do is meet—no, exceed—the incredibly high bar set for us. But Ms. Shen is right: The public's attitude is changing. The industry is in a period of growth and rebirth, and perhaps a restaurant of this scale and style is no longer sustainable."

She felt Sixto's gaze and she met it; he looked serious. *This was it.* This was their moment. This was her dream come true. If she wanted it.

Geoffrey held his hands together in front of his chest. "Jarrod and I have spoken at length about this, and we both agree that the right thing, the responsible thing, is for Brown Butter to close."

"Wow," Effie whispered.

"Whoa." Ernie squeezed her hand tightly.

Across the room, Sixto looked smug, and turned toward Jean-Claude. "Let's finish that conversation at Gert's," Effie heard him say, then watched Jean-Claude's right eyebrow arch toward his hairline.

The room quickly swelled with the voices and shouts of the restaurant's staff.

"Hey, quiet please," Geoffrey repeated again. Next to him, Jarrod continued to study the floor. "I want to be as professional and efficient about this as possible, so the majority of details about this transition are going to be shared with you via email. The closure is effective immediately. You will all receive two weeks' severance pay, and, of course, letters of recommendation as needed."

Ernie's elbow met Effie's ribs, and she followed his gaze to Jarrod, whose face was Flamin'-Hot-Cheetos-red.

"What about *him*?" Jersey the bar manager's voice rose above the crowd.

Jarrod opened his mouth but was silenced by Geoffrey's hand on his shoulder. Geoffrey cleared his throat and spoke the next sentence to the back of the room, where the ceiling met the wall. *Coward*, Effie thought. *Look us in the eyes when you say it.* "Jarrod will be taking on the role of head chef at Black Garlic, our relaxed-casual Asian-fusion restaurant in the Berkshires. And we both thank you all, from the bottom of our hearts, for the service, care, and love you've put into Brown Butter."

"No!"

"Unreal!"

"Unfair!"

"Dirty!"

"Insane!"

The shouts clattered together against one another, angry and hot. A few of the servers were waving their hands, trying to get Geoffrey's attention. The back-of-house staff—except for Sixto—all looked dejected. The fight was over. It hadn't begun, really. Brown Butter never stood a chance.

Chapter Thirty-Seven

Later that evening, Effie sank into her papasan chair with a glass of iced tea. She'd taken one of Ernie's dimple mugs from the boathouse, and she pressed her thumb into the crevice now. After a luxurious sip, she set the mug on the floor, and gritted her teeth. She wanted to give Sixto her answer that night. She just hoped the call she was about to make would be as helpful as it was going to be painful. She burrowed into the chair even deeper, fished her fully charged phone out of her pocket, and video-called her mom.

Susan answered after two rings. She was in her home office. It had been years since Effie had visited, but she remembered the red-orange walls, the big window overlooking a park. It was the room she stayed in when she used to visit, sleeping on the pullout sofa and reading chapter books to Ingrid until their eyes closed.

"Sweetie?" Her mother studied the screen over tortoiseshell glasses. "Is everything okay?"

Effie wanted to laugh. Wanted to laugh at the term of endearment, which sounded stilted and odd, at her mother's assumption a call meant something was wrong, and at the fact she was dead right.

"Yeah," Effie said, feeling a lightening in her heart. Everything was already imperfect. But still good. There was nothing left to fear. No matter what her mother's answer was. "I just have a question for you."

"Hold on," her mother said, situating her phone on a small tripod. She sat back and wrapped a pashmina shawl around her shoulders. "Okay, I'm ready. Wait—is it about my clothes and books? I told your sister to divide them between you. Consider it an early inheritance present."

"No, it's not about that," Effie said. "But thanks. I took your orange dress." Her mother nodded imperceptibly. She was not a cold woman, but she was not a warm one, either. At least she seemed to be on a more even keel since moving away. Effie's chest rose and fell, and then she asked, "Why did you leave? Was it Alder Isle, or was it us?"

"Oh . . ." Her mother's voice came out soft and surprised. "I thought we were clear about this, your father and I, when we separated."

Effie shook her head. "Whatever you told your fourteen-year-old and four-year-old kids was probably not the truth. At least, not the full truth. But I'm ready to hear it. So. Why'd you leave?"

Her mother took a sip from a glass of water and looked at the camera seriously. "Well, it was neither. The island or my family. Nothing pushed me away from Alder Isle, Euphemia."

"Effie," she corrected. "I prefer Effie."

"Effie," her mother repeated. "I left because it wasn't possible to have my career on Alder Isle. I loved—love—you all dearly, but I'm just not *me* without the newspaper. Without reporting, writing, travel. I needed to be here, in Chicago, to feel whole."

"Huh," Effie said. That wasn't the answer she was expecting.

"Has this been on your mind all these years? I'd hate for you to think I didn't want to be around for you."

Effie bit back another laugh. Whether that was her mother's intention or not, that was exactly how Effie felt. "Sort of. I always assumed that it was some combination of us and Alder Isle that you hated so much. In some inherited way, I internalized that. It's like . . ." She trailed off, trying to put the rest into words. "It's like I hated it because I thought it pushed you away."

Her mother nodded thoughtfully.

"And now, I'm at this precipice. When I came back for the summer, I reconnected with Ernie. You remember him? Ernie Callahan. My childhood best friend. His dad was . . ." Effie took in her mother's blank look and sighed. "You know what, it's not important. I fell in love with him this summer. Actually, I realized I've loved him for years. He makes me feel calm and complete and safe in ways I never thought possible. He's mine. I'm his." It felt good to be saying this out loud, although the words were mostly for Effie's own benefit. She was working out how she felt as she spoke. "I want to be with him, but I'm afraid I'll eventually freak out and leave . . . like you did."

"Oh, Eu—Effie." Susan was leaning closer to the camera, and

Effie could see her own ice-blue eyes mirrored in her mother's. "Let me tell you one of life's secrets. Everyone has their *thing*. For me, it's work. I blame Betty Friedan for that, but it's what drives me. Your father, it's his projects; his creativity. He needs those fiddly things to feel inspired and purposeful."

"I think Dad's thing is *you*."

"Ha! No."

Effie let it rest. No sense in mentioning the photo shrine in the kitchen.

"Your thing can't be another person. It's dehumanizing. And dangerous. Anyway. I was saying. Your sister has always thrived on the acquisition of knowledge, on the pursuit of mastery. You see what I mean? If you have your thing, you can survive just about anywhere, in any situation. But lose the thing and you're good as dead." Effie wore a worried look. "Oh dear. Perhaps that was a bit dramatic. But it's the way I remember feeling so many years ago. My thing is reporting. I couldn't do that there, not in the way I wanted. So I had to leave. Your thing is your restaurants, no? Ingrid told me you had found one there on Alder Isle. Brava! See, you've sorted it. Be with your lovely little boyfriend and do your cooking, and you'll be all set." Susan looked immensely pleased with her tidy parenting.

"It's not restaurants," Effie said, feeling the weighty truth of the words as they left her mouth. "It's never been restaurants."

"Oh, well . . ." Her mother looked disappointed at not wrapping up the threads as neatly as she'd assumed. "What is it?"

"I don't know," Effie said. "I honestly don't." Her eyes skimmed over the room and landed on the digital clock. A rainbow-colored Lisa Frank tiger's paw pointed at the time. It was late. "I've got to go, Mom. Thanks for the . . . chat. It was helpful."

"Really!" Her mother's response betrayed surprise. "Well, I'm pleased. Ring anytime. Don't be a stranger."

"Okay," Effie said, and ended the call. She sent a frustrated sigh into the corners of the room. She had her answer.

And a new question.

Effie Olsen no longer wanted to be a professional chef.

She was good at it, and some days she even enjoyed it.

But it had never been her thing. And after years of doing the work, she was finally able to see with clear eyes the toll it took on her. Working in restaurant kitchens had hardened her in ways she wasn't proud of. The job stole her spontaneity, and it sapped her spirit. Perhaps once, long ago, the act of feeding people gave her enough joy to make up for everything it stole. It wasn't like that now.

The summer had been one of contradictions. There had been moments when she felt irretrievably far from herself. When she felt like she didn't know who she was at all. Those moments came in busy dinner shifts, when she heard her own voice rise above the clatter of pots and pans. When she looked at the clock after a long shift and realized she hadn't eaten a real meal for almost twelve hours. But there were many more moments when she felt entirely at home in her own body. Like she had not just come home to Alder Isle, but to herself, too. Moments when she laughed so hard, her sides ached. When she surprised herself. When she felt free and easy and light. When she cherished the friendships she had begun to cultivate. Moments, she realized, that all had one person in common. *Ernie.* If only a person could be your thing! Now that she had let him in all the way, loving Ernie was so big, so enveloping, she thought it could feed her forever. But was it enough? Her mother didn't seem to think so. And she would know.

Effie Olsen would not be a partner in the new restaurant. She wouldn't be a chef at all. But if she was going to stay on this tiny island forever, she had to figure out what would feed her soul.

Telling Sixto about her decision wasn't as heartbreaking as she thought it would be. He was kind and said, "It's okay. Sometimes it's just not right." That was what he'd told her weeks ago, while they scrubbed Brown Butter's stainless steel. She was glad he understood. "Besides," he added, "it's not like I'm going to be mad about being top dog." She laughed and fist-bumped him.

The purchase of the beautiful old building on Main Street moved forward quickly. Ingrid offered asking price with a generous down payment and the broker made efficient work of the deal. Jarrod had left with Geoffrey the night of the meeting, and Sixto got to work the day they closed on the sale, just over a week later. He wanted to open the restaurant officially on October 1st, to capture as much business and media attention as possible before winter settled in. It was a fresh start for so many people. He had convinced almost the entire staff to stick around, including the kitchen brigade. Minus Effie and Ernie. Plus Chad!

Sixto had renamed the restaurant, but he wouldn't reveal the secret to anyone except Ingrid. ("It's *really* good," she told Effie half a dozen times before biting her tongue and squealing in excitement.) The big windows of the restaurant were covered with brown butcher paper, so the staff could do the work of reimagining the space.

For the next month, it seemed as if all of Alder Isle was pitching in to make the opening a success. Dahlia arranged endless variations on late-summer bouquets for Sixto's approval. Kit did new paintings. Jean-Claude and Sixto refined the menu with daily tastings. Effie was always invited, and she always came, offering enthusiastic praise to the sopes with wild mushrooms, to the braised pork pozole. She was happy to be included in the process. It gave her something to anchor her days so she didn't feel entirely adrift, using Ernie as an excuse and a distraction from the troublesome pursuit of discovering her *thing*.

And Ernie was busy—awfully busy—too. He went to Lake's house most days to shape the plates and elegantly shallow bowls Sixto had commissioned. Their look was slightly different than his previous style, and Effie thought it showed growth and maturation as an artist. The surfaces were still textured, but the lips and edges were smooth and clean. The glaze he'd chosen was a pale sage green with soft brown speckles. The pieces were lovely and sweet, and creating them made Ernie happy. Which made Effie happy. She went with him sometimes and chatted with Lake over lunch while Ernie worked. The two women had more in common than she'd originally assumed, and she looked forward to their time together.

Even Effie's father was involved in the restaurant's rebirth. He had gone all in on the creation of a new ice cream flavor, which would be featured on the dessert menu. Although everyone loved beach plum swirl, it wasn't quite right for this new venture. When she wasn't at Sixto's tastings or spending time with Ernie, Effie joined her father at Meadowsweet Scoops, helping him mix new batches and twiddle with flavors. He seemed so bright, so pleased to be tinkering, and Effie was happy to see it. Happy to be there to witness it.

But she hated how chaotically her mother's words rattled around in her head wherever she went. Hated how figuring out what she didn't want brought her no closer to what she did. Hated how, on an island full of friendly people, she still felt alone and isolated in her uncertainties and insecurities. Loving Ernie was big, and real, and so, so good. But it wasn't everything. And sometimes, as she lay awake long enough to watch the moon set into the harbor, she worried it wasn't enough.

Ernie was an excuse not to leave Alder Isle. He was part of building a life here. What she needed was a reason to stay.

Chapter Thirty-Eight

Half a week before Sixto's restaurant opened, Effie was helping Ernie do inventory on his new collection of plates and bowls. She was marking down quantities of each form with a clipboard and pen while he inspected each one for blemishes and glaze imperfections, then set them into organized sections. It had taken them almost two hours, and they finished the job standing in the middle of the boathouse surrounded by dozens of pottery piles all over the floor.

"One or two more days of work and you're golden," Effie said, tucking the pen into her back pocket. "I'm proud of you."

Ernie's smile brightened. "I'm proud of me, too. I think I'm going to make another few sets and ask Sixto if I can sell them at the restaurant. For people to remember their meal there."

"I love that idea." Effie stretched her arms over her head.

Ernie caught her hands in his and floated them down beside her waist as he touched his lips to hers. "I love you."

"Why?" she said, her voice bubbly. She turned her head and gave him the side of her neck.

His mouth brushed down her cheek and landed on the soft underside of her jaw. "Because you're a very, very helpful studio assistant." His hands found her pocket, and he slid the pen out. It landed on the floor with a small clatter. "Even if you think you can get away with stealing my equipment."

"Maybe I stole it on purpose," she said, her laugh mingling with his. "Maybe I was hoping to be reprimanded."

They had slept together enough times that their intensely intimate lovemaking had transitioned into something lighter and more playful. Each time they met each other in that way, they were exploring what they liked and what felt good. Testing the limits of what was sexy and what was silly, and what was both. It had quickly turned into Effie's favorite game.

He gripped her forearms and held them against her body. Her breath quickened and his deepened. His voice came out low and authoritative. "You think that's what you want. We'll see." He released his grip and spun her around, then wrapped his arms around her waist. His fingers met at her buttons, which he loosened easily. He shimmied her shorts and underpants over her hips, and they both watched them fall to the floor. "Will you get on your hands and knees for me? And close your eyes?"

She stepped out of the pile of clothing and did what he asked. And then she waited. It felt like a very long time, although it couldn't have been more than half a minute. When his knuckle brushed the top of her thigh, the sensation came as a surprise, and she shuddered. He slid his hand upward and began teasing her in frustratingly slow strokes. His touch alternated between his first two fingers and his thumb, but he refused to explore further than her edges.

"Ernie fluffing Callahan," she said, lowering herself to her elbows and raising her rear higher. "Are you going to touch me for real or not?"

He slipped his hand past her center and up to the tiny spot where all her pleasure and excitement gathered. "This is real." He was making small, fast circles with his fingertip. "But it's all you're getting." She huffed. "For now." He said the last two words with his other hand at the nape of her neck.

They kept on like that, her eagerness swirling out from her center until her entire body was tingling with need. She pushed her hips back, letting him know that she was done waiting. He held on to her waist and pulled her close to him. She could feel how ready he was, too.

It was just a second of waiting, maybe two, while he put on a condom. But it was enough time for Effie to feel the panic of not having him. She couldn't imagine a life without Ernie's touch. Without their inside jokes. Their shared history, and the rest of the story they would write together.

She had to keep this. Protect it. At all costs.

She had to find her place on Alder Isle, so she could stay with him.

"Do you . . ." Effie gasped and gripped her palms and knees against the jute rug as Ernie pushed himself into the deepest part of her.

"Do you . . ." She couldn't finish the thought with him moving inside her like that. Ernie chuckled; he knew it.

"Hey, hush, Eff," he said, guiding her upright with his palm over her chest. "I'm over here trying to fuck you properly." Laughter twirled around in her mouth as a sensual feeling overtook the rest of her. "Arch your back for me." She did, and he tilted his hips toward her, and she saw rocket ships, shooting stars bouncing all over the walls of the boathouse. His hands roamed over her belly and rib cage as he moved faster. She floated her arms upward and caught the back of his head in her palms.

He switched his rhythm, moving in slow, thick circles inside her.

"I like that," she murmured, adding his name in a whisper just loud enough for them both to feel its effect on him.

"I love that," he said. "I love hearing my name on your lips when I'm inside you."

"You have me," she said, turning her head to catch his mouth. He gave it to her, and she softened.

"I know I do," he said gruffly, and she pulled away a bit, in mischievous defiance. "And you have me," he spoke the next words more softly, at her ear. "You always have. You always will."

She swallowed a cry as they both found their release and tumbled onto the rug. They lay there as the sun traveled across the sky and dipped down into the water. And finally, once it was dark and Effie's stomach rumbled, Ernie guided her upright, kissed both of her shoulders and then her chin, and then her mouth, and he asked her what she'd been trying to ask him earlier.

He knew, though. It was the same type of question she asked him every day.

Do you think making ice cream sundaes at Meadowsweet Scoops could be my thing?

Do you think waitressing at Gertie's again could be my thing?

Do you think the grocery store deli counter could be my thing?

The secondhand store?

The souvenir shop?

Dougie's lobster roll truck?

Bartending?

No. No. No, no, no, no, no. The thing about things was they were in short supply on tiny islands off the midcoast of Maine. Everybody else already had their things. What Effie had was a bag of knives and a boyfriend she loved. She was still in search of *her* thing.

Any dinner requests?" he asked her, pulling on his gray sweatpants. He fiddled around in the kitchen cupboards.

"Naw, you choose," Effie said, slipping into the bedroom, where she now kept a few extra pairs of underwear. She put one on, then slipped into one of Ernie's shirts and his plaid pajama pants, and sank onto the couch. "What I was trying to say before you very selfishly, rudely distracted me was, do you think being a journalist could be my thing?"

"Like Carina Shen?" He set a cutting board on the counter.

"Yeah. Or my mom. Maybe the *Alder Isle Gazette* would hire me as a restaurant critic." She thought, tallying the total number of restaurants on the island, and stopping shy of six. "Or I could write about high school sports. Or something. Maybe I'd like it."

"Maybe you would," Ernie said. He was always encouraging when she started on this line of questioning, but the responsibility to find her thing was her own. Sometimes she envied him for how easily he'd transitioned from a lobster-thing to a pottery-thing. And speaking of: Ernie closed the refrigerator door and turned around, a lobster in each hand and a dimpled smile on his face.

"Oh my God!" Effie laughed. "Please tell me you planned this. Actually, don't. It's funnier if you just happen to have a thousand lobsters knocking around in your fridge."

"Not a thousand; two. And yes, I got them earlier today. As I told you at the beginning of the summer, this is an adult fridge. Full of beer *and* green vegetables *and* low-fat dairy products *and* live lobsters."

"Well, yay. Thank you. Wait!" Effie looked at the calendar stuck to the door with a tack. It was a Monday. "Is this the last item on the bucket list?" Existential life questions and job security quandary temporarily set aside, she pulled a large stockpot from on top of the refrigerator and began filling it with water. The action felt ingrained, like she'd never left Maine in the first place.

"It is. Although I really wanted to take you out on a boat. That would have been a much cooler ending. And more expensive. If you remember, I got fired from my job."

"At least you found a new one," she grumbled, turning off the tap.

Ernie set the lobsters on the cutting board and wrapped her up in a hug. "I'm lucky. For a million different reasons," he whispered in her ear. Effie side-eyed one of the lobsters, crawling toward freedom at the edge of the board. "But pottery isn't a magic bullet. Neither was being on the boat. Or working in the restaurant. It was a job. A way to make money. Insofar as I have a thing, it's our thing. What we have together. The feeling of your eyes on me, of my arms around you. The sound of your laughter, and the way it turns into a snort when something's really funny. The ways in which we're different, and the ways in which we fill in each other's gaps. How you light me up when I'm down, and I cool you off when you're fired up." The lobster had made it all the way to the corner of the countertop and seemed to be considering its next move. "The way that just being next to you—feeling you slip your hand into mine—makes me feel safe."

"You make me feel safe, too," said Effie, stepping out of his hug to pick up the lobster and deposit it back on the cutting board. It immediately began its journey once more.

"Well, there you go," Ernie said. "That's just one of the dozens—hundreds?—of ways in which we're there for each other. You've taught me so much. Not just about running and cooking and superficial stuff. But about who I am and what's important to me." He continued: "When we were younger, and I had the hots for you—" Effie snorted. Ernie smiled slyly and kept talking. "I didn't realize any of this. I didn't realize how well we complement each other. I just wanted to hang out with you forever and be able to kiss you, too. It's pretty great that we get to do all of the above."

"It only took us a decade and a half to get there." Effie returned to his arms, this time cramming her head into the crook of his neck. She heard a *thud* and tensed.

"It's okay," Ernie said, reaching behind him. "He fell on top of the trash can. He'll live. For a while longer, anyway."

For once, Ernie's jokes didn't make her feel light. He was right, of course. About all of it. But it was so easy for him to say from where he was sitting, with a job and income stream. On an island he'd always loved, had never tried to leave.

"Besides," he said, taking a quick beat to brush his lips against her forehead, "who says your mom is right? Who says you need to have a thing? When was the last time you followed somebody else's dumb rules anyway?"

She stood on her tiptoes to kiss the edge of his lips. That was interesting food for thought. The last time she felt free enough to create her own destiny was, well, sixteen years ago. "Fair enough. But I still need a *job*."

"We'll figure it out," he said, retrieving the lobster and turning the stovetop's flame to high under the stockpot. As Ernie busied himself with the butter, Effie began finely chopping parsley leaves. That word, *we*, made her feel calm and steady and—for the first time in a long time—hopeful.

For now, there would be fresh lobster and melted butter and cold bottles of Maine beer and potato salad and dinner rolls and a big, green salad and another perfect sunset in a sleepy island town full of old-growth alder trees and good, kind people.

The present moment was all Effie had, but for a few hours, it was more than enough to fill her up.

Chapter Thirty-Nine

The rest of the week finished with Maine being quietly perfect in every single way. Friday evening arrived with a sparely warm breeze and the electric feeling of a town on the precipice of something. At six o'clock, Effie dressed in her mother's old sundress, a leather bomber jacket, and a pair of black Blundstone boots, and walked down the stairs to the kitchen where her father was waiting, dressed in a gold corduroy suit and a skinny necktie. *Oh, Dad*, she thought.

"Oh, Dad," she said. "You look great."

"Thanks!" he said, doing a quick catwalk strut to the dented old refrigerator and back. "Still fits, can you believe it?"

"I cannot," she agreed, and held out her arm. He linked his through it. "Shall we?"

The two of them walked the few blocks to Ingrid's, where she was waiting on the front porch in a miniskirt and oversized sweater. She stood, smiled, gave a little shout, and joined them.

And then the Olsen family walked to a brand-new restaurant on Main Street, where they had a table reserved for opening night.

"Fénix," Effie read aloud under the weathered wood sign hanging from wrought iron. "As in, phoenix? Born from the ashes?" Ingrid nodded. "Wow, that's good."

"*He's* good," Ingrid said, pointing at her boyfriend through the window. Sixto was wearing clean chef's whites and talking with a table of diners in the front of the restaurant.

Effie gave her sister a big smile. "You must be so proud of him."

"I'm proud of everyone, of the whole world!" Ingrid said, young enough to really mean it and sincere enough to pull at Effie's heartstrings. She laughed, and so did their father. And then they walked through the doors for their dinner reservation.

Mick and Ernie had already arrived and were seated at a rectangular table in the middle of the dining room, the one that used to sit underneath an iron-and-glass chandelier. Sixto had done some redecorating in the month's flurry of work, and now the lighting was bright and inviting, with cheery fixtures and colorful bulbs that bathed the walls in appealing shades of red and purple. Latin pop music played from the sound system, and the room smelled like fresh herbs and chilies and slow-cooked spices. Dahlia's arrangements of asters and anemones sat prettily in the new bud vases Ernie had made. The old paintings were gone; in their place were framed pieces that depicted the restaurant in every season. The paintings were a departure from her typical style, but Effie could still recognize Kit's passion in them. Brown Butter may have employed many of the island's residents, but Fénix celebrated every one of them.

Both Ernie and his father stood as the Olsens approached

their table. While Mick and Samuel shook hands, Effie gave Ernie a kiss and an appraising nod. He was wearing dark denim and a button-down under an olive-green cashmere sweater. The shirtsleeves had been rolled up over his sweater, hinting at his collection of forearm freckles. "You look hot," she said, and he rolled his eyes at her, then motioned she twirl around for him.

"I love everything you wear, but this dress has got to be my favorite," he said.

"You only like it because I wore it the first time we slept together," she whispered, her lips at his ear.

"I only like it because you look like a goddess and you're perfect," he corrected her. She gave him a teasing look, but felt effervescent as they took their seats.

"How many you got on the books tonight?" Ernie extended his hand as Sixto approached the table.

"We're at full capacity," Sixto said with a proud smile. Carina had covered the restaurant's rebirth and rebranding in a new article the week prior. It was that article—which included a *No comment* from Jarrod and Geoffrey—that triggered a landslide of new reservations for opening night. Some were from diners who had been planning on coming to Brown Butter. Others were seasoned chefs from around the country. And this time, plenty more were locals.

After ordering enough food to cover the table and then some, the Callahan-Olsen party had finally eaten their fill. Nikki, who'd stayed on as lead server, had just dropped off dessert menus and they were all debating flan versus Samuel's new goat-cheese-and-sour-cherry ice cream versus a platter of traditional Mexican cookies when Effie had a realization. "We never spent time together, both our families, when we were young."

"That can't be right," said her father.

"It's true and it's sad, because you're all so important to me," said Effie, who was speaking freely thanks to the mezcal margarita she had just finished. "But I admit that for a while, I felt guilty. Like I was keeping the two parts of my life separate." She looked to Mick. "Like I was a burden to you when I was a kid. Going over to your house all the time, eating your food, sleeping over. I felt guilty that I needed more parenting when I had a perfectly fine father at home."

"Wow, thanks," Samuel said, feigning hurt. His eyes were mirthful though.

"We loved having you with us," Mick said.

"Sure did," Ernie added, and squeezed Effie's knee.

"It takes a village to raise a kid," Mick said, a sentiment that caused Samuel to raise his glass. "It takes a village to be an adult," he added. "Your father was there for me a few years ago when I was sick. Came over, kept me company. Kept me fed. Mostly French toast, but who's complaining about that?"

Effie looked to her father. She hadn't known. But then, she hadn't asked. Her heart swelled with emotion.

"You've always been a part of the Alder Isle family. Even when you were gone. We'd do anything for you," Mick said. "Most of all, my boy." He touched the edge of his glass to Ernie's. "We wouldn't be sitting here, together, if it weren't for him."

"We wouldn't?" said Ingrid skeptically.

"We wouldn't?" echoed Effie.

"Was I not supposed to say that?" asked Mick, his palm cautiously running over his brush buzz cut.

"It's okay, Dad," Ernie said, then took Effie's hands in his own. "It's time I shared anyway."

"You know what? We should get another one of those mezcal things," said Mick, and he and Samuel promptly made their way to the bar area. Ingrid mumbled something about wanting to check in on Sixto. And then they were alone, and Effie was quiet, and Ernie began talking.

"I'm the one who contacted Carina in the first place. Soon after you came back. I created a new email address and didn't sign my name. All I said was that things were not quite what they seemed at Brown Butter, and the head chef may be lying to diners." He hadn't let go of her hand, hadn't stopped rubbing it. "I almost broke down and told you at Dahlia and Kit's dinner, when Kit said that thing—that if Jarrod got fired, you would be promoted. Because that was exactly why I did it: get rid of him, and you could have everything you wanted. The job of your dreams. Another chance. I thought I was doing the right thing."

"The job of my dreams on *Alder Isle*," Effie pointed out, her brain slow to catch up with the rapid pace of her heartbeat. "Are you sure my staying here for good had nothing to do with your decision?"

Ernie shook his head, then nodded it. "I'm . . . not entirely sure."

"Why didn't you go to Geoffrey first?"

He laughed. "Like that would have changed anything."

She furrowed her brows. Fair. But also . . .

"I wouldn't have done it if I didn't see how happy you looked in the kitchen. I had no idea you were suffering so much. All I saw was you coaching Anika after Jarrod destroyed her confidence. The way you softened your phrasing to give B.J. advice in a way he'd really hear. How you adapted lesson plans with Chad to keep up with the pace he was setting for himself. I know you dread social interaction, but this seemed different. Maybe because it was purposeful? Intentional? Eff, you just seemed so bright, so alive, so . . . yourself."

They sat in silence. Finally, she raised her eyes to his. Ice blue and warm gray. Salty and sweet. Fiery and cool. "You haven't changed at all," she said. "Have you?"

Ernie's jaw was set, not out of anger but a gathering sadness. "If you just let me explain. If I can just—"

Laughter gathered in her throat, then sparkled on her lips. She scooted her chair to face his. "Ernie! I'm not mad!" She gripped his cheeks with both hands and kissed him firmly on the mouth. They were so close, his freckles blurred and all she could see were the crinkles at the edges of his eyes. She kissed him again, quicker and livelier, and moved her lips to cover his nose, his temple, his forehead, the tip of his chin. "You're a genius."

"I am?"

"You are. Or else you just know me better than I know myself," she said, grabbing his hands once more. "I've been doing mental Cirque du Soleil to figure out my thing, and you've known it all along!"

"I have?" Ernie said.

"You have," Effie confirmed. "And I love you for trying to make it happen for me."

"I'm so glad. But can I ask a possibly embarrassing question?"

"Anything."

Ernie grinned sheepishly and his dimple settled in deeper. "What's your thing?"

"Ernie Callahan, I'm going to teach people how to cook."

Chapter Forty

Although she hadn't always known it, Effie was a born teacher. She was dynamic and thorough, intuitive and a good leader. She was that way at age sixteen and as a professional chef, and she still was now. Empowering other people in the kitchen had always been her favorite part of the job, the part that kept her drive alive. So why couldn't she take that and run with it? There wasn't a single thing stopping her. She could rent the kitchen from Sixto when the restaurant was closed. Or find her own space. She could teach Chad and Anika. And the other residents of Alder Isle. Or tourists. Or whatever! She didn't need to know all the details right now. She knew where she belonged and who she loved and what she liked to do. That was enough.

It was everything.

Ernie stood and scooped her up so enthusiastically her feet left the ground. "It's perfect."

"It's my thing!" she cried.

"It's your thing," he agreed. "And that makes this next part so much better. Come with me." He held her wrist, the way he had back during the rainstorm at Top Spot Mountain, and he started to pull her toward the door.

"Wait!" she laughed, feeling giddy. "The bill! We can't skip out on Sixto."

"It's all good," Ernie said, making eye contact with their fathers at the bar and giving a nod. "It's covered."

Effie was just about to protest further when he put a finger to his lips. "Wait and see." He led her out of the restaurant and down Main Street. He led her past her father's ice cream shop and the library and The Gull's Perch and Son of a Wharf and This Man's Trash. The air smelled like shellfish and seaweed. The evening sounded like hermit thrushes and distant laughter. Ernie led her all the way to the harbor, and then he said, "Let's go out on the water."

Effie gasped. Tied to the pier was a small boat with a seaworn black hull. Next to the boat, waiting on the dock, was a neatly folded Pendleton blanket.

There was no picnic basket. No sleeve of crackers or wedge of cheese. No fancy little knife. No bottle of champagne. But there didn't need to be. There was Ernie and the promise of a future for both of them on Alder Isle.

"One sunset boat cruise for two, coming right up. No way was I going to close out our bucket list with a lobster dinner in my tiny kitchen. And even though summer's over, we're just beginning." He kissed her, then rubbed the tip of his nose against hers. She hugged his waist and looked out at the boat. "It's

Dougie's," he said. "On loan. We have to return it by four tomorrow morning. But if we're still out on the water at that point, something has gone terribly wrong." He helped Effie into the boat, and she accepted the blanket. She set it neatly on the seat next to the captain's chair and stood at the bow. Ernie turned on the lights and unmoored them and started the engine. And then they were off, into the warm glow of the evening sunset.

They drifted for a while, close enough to the harbor to see the winking lampposts but far enough to feel like they were sharing a secret. Effie let the air tousle her hair as she closed her eyes and tried to memorize how the night tasted, how it felt.

She steadied herself with her palms on the boat's smooth edge, and allowed herself to dream. She would use the money she'd saved this summer to start her own business; to buy an extra set of knives and equipment for her students. She'd advertise in the local paper, and on the neighborhood email message board. She'd move in with Ernie. Or maybe they'd get a new place, big enough for them and for a dog. A cat? A goldfish? They'd get a place big enough for a dining table, and they'd invite Kit and Dahlia over for dinner, and Ingrid and Sixto, too. She would take a couple months off each year to travel with Ernie. To show him the places she had been, and to discover new ones together. She would cheer him on as his pottery business grew, and together they would find their places within the community, both together and individually. She would find a therapist, and she would do the hard work, whatever it looked like and wherever it brought her.

The breeze kicked up into a marine wind, and she shivered. Behind her, she felt Ernie unfold the blanket and drape it over his shoulders. He wrapped his arms around her, the blanket enveloping them both. His hand found her own, then her hand found a smooth, round piece of metal with a large stone in the center.

"Oh!" Effie opened her eyes and looked at the ring in her palm. Her face felt wet and warm. She lifted her fingertips to her cheeks. Tears: so many they were pooling at the corners of her lips. He pressed the pads of his thumbs to her cheekbones, and any tears he wiped away were immediately replaced. "I'm sorry, I can't stop crying!" It wasn't the most romantic thing to say before a marriage proposal, but it was the first thing that came to Effie's mind.

"I'm not in a hurry, Eff. This has been sixteen years in coming."

She laughed then, and her tears slowed enough for her to see his reassuring gaze through the shine.

He wrapped one arm around her waist and pulled her closer, so their foreheads were touching. She held the ring up and together they studied it. The band was hammered gold. In the middle was a pale blue sapphire, cool and clear and set in a full bezel. It was the most beautiful thing Effie had ever seen. It was like it'd been made just for her.

"I know I tried the whole 'declaration of undying love' thing before, but I've learned a few important things about you since then," Ernie said. "One: don't bring champagne." Effie snorted and tried to cover it up as a laugh. He continued, gently taking the jewelry from her. "The ring I almost gave you at eighteen was for the girl I wanted you to be." She sniffled. "This is for the woman you are." Her took her left hand. She let her fingers unfurl from where they'd been pressing into her palm. He set the ring onto the tip of her fourth finger, and paused at her first knuckle. She nodded. He smiled, then slid it all the way down. It *had* been made just for her! It was snug and comfortable against her skin. It felt right.

"Well, I'll be. A perfect fit," Ernie said. "What do you have to say about that, Effie Olsen?"

She threw her arms around his neck and kissed him like a woman in love. She kissed him like she'd wanted to all along, like she hoped to for the next fifty years, wherever they lived and whatever they did. "Ernie Callahan," she said. "I thought you'd never ask."

Epilogue

On a Monday afternoon six months later, Effie and Ernie Callahan stepped off the ferry onto Alder Isle. He was pulling a large piece of wheeled luggage; she was holding a backpack the opposite way, close to her chest with her arms cradled protectively around it. Ernie looked at his watch and let the suitcase rest on the sidewalk. "He should be here any minute."

They had just arrived home from a two-week trip to Greece—a belated honeymoon. Dahlia had taken the ferry with them on their way out and driven them to the airport. Sixto had promised to pick them up when they arrived home, but it had docked a bit ahead of schedule. The damp April air felt frosty after fourteen days soaking up the Santorini sun, and Effie shivered, pulling the sleeves of her wool sweater down over her hands.

"Am I late? Shoot, I thought I was early!" Ingrid's voice reached them before Sixto's sedan did. She parked, then hopped out and hugged them both. "Sixto's tied up at Fénix." She tossed the suitcase into the trunk of the car, then reached for Effie's knapsack.

Effie yanked it away and tsk-tsked her sister. "Fragile cargo in here *thankyouverymuch*." She had smuggled back half a dozen orange-and-oregano cured sausages wrapped in her running socks and fisherman's sweater. "What's going on with the Northeast's Best Chef?" she asked, referencing the title bestowed upon Fénix from the James Beard Awards's annual list. It had dropped the day they'd left for Greece, so a delayed celebration was in order.

"Filming an episode of *Dinner Story*," Ingrid said, waiting a dramatic beat for their reaction.

"Nicely done, Sixto," Ernie said, and placed his hand over Effie's knee. *Dinner Story* was a hot Netflix series that profiled up-and-coming professional chefs. Effie was grateful for his touch, and set her hand on top of his. Even though she didn't regret leaving the restaurant industry, there were sometimes pangs of sadness for the opportunities she'd given up. Ernie knew that, and the acknowledgment from him was reassuring enough to pull her out of it.

"Yeah. He's basically the best," Ingrid said, turning onto the Cleary Island bridge. "So. How was your honeymoon?! More or less exciting than the wedding?"

Effie and Ernie looked at each other and shared a secret smile. They had gotten married in the beginning of November, a month after he proposed. They had agreed they didn't want an extravagant wedding that took a year to plan—not after waiting sixteen to come together. Dahlia and Kit offered their rambling house and beachfront property for the ceremony and reception, and

Sixto catered the meal with a buffet of dishes inspired by Brown Butter, Fénix, Alder Isle, and Effie and Ernie's story. There was an herby salad made with heirloom beans, creamy bucatini with big pieces of lobster-claw meat and lots of fresh chervil, and upscale tuna noodle casserole. (Dahlia had suggested they drizzle it with truffle oil, which made Effie howl with laughter.) For dessert, Samuel hired Jessalyn from The Gull's Perch to scoop cones of blueberry lavender and Grape-Nuts ice cream, with all the toppings. Ernie had worn a pair of slim-fitting chinos with a button-down and a tailored blazer. Effie had worn a white wide-legged jumpsuit with a fitted waist and a pair of dressy ballet flats. Her bouquet was made by Dahlia, of course: Japanese pokeweed and pampas grass tied together with a piece of matte ribbon. Dozens of their friends and family had come. They had hooked up a phone to a speaker, and everyone took turns playing DJ. Guests danced late into the night, and some even stayed awake until sunrise, when Kit set out a spread of bagels and hot coffee and apple-blackberry pie. It had been a beautiful wedding.

But it wasn't their first.

As soon as Effie said yes to Ernie on the boat, she knew she didn't want to wait. The next week, they got a marriage license, got in Ernie's truck, and drove to Portland where they tied the knot in a civil ceremony attended by two strangers they'd met at the old-timey gas station coffee shop that morning. None of their friends in Alder Isle knew about the real wedding, and Effie and Ernie intended to keep it that way. After all, they reasoned, secrets are hard to come by on a tiny island off the midcoast of Maine with a full-time population of fifteen hundred.

"Can't choose, little sis," said Effie. "Honeymoon was great. Lots of beach time, despite the fact *someone* demanded we start every day with a run through the countryside." She gave Ernie a fake-annoyed look, and he winked at her. They had both agreed their daily runs had become an anchor for their relationship, especially when life got busy. Effie continued: "It was also really nice to take a break from work." Effie's cooking classes had taken off around Christmas when she ran a two-for-the-price-of-one special. She'd also invested in a camera and tripod, and was now teaching virtual classes that had received a shout-out in *New York* magazine. And just two days ago, an email from MasterClass had arrived in her inbox: they were interested in producing a series around "true seasonal cooking" with Effie as the instructor. She had briefly read the offer during their last Greece beach day, but decided to shelve it until she returned home. She hadn't even told Ernie, although she would soon. It was just one of those secrets she wanted to cherish.

"And how's tricks with the pottery biz?" Ingrid asked, parking the car in front of Ernie and Effie's small white farmhouse. It was seven hundred square feet, wind-worn with a wraparound porch, and just right for right now. "Your Etsy site hasn't crashed due to lack of unfulfilled orders?"

"Ha," Ernie said, unbuckling and stepping out into a wild gale that carried with it angry, cold drops of sea. Together they gathered their luggage and ran into the house. Once they'd shut the door against the weather, Ernie shrugged off his coat and took Effie's and Ingrid's to the mudroom. Effie walked straight to the old Mr. Coffee and began filling it with grounds and hot water.

"Etsy shop is chugging along, but Geoffrey Goldman actually just contacted me," Ernie said. Effie waited to see her sister's reaction. The wide eyes and open mouth matched Effie's expression when Ernie had told her.

"Ever since the *Times* story specifically called out the serveware, I've been fielding calls from restaurateurs all over the country. It's embarrassing. For them, I mean. The fact that they think I'm actually good at this."

"You are very good at this," Effie said. "But I mean it: you had better double what you charged Sixto if you take the job from Geoffrey."

"It's not for Jarrod's new restaurant, is it?" Ingrid settled into one of their mismatched dining chairs.

"That would be hilarious," said Effie. "But you hadn't heard? He's no longer working for Geoffrey at all. He went corporate. Does catering for some big event center in Vegas now. At least that's what B.J. said, and he seems to know all the gossip. I'm sure it pays well, but it sounds pretty soulless." Ingrid nodded and for a few minutes, they all just listened to the machine's steady drip. When it beeped, Effie and Ernie stood at the same time, laughed, and fixed cups of milky-sweet coffee for everyone.

"Yay for him," Ingrid said, accepting one of Ernie's textured mugs.

"Yay for you," Ernie said, and Ingrid glowed. She was halfway through writing a book about investing basics for Generation Z.

"Yay for us," Effie said, and lifted her mug to cheers her husband and her sister. She took a sip and felt warm from the inside out. She had Ernie and she had her family. She had friends, a job that lit her up, and ambition to keep striving. She had such a full, happy life. There was just one question left to answer.

"So," she said, setting down the mug and opening the door to the pantry full of spaghetti, canned vegetables, and spices. "What's for dinner?"

Acknowledgments

Stupendously large thanks to my agent, Sharon Pelletier. Your support, guidance, patience, and appreciation of a quality Harry Styles GIF is unparalleled.

I feel so lucky to have landed at Berkley, and to be working with a crackerjack team. My editors, Kerry Donovan and Mary Baker: your insights and suggestions make my writing better, cleaner, and more exciting. Our time together has taught me an immense amount about crafting a work of fiction. Thank you to my production editor, Alaina Christensen, and my managing editor, Christine Legon. Thank you to Courtney Vincento for proofreading *Effie*. Thank you to my copy editor, Meg Gerrity, for such thorough attention to detail. Not only did you wrangle my grammar into shape, but your thoughtful timelines and character notes were helpful in weaving a cohesive narrative. So many thanks to the marketing and publicity team, Yazmine Hassan and Anika Bates, for working tirelessly to get my books in the hands of people who will love them. To Mallory Heyer and Rita Frangie Batour for drawing and designing the covers of my dreams: I just love how you bring my characters and their worlds to life. Your artistry is better than my imagination could ever be.

Thank you to the libraries and independent bookstores that stock, sell, share, and circulate my books. I am especially indebted to the Onondaga Free Library, Golden Bee Bookshop, and Parthenon books in New York; and the Stowe Free Library and Bear Pond Books in Vermont.

I am grateful to Hill Farm by Sagra and The Constance Inn for hosting me and providing comfort during periods of intense, focused writing.

Thank you to all the chefs who taught me how to cook, with special commendations to all the ones who made me cry in the walk-in (Walken) cooler.

Julie: Without you, I'd never have set this story in Maine. Thank you for providing the inspiration and research materials, and for giving manuscript feedback. Additionally, without you, I wouldn't have grown and learned so much about being a balanced, healthy human. Without you, I'd have no one to chat with over text and Instagram at the same time. You're my favorite forever friend.

Jen: Thank you for being willing to be my first reader for life. I value your opinion, but even more so, your friendship. Your steady, loving presence in my life is a gift for which I have no words (beyond the ones I just put on this page).

To Erin: Thank you for hosting me, and for teaching me all about island life. My time at "Alder Isle" remains one of the most formative experiences for me as a writer, and I know it was deeply influenced by your beautiful space and top-tier hospitality.

Rachel: Sometimes I still can't believe how lucky I was way back in 2013. Your trust in my abilities—and potential—still drive me forward.

Thank you to my family: Mom, Dad, Sasha, Josh, and Anna. I love sharing the writing process with you. Thank you for always being willing to cheer me on and cheer me up in our text chain. And for buying my books, even though you know I'd give you extra copies for free.

Thank you to Cedar, even though you won't read this on account of being a dog. But you're *my* dog, and your companionship during the writing and editing process is vastly appreciated. I'm sorry that walkies are sometimes shorter when I'm on deadline.

To Margot and Ellis: Thank you for brightening my days, making me laugh, and helping me to see the bigger picture.

To Matt: Thank you for you. Thank you for believing in me and in us.

Keep reading for an excerpt from
Rochelle Bilow's

Ruby Spencer's Whisky Year

available now!

The next day, Carson delivered the rest of Ruby's haul in his truck. Thankful for any excuse to procrastinate writing her cookbook proposal, Ruby opened her notebook to the page where Carson had drawn the plan and written instructions.

It's not that Ruby didn't know her way around a hammer. She had lived alone for years, after all, and pictures don't hang themselves. It was just that building a raised garden bed with a hinged top was way more complicated than it had seemed yesterday, standing at the counter with Carson. But it was either that or stare at the judgmentally blinking cursor on her laptop. She tied her curls back into a quick braid and got to work.

After clearing away a four-by-six-foot patch of weeds and long grass near the path that connected the Cosy Hearth and her cottage, Ruby lugged the untreated wood—thankfully, already cut to size—to the site, and set the pieces on their sides in the shape of a rectangle. She reviewed Carson's notes: *Use screws to secure the framing.*

Ruby grabbed the first screw and set its tip against the piece of wood where it met its neighbor. "Eek!" she squealed a little, both in fear and the thrill of doing something hard and good. She aligned an electric drill over the screw and pulled the trigger. The screw made it halfway in before the wood started splitting apart at various points. The plank looked like it was in danger of completely splintering. "Eek," she said again, more quietly this time.

"You didn't ask advice but—if I were you, I'd mark the places you mean to screw before doing it. And predrill the hole."

Ruby turned around, still in a squatting position, the drill still in her hand. Leaning against the cottage was a well-built Scot with a truly heroic beard. Brochan. His facial hair was trimmed neatly around his mustache and well maintained at the edges, coming to an unruly rounded point about an inch lower than his chin. It was a *great* beard (not that she was a connoisseur or anything). The man attached to the beard was at least a foot taller than Ruby, wearing a white linen shirt rolled up at the elbows, the hem grazing the waistband of his gray canvas work pants. His facial bone structure was strong; but the presence of round, ruddy radishes for cheeks made his features seem kind, rather than severe. Clearly he'd spent much of his life outdoors; the time was showing on his skin, with deep creases around the outside edges of his eyes. Which were almost black. His hair was thick and the color of good dark chocolate, just long enough to tuck behind his ears. Which it was. Tucked behind his ears. And that beard. Ruby couldn't tear her eyes from it. It managed to somehow look full and bushy without being wild, and there were hints of red around the edges.

Eek, squealed Ruby internally. How long had she been staring? Long enough to drink in all those details. Long enough to become creepy? Definitely.

"I did not . . . ask for advice," said Ruby, "but I'm also not about to turn it away when it shows up at my door. I mean, in my garden." She blushed and her neck felt hot. The man stood there, in no apparent hurry to make the situation less uncomfortable. He crossed his arms and waited for her to speak again. Ruby caught a glimpse of the roped muscles that snaked along his forearms. They were strong, but not grotesquely big—his muscles—and looked like they'd been formed with years of manual labor. They were not the kind of muscles built on barbells and rowing machines. *Wait.* Had she just done a flirt? No. Impossible. She was merely caught off guard. *Slow it down, girl,* she thought. *Introduce yourself. Before this gets any creepier.*

"What I meant was, thank you. That's probably very wise. Is it obvious I've never done this before? Ha. I wanted to grow some vegetables over the summer, but judging from the weather lately, they'll need all the help they can get." Ruby shivered as a breeze picked up, and wished she had dressed in more than a thin tank with her trusty leggings. "Oh! I'm Ruby. I'm renting the stone cottage from Grace. You can call me Roo, though. Everybody does." *Awkward, just stunningly awkward.*

The man laughed and kept his post against the cottage. "Brochan."

Ruby set down the drill and stood. Brochan kept leaning and smiled. Ruby waited. Brochan waited longer.

"Brochan." Ruby took the word in her mouth, attempting to gently roll the *r* in the way he had.

"Brochan," he repeated it, correctly this time.

"Brochan," Ruby tried again.

"Call me Broo," he said.

Ruby giggled. Was *he* flirting? Um, how old was she? Twelve, apparently. She extended her hand. "I'll work on it." He took her palm and squeezed, rather than shook. She let her gaze travel briefly along the length of his arm to his chest and collarbones, which were carpeted with thick dark hair. *Brochan*. That name. This man. The last *lad* to spend a night at the stone cottage before her arrival. A man who could hold his scotch. A man who, by nineteen, had already felt tortured by memory. Probably a super great person for her to get involved with!

Both Neil and Carson had made it seem like there was something mysterious, or secretive, about Brochan; but as Ruby studied his face, she couldn't notice anything weird or unnerving. He didn't seem like a serial killer or town drunk (the town drunk was probably Neil, all things considered).

"Are you from here? I mean—Thistlecross. Not the cottage," Ruby asked and attempted to cram her hands into her pockets before realizing she was in leggings and had no pockets.

"Yes," said Brochan, squatting down and looking first in the direction of town, then back at the cottage. He picked up the drill and gave it a quick whirr. "I'm from here." Motioning for Ruby to join him, he flashed a smirky grin, and the corner of his mouth turned up at the same time his eyes brightened. "Now. Let's make a home for those lettuces of yours."

Author photo by Amelia Marie Photography

Rochelle Bilow is a food and romance writer who previously worked as the social media manager at *Bon Appétit* and *Cooking Light* magazines. A graduate of the French Culinary Institute, she has also worked as a line cook, a baker, and a wine spokesperson. Her books include *The Call of the Farm*, a swoony farming memoir; and *Ruby Spencer's Whisky Year*. Raised in Syracuse, New York, Rochelle now lives in northern Vermont.

VISIT ROCHELLE BILOW ONLINE

RochelleBilowWriting.com

RochelleBilow

BilowRochelle